A lover of fairytales and cowboy boots, **Lauri Robinson** can't imagine a better profession than penning happily-ever-after stories about men—and women—who pull on a pair of boots before riding off into the sunset...or kick them off for other reasons. Lauri and her husband raised three sons in their rural Minnesota home, and are now getting their just rewards by spoiling their grandchildren. Visit: laurirobinson.blogspot.com, facebook.com/lauri.robinson1 or twitter.com/LauriR.

# STOLEN KISS WITH THE HOLLYWOOD STARLET

Lauri Robinson

**MILLS & BOON**

First Published in Great Britain 2019
by Mills & Boon, an imprint of HarperCollins*Publishers*
1 London Bridge Street, London, SE1 9GF

© 2019 Lauri Robinson

ISBN: 978-0-263-26932-1

MIX
Paper from
responsible sources
FSC® C007454

To my sister-in-law Jeannette.

An angel among the living.

# *Chapter One*

1927

*Look out, Los Angeles! Shirley Burnette's rolling into town!*

Shirley giggled at her own thoughts. Could almost hear Pappy saying them.

He used to say, "Look out, Shirley's up and at 'em," every morning without fail.

Nose glued to the window, she was enthralled, so thrilled her own breath kept fogging up the glass. Swiping the glass clean, she felt her excitement rise higher and higher as she watched the buildings roll by.

Big ones, little ones and those in between.

Los Angeles.

Hollywood.

The place where dreams came true.

No more washing dishes. No more shucking

corn. No more mucking out stalls. Nebraska was half a nation behind her, and that's where it was going to stay.

The train whistle, a screech that could make the hair on your arms stand on end, sounded like bells straight out of heaven to her. She'd waited years to hear that sound.

Years and years.

This wasn't just her dream, it had been her mother's, and she had to make it come true. No matter what.

There had been times she'd wondered if that was possible, especially four years ago, when Pappy had died. That's also when she'd focused on making it come true even harder. She'd tucked away every spare penny she'd made working for Olin Swaggert, and made sure none of the overgrown thugs he called sons didn't get their grubby hands on it. She made sure they didn't get their grubby hands on anything else, too.

Olin kept saying that she was bound to fall in love with one of his boys, get married and live right there on that pig farm forever.

She'd assured him that would never happen.

Never.

Ever.

A lot of lazy dewdroppers, that's what the entire clan of Swaggert boys were, and more than once she'd wanted to throw in the towel. The only reason she hadn't was because Olin had paid her. The Swaggerts were one of the few families who could afford to have a live-in worker.

Live-in because, thanks to some city slicker lawyer, as soon as Pappy had died, the Swaggerts got the farm. Lock, stock and barrel. The lawyer claimed Pappy had owed Olin money. Lots of it. She'd argued that, but that hadn't done a wit of good. In the end, she'd been left with no place to live. No place to do much of anything. Olin had offered her a job—out of the goodness of his heart, that's how he'd put it.

A heart like his didn't have any goodness. He'd known how badly it had hurt her to see the house she'd grown up in, lived in her entire life, torn down, but that hadn't stopped him from tearing it all down and plowing up the land.

Corn. That was all that was there now. A field of corn.

That lawyer hadn't had a heart, either. He'd refused to listen to a word she'd had to say. So had the sheriff, who'd ordered her out of the house. It had been hard to swallow, that there was nothing left of her family. Other than memories and a dream, so with no other options, she'd taken the job with the Swaggerts and turned her focus to saving up the money to get here. To where the only thing she had left was sure to come true.

Los Angeles. The City of Angels.

It was fitting. A girl who sang like an angel should live in the City of Angels.

People had been saying for years that she sang like an angel. Pappy, of course, and other family members before they'd died, but town folks had said it, too.

Granted, the population of Roca, Nebraska, was little more than two hundred, but a couple of churches in Lincoln had paid her to sing at funerals. Donations. She'd gotten donations. Piddly ones. But money was money and every penny she'd earned had brought her one step closer to this day.

She was here to become a singer. Sing like she and Pappy used to. Sing like her mother had, years ago, when she'd been young and traveled the country. That's how her mother and father had met. He'd heard Momma sing at a playhouse in Lincoln. Within two shakes of a cat's tail, they were married and Momma moved to the farm.

Pappy had claimed that Momma had never regretted that because she still sang all the time. Just not on a stage. Shirley couldn't say if that was true or not. She'd been young when her parents had died. Sometimes, late at night when it was dark and quiet, she could hear her momma singing inside her head and her heart. That's where her singing lived, inside her, where no one could take it away from her.

Pappy had said that, as a baby, she'd never cried. She'd sung instead. Sung her lungs out from the day she'd been born. He said it was in her genes and that she'd grow up to be just like her momma. A singer. A famous one, like her momma had dreamed of becoming before she'd married her father.

That's what she was here to do. Become a singer. A famous one. She would learn how to dance, too. Really cut a rug. Had to. The two, singing and dancing, went hand in hand.

Oh, yes, she was going to sing and dance, and live and laugh!

The train jerked and bucked as it rolled into the station, and she swiped away the fog on the window one last time before straightening the collar of her blue paisley dress and picking up her purse, ready to get her first real look at her new world.

An entire new world that was there for the taking. Her taking. Like apples hanging on a tree ready to be plucked.

Life is good. When you make it that way.

Smiling at her own thoughts, Shirley was first in line, standing at the door, when the heavy metal was slid aside. She rushed down the steps, wishing she could twist her head like an owl. There was so much to see.

Buildings that went so high into the sky a person could dang near touch the clouds if they were to stand on top of one, and cars, more than she'd seen in a month back in Nebraska, and people. Tall ones, short ones, skinny ones, fat ones, old ones, young ones…just all sorts. All sorts!

*We're here, Momma. The place where our dreams are going to come true!*

In an attempt to quell her enthusiasm long enough to collect her luggage, she gave herself a nod and leaped off the edge of the train station platform.

A second later she comprehended the baggage compartment was in the other direction, and had to step back up on the wooden platform and follow the crowd heading that way.

That didn't faze her.

She was too happy.

Too free.

Shirley stood in line, tapping a toe and looking in all directions, until it was her turn. Then she collected her suitcase, thanked the man wearing a bright blue coat with shiny brass buttons and spun around while filling her lungs with California air.

Full of train smoke, the air stuck in her throat. She had to cough three times to clear her passageway, and wipe aside the tears the coughing caused.

But none of that fazed her, either.

Nothing could.

Her ordinary life was over.

Or soon would be. Her first order of business was to find a job. The money she'd saved was down to a pouch of coins and a few bills.

She wasn't overly particular, and certainly wasn't afraid of hard work. Things took time; she fully understood that. Becoming a singing sensation would be no different. Until then, she could only imagine that no matter where she got a job, it would be wonderful. It had to be. This was California!

Swinging her purse in one hand, her suitcase in the other, she headed toward the blocks upon blocks of tall buildings. Made of brick and concrete, every building was connected to the next one. The entire block was that way. Every block for as far as the eye could see. Some buildings were tall, some short, some had arched windows and decorative dormers, others just had rows and rows of windows.

Ten. That one building had ten rows of windows! She couldn't help but wonder what could be behind all those windows, and scurried forward, rushing across the street to the next block. The first floors of most every building were businesses, all sorts of them. One sold only shoes. Another cigars and tobacco. Another one sold cakes.

Just cakes?

She stepped closer and peeked in the big window. Sure enough. That's all that was inside there. Cakes. And people buying them.

People. Good heavens but there were people everywhere. Dressed in fancy suits and work clothes alike. Men, that is. The women, they all had on stylish clothes. Not simple dresses like the one she was wearing. Someday, she'd have dresses like they were wearing, but she wasn't going to worry about that. Not today. Not when there was so much to see.

Like that cake shop.

Who'd have thought a store could sell nothing but cakes? That was truly fascinating.

Everything was fascinating.

There were big signs, like the one about selling nothing but cakes, everywhere. In all the windows. On the storefronts and on the sides of the buildings, even sprouting out of the rooftops like an old man with only a few strands of hair sticking straight up.

Billboards. That's what those signs were called. She'd seen pictures of them in magazines. Every chance she'd got the past few years, she'd popped into Lester Frank's store and read those magazines cover to cover. When she had time to read. Other days, when she had to hurry or be left behind by one of the Swaggerts, she'd just looked at the pictures. Every last picture before she put the magazine back and bought the items on her lists.

The pictures in those magazines looked just like everything around her.

Everything.

Except those pictures had been black-and-white. Here, everything was colorful.

Right down to the automobiles parked along the curb and those buzzing up and down the street. They were red, green, yellow, blue, silver, even white. Why, there was hardly a black one to be seen.

Back home, they'd all been black.

Dull black cars. Just like her life had been. Dull. Colorless.

Happiness bubbled inside her. She was here. Truly here! And everything about her old life was behind her.

All those colorful cars, of all different makes and models, were something, but the roads, they were amazing. These roads weren't made of dirt like back in Nebraska. No, sirree! They were paved. And the sidewalks concrete. Her heels clicked against it as she walked.

That made her smile.

Everything made her smile. She spun in a circle, looking up at all the signs, around at all the stores and cars and down at all the concrete. It was all she'd dreamed it would be.

Stopping before she made herself dizzy, she

drew in a breath and set her focus on her first necessity.

Money made the world go around and she needed to find a way to make a few bucks— seed money—to get her world spinning.

Her smile increased upon noticing a newspaper stand across the street.

Ask and you shall receive!

She stepped off the curb and walked between two parked cars. When there was a break in traffic, she took the opportunity and hurried forward to cross the street.

Out of nowhere, a sound, or flash of color, had her looking left.

A big red car was barreling right at her.

Shirley leaped backward, but her feet went out from beneath her as a screech the likes she'd never heard before scared the very soul out of her body. The next second, her rump landed on the pavement so hard her teeth nearly rattled out of her mouth.

Walter Russell shut off the engine of his Packard at the same time he threw open the door. Thank goodness the roadster had mechanical brakes on all four wheels, otherwise he would have hit the woman. He didn't think he had hit her, but couldn't see her over the hood. She'd gone down while his brakes were squealing like a stuck hog.

Where had she come from? It was as if she'd shot right out in front of him on purpose.

He rounded the front of the car, saw her sitting on the pavement and ran closer. "Are you all right? Are you hurt anywhere?"

Eyes wide and mouth open, it was a moment before she shook her head. "My behind is throbbing and my teeth are stinging 'cause this here pavement is a hell of a lot harder than dirt. I can tell you that. And hotter. Boy-oh-howdy but it's hot. That sun is doing its job."

He held back a grin, because it certainly wasn't funny. Not even her thoughts about the pavement. She just looked so cute, so startled, sitting there, shaking her head.

Walter gave his head a clearing shake. "Here," he said, taking ahold of her arm. "Let me help you up."

She pulled her arm away. "I can get up all on my own. Been doing it every morning since the day I was born." She let out a tiny giggle. "Well, dang near since then."

He stepped back as she planted her heels and palms on the pavement, then arching her back, she literally leaped upright. It was a smooth, somewhat graceful movement, just one he'd never seen done before. And wasn't overly sure he'd seen it this time. She was a little thing. The top of her head barely came up to his shoulders. That could explain why she was so agile. How she'd hopped up off the ground like some acrobat in a circus show.

"Hand me that suitcase, would you?" she asked, nodding toward the Packard as she picked up her handbag.

He spun, and frustration washed over him. The suitcase had landed on the hood of his roadster. His brand-new roadster. He'd owned it less than a month. Gingerly, he lifted the hard-sided suitcase off the hood, checking to make sure none of the bright red paint had been scratched.

It didn't appear to be. The chrome Flying Goddess of Speed hood ornament appeared undamaged, too, so did the big chrome headlights on both sides of the ornament.

"Well, give it here," she said. "Why'd you try to run me down like that?"

Walter handed her the suitcase as more frustration filled him. "Run you down? I wasn't attempting to run you down. I'd just pulled away from the curb and you jumped out in front of me. There is a city ordinance against jaywalking. You can be arrested for that."

"Arrested?" She took a step back. "For what?"

"Jaywalking."

"Ain't never heard of that." A deep frown wrinkled the smooth skin between her brows. "What is it?"

"Jaywalking?"

She nodded.

Between her accent and knowledge, it was apparent she was not from California. Had most likely just stepped off the train from some Midwest town. That was where most of the newcomers came from. The center of the nation. He'd been born and raised there, smack-dab in the middle of nowhere, and had been happy to leave. "It means you can't cross the street in the center of the block. You have to walk to one corner or the other."

She looked up the road, and then down it, before turning to look at him again. "Now, why would I want to walk all the way to that there corner?" She pointed up the street. "Or all the way down to that there one." She pointed to the corner behind him. "When where I want to go is right there." She pointed directly across the street. "Makes no living sense to me."

Yes, she was most certainly from the Midwest. Walter pointed to one, then the other corner. "Drivers know to watch for pedestrians at the corners." He then pointed at the road before her. "Not in the middle of the road."

Her short blond hair bounced as she shook her head. "Well, they better learn to. It ain't that hard.

Folks back home do it all the time." She gestured at his car. "You need to learn it, too."

A horn honked. "Get out of the road!" a driver shouted while steering around the Packard.

Walter ignored the driver. "No, you need to learn not to jaywalk. Better yet, why don't you just walk back to the train station, on the sidewalk, and go back home."

Her eyes, a deep blue, narrowed and darkened as she planted a hand on her hip. "I just got here and no one is going to make me leave."

A part of him felt sorry for her, the other part was thoroughly disgusted. Not by her, but by what she expected. Los Angeles was full of newcomers. Just like her. All dreaming the same dream. "Look around. The streets aren't lined with gold and the beds aren't made of rose petals." That was what the magazines made people believe, and believe they did. "Go home. You'll be glad you did."

"No, I won't. I came here planning to stay, and stay I will."

"Plan on becoming a star, do you?" He huffed out a breath. That wasn't a dream. It was a nightmare. One he was still living.

"No. A singer." She squared her shoulders. "Folks back home say I got the voice of an angel."

He shook his head. She'd find out sooner or later, so he might as well tell her. "There are no angels in Los Angeles." Just a lot of devils. He personally knew several of them.

She lifted her chin a bit higher. "There are now."

He should just surrender. Leave her to her head-in-the-sky dreams. "Where are you from? Kansas? Oklahoma?" Her accent wasn't deep enough for Texas.

"Nebraska. And I ain't going back."

He remembered wanting to leave that state, and had left it, only to discover there were times that he wished he'd ended up someplace other than here. Burying those thoughts, he asked, "Why?"

"Because I'm a singer." A tiny frown formed over the bridge of her nose. "At least, that's what I'm going to be. Soon. Real soon."

Another car honked, the driver shouted, shaking a fist while driving past.

There was nothing he could do to change her mind. That was for sure. So there was no use trying. He should have known better right from the beginning. "You keep jaywalking, and you'll become an angel, all right." He pointed toward the sidewalk. "Walk to one corner or the other before you try crossing the street again."

She shook her head. "I tell you, that there is about the craziest thing I ever did hear."

He took a step toward his car, but stopped, looked at her again. She was cute with her big blue eyes, blond hair and catalog-ordered dress. Cute enough to catch attention. He didn't like the thought of that, but it was a reality. She was of no concern of his; however, he knew one thing for sure. "You won't get a singing job here."

She puffed up like a hen shooed off its nest. "You can bet your darn tooting boots I will."

He lifted up a foot, showing her a shoe. "I'm not wearing boots. No one here wears boots. And no one is going to hire you to sing speaking the way you speak."

"Speak—" Her eyes narrowed. "What's wrong with the way I talk?"

"Nothing." He let out a sigh because being rude wasn't his way, but neither was lying. "In Nebraska. But California wants the entire nation to believe everyone here is sophisticated. A cut above the rest, and you sound like you're a country bumpkin straight off the train. Which you are." A solid stab of guilt hit his stomach at the way her face fell. However, a little disappointment now was nothing compared to what she was going to experience. "Go home," he said earnestly. "Just go home."

She spun around. "You go home."

A heavy sigh escaped as Walter watched her march between the cars and back onto the sidewalk. He couldn't help but think how another beautiful woman would soon be gobbled up by the evils that be, and that there wasn't anything anyone could do about it.

Trying one last time, he leaned against the side of his car, and shouted, "It's not here. Whatever you hope to find, it isn't here."

She looked at him and spread her arms wide. "Hope? Hope is everywhere. You should go get yourself some."

## Chapter Two

❧◉❧

The clicking of her heels on the concrete no longer made Shirley smile. She was too mad for that. He had to be the rudest man ever. Almost running her down with his big red car, and telling her to go home 'cause there's no hope here.

Fool.

Hope was everywhere. Like dreams. You just had to snatch it up and hold it inside. Without it, there was no point in living. Hope was all she'd had for years; it's what kept her going after she'd lost everything, everyone. It was what had brought her all the way to California. He was wrong. Hope was here, all right, because it was inside her. If a person didn't have hope, they didn't have anything. He needed to learn that.

"There ain't nothing wrong with the way I talk, either," she muttered under her breath.

Goose bumps rose up on her arms as she remembered Miss Larsen, the schoolteacher she'd had for only a short time. Pretty and young, Miss Larsen had been from out east somewhere, and had talked so funny the kids had teased her. Teased her so much she'd left.

Miss Larsen had said that *ain't* was not a word. They'd all thought she'd been wrong. The silliest teacher ever.

"Excuse me."

Shirley turned, but the person who'd spoken stepped past her into the street. So did others. She looked left and right, twice, and then followed. Others followed her, and they all made it across without anyone getting hit. The cars stopped, letting the last few folks make it all the way to the sidewalk before the cars started moving again.

She looked up and down the blocks. The only place people were walking across the streets were at the corners.

Dang.

Huffing out a breath, she shook her head. Just because he was right about that—jaywalking—didn't mean he was right about everything. Him in his fancy black-and-white suit. Even his shoes had been black-and-white. Shoes like that weren't made for working. That's for sure. Neither was that fancy suit, even though it sure made him look nice. So did his hair, the way it was trimmed and combed over to one side. She'd only seen men who looked that spiffy, that handsome, in magazines. There hadn't been a hint of a whisker on his chin. Matter of fact, his face had been so pleasant to look at she'd kept trying not to look at him because for some silly reason it made her heart pitter-patter.

She wasn't here for pitter-patter. She was here to sing.

Turning about, she walked toward the newspaper stand. It sure seemed like a waste of time to walk all the way to the corner, then across the street, and all the way back down this side of the street, but if that was way folks around here did things, she'd just have to get used to it.

That wouldn't be so hard.

A few minutes later, she decided crossing the street at the corners was downright easy compared to deciding what newspaper to buy. She'd never seen so many. In the end, she picked the one with a picture of a big building on the front page and a headline about a new theater that would open soon. The man selling the newspapers said that building was only a few blocks away, so that paper seemed like a logical choice.

She paid the man, tucked the newspaper under her arm and walked down the block to where a sign said the soup of the day was tomato.

The inside of the café was red and white everything, right down to the floor. She found a seat at a white table and sat down on a red chair, smiling at how bright and cheery everything appeared. Far cheerier than that man driving the red car. He had been nice looking, though. Far nicer than any of Olin's sons. It could have been his suit. She wasn't used to seeing men in suits.

"What can I get for you?"

Shirley glanced up at the woman with a red scarf tied around her dark brown hair. It was tied with a big red bow smack-dab in the middle of the top of her head. It looked spiffy. Shirley figured she might have to tie a scarf that way on her head. She'd have to buy one first. Which meant she needed to get a job.

"I would like a bowl of soup, please, and a cup of coffee," she said, and then held her breath, waiting for the woman to comment on the way she talked.

The woman smiled and nodded. "Coming right up."

Shirley smiled, too, mainly to herself. That man didn't know what he was talking about. Determined to forget all about him, she laid the newspaper on the table, but then, just out of curiosity, scanned the entire front page for the word *ain't*.

By the time a bowl of soup and cup of coffee were set on the table, she'd skimmed the entire newspaper and hadn't found the word. Not once.

That was fine, she didn't need that word, anyway. Pert-near never said it.

She scanned the newspaper again while eating her soup.

"Well, gal-darn it," she whispered.

The soup was gone, except for a small amount on the bottom. She grasped the bowl with both hands, but then looked around the room. Others had bowls of soup, but none had picked up the bowl to drink the last bits, so she slid her hands off the bowl and folded them in her lap.

She watched and listened to other people, especially a woman dressed in a dark blue dress and wearing white shoes.

"More coffee?"

Shirley nodded and slid her cup to the edge of the table.

"New to town?" the waitress asked as she poured the coffee.

"Yes, I am," Shirley answered, conscious of how she sounded. She didn't sound like that other woman, that was for sure. "I truly am," she added, focusing on sounding less like, well, a country bumpkin.

"If you're looking for a job, Mel—he owns this place—is looking for a dishwasher."

If felt as if someone had just kicked her in the stomach. Washing dishes. Beggars couldn't be choosers, but she'd washed dishes her entire life, and had sworn she wouldn't do that again. Not for someone other than herself.

Once again, trying to make herself sound different, sophisticated, Shirley nodded. "Thank you, I will keep that in mind." She'd heard the woman in the blue dress say that just a few moments ago. Then a hint of excitement fluttered across her stomach. If the waitress knew about a dishwashing job, she might know about other ones. "Do you know of any singing jobs?"

The waitress shook her head. "No." She nodded toward a man sitting at a table. The same man who'd been talking to the woman in the blue dress. She'd left, but he hadn't. "Roy would be the man to talk to about that." The waitress slid the coffee cup back to the center of the table. "Coffee and soup's fifty cents."

Fifty cents? Shirley picked her purse up off the floor. At these prices she'd be broke in less time than it took to sneeze. She counted out the change and handed it to the waitress. "Thank you."

"Good luck to you."

As soon as the waitress walked away, the man rose from his chair and walked over.

"I couldn't help but overhear you say that you're a singer." He pulled out the chair on the other side of her table. "Mind if I sit down?"

Shirley's insides leaped so fast she almost flew off her chair. "Yes, I am a singer." He was wearing a suit, like that fella that had almost run her down with his big red car. She peeked around the edge of the table. He wasn't wearing boots, either. She wouldn't hold that against him. Nodding at the chair so he'd go ahead and sit down, she added, "Been singing my entire life."

The guy with the red car, his hair had been the color of sand; this fella's was as dark as garden dirt. So were his eyes, and he had a pointed jaw. Made her wonder if it was on account he rubbed it so much. That's what he was doing now. Rubbing his chin.

"Tell me about your experience," he said, still rubbing his jaw.

"My experience?"

He smiled. "Yes. Singing. Where have you sung before?"

"Oh." She waved a hand. Should have known that's what he meant. "Everywhere. While cooking, cleaning, gardening, working in the barn, feeding the hogs. I just sing all the time. Have for as long as I can remember."

"I see."

He leaned back in his chair and stared at her so hard she wanted to make sure her collar wasn't flipped up or something. She was about to check when he gave a slight nod.

"Have you ever sung in front of people?" he asked.

"Oh, sure. Every Sunday I could make it to church." Wanting him to know how good she was, she continued. "Folks there said I had the voice of an angel. Churches up over in Lincoln had me come sing at funerals whenever I could make it."

"Lincoln?"

She nodded. "Lincoln." The way he frowned said he might not know where that was, so she added, "Nebraska."

"Oh, yes, Nebraska. I've heard of that." He folded his arms across his chest. "How long have you been in California?"

"Since the train I just got off crossed the state line." Her heart shot into her throat as he glanced at the door. Afraid he might leave, she asked, "Wanna hear?"

"Hear what?"

"Me sing." Before he could say no, she drew in a deep breath and let the words flow. "Amazing grace, how sweet..."

She continued through the third verse, then, repeating the final line, she held on to the notes while letting her voice slowly fade away. Others back home liked how she'd always done that.

Folks here must, too, because everyone in the café was looking at her and clapping. Excitement fluttered inside her stomach. She smiled and nodded at them, and then turned her full attention to the man sitting at her table.

"That was very good," he said when the clapping stopped.

"I know." Folks had been telling her that for years. "That's why I'm here."

Smiling, he nodded. "What is your name?"

"Shirley. Shirley Burnette."

"Well, Miss Burnette, I'm Roy Harrison." He stretched a hand across the table. "It's very nice to make your acquaintance."

She gave his hand a solid shake. "You, too, Mr. Harrison."

He leaned back in his chair again. "Miss Burnette, I'd like to offer you the opportunity to audition for some people I know. I'm confident once they hear you, they will offer you a job."

Her heart nearly stopped right then and there. At the exact same time happiness burst inside her. She'd never been so happy in her entire life. If she hadn't been sitting down, she'd be jumping up and down like a baby bird learning to fly.

"Do you have accommodations?" Mr. Harrison asked.

Still trying to stay seated, for the excitement inside her was getting harder and harder to control, she held her breath for a moment. "Accommodations? You mean a place to stay?"

"Yes."

"No, sir, not yet."

"Well, Miss Burnette, I can help with that, too."

*Oh! Glory be! California is the place to be! Ain't even— No, haven't even been here a day and already have a job and a place to live. That guy in the red car might have been right about the boots and the jaywalking, but he sure was wrong about everything else.*

Walter couldn't get the sassy, country-bump-kin blonde woman out of his head. It had been over two weeks but she was still there. On his mind. He was worried about her. About where she ended up. He'd like to think she'd taken his advice and gone back home, but he highly doubted that. She was too determined to do anything that reasonable.

He'd known another woman like that, and she was dead. It had been four years now; the days had gotten easier, but other things, namely the guilt, had gotten worse. In hindsight, he would have done things differently. Given her the divorce she'd wanted. Maybe then Lucy would still be alive.

He'd been so determined, so set on having everything he'd wanted that he'd not taken the time to realize she hadn't wanted the same thing. That their marriage had been destined to fail from the start.

That had been exactly what he hadn't wanted to face.

Failure.

He'd failed once before with Theodore, and like it or not, ultimately, he'd failed with Lucy, too.

"Mr. Russell, do you not care for the beef?"

Walter glanced up, forced a smile to form for Mrs. McCaffrey. "No. I mean, the beef is fine. Excellent. I just find I'm not hungry this evening."

The twinkle faded from her green eyes as her frown added more wrinkles to her usually jolly face. "I do hope you aren't coming down with something."

She was one in a million. Finding Mrs. McCaffrey was one of the things he had done right. She was the best housekeeper in the state, and he was lucky that she'd stuck with him through thick and thin. Her husband had died many years ago, and having no children, she'd dedicated herself to taking care of others. He'd hired her six years ago, before he and Lucy had gotten married, which had proven insightful on his end because Lucy had wanted nothing to do with housekeeping.

Of course she hadn't. She'd been a star.

He muffled a sigh. "I'm fine. I just had a late lunch. I should have telephoned you, but the afternoon got away from me. I do apologize."

Mrs. McCaffrey waved a hand and then lifted the serving dish holding several slices of roast beef off the table. "That's nothing to apologize about. You're a busy man. The most sought-after lawyer in all of Los Angeles. And this beef will keep just fine for tomorrow night."

Walter nodded. "I'm sure I'll be hungry tomorrow night." He hadn't had a late lunch; he just wasn't hungry because his mind was on that girl from Nebraska. He hadn't been back to that state since he'd left over ten years ago. Not that she was making him homesick. He hoped she was homesick, though, and that she had already gotten on an eastbound train.

It was all rather foolish and out of the ordinary for him to be so worried about a stranger. He'd met hundreds of young women over the years, and never thought twice about the decisions they made. Because those had been their decisions, just like the ones she made were hers—that woman from Nebraska with her short blond hair and big blue eyes.

She didn't look like anyone he knew, nor did she remind him of someone, of anyone, so there really was no reason for his fixation.

Then again, he'd never almost run someone over before, either.

"Would you care for a piece of cake and a cup of coffee?" Mrs. McCaffrey asked, returning to the dining room.

"No, thank you." He stood. "I have some work to finish."

She pulled the serving spoon out of the potatoes and waved it at him. "You shouldn't work so much. It's not good for the soul."

"Someday I won't," he said, just to placate her. In all honesty, there was nothing else for him to do. It was a good thing that his clients kept him busy. In more ways than one. Being a lawyer for the rich and famous was a time-consuming job, but also one that had created a bank account that was far beyond what he'd ever have imagined.

Money hadn't been the reason he'd gone into this profession, but he certainly couldn't complain over how profitable it had become.

He strolled out of the dining room and down the hall to his home office. The house was big, five bedrooms upstairs, and one downstairs—a suite of rooms—off the kitchen, which was where Mrs. McCaffrey lived. There were other rooms on the main floor, but other than the dining room and his office, he rarely entered them.

There had been a time when he'd imagined this house full of children. A family. A real family. That's what he'd wanted. Why he'd bought this house. A family like the one he'd had before he'd become an orphan at the age of ten.

That had been eighteen years ago now. He could barely remember what his parents had looked like, but he remembered that they'd loved him. And his little brother, Owen. He remembered the storm, too, and the flash flood. Parts of it. Especially being so cold that he didn't think he would ever warm up.

It had been that way at the orphanage, too. Cold. Bitterly cold. A few months before he'd turned sixteen, he and Theodore Grahams had decided they'd had enough of being cold, and enough of being farmed out as day laborers to people who expected orphans to work harder than anyone else, so they'd escaped. Hopped on a train, and rode it to the end of the rails.

That happened to be California, and that suited them both just fine.

They'd found work on the docks, and thought their futures were as bright as the sunshine. It had been, for a few months. Until Theodore, big for his age, got in a fight with another dockworker. A serious fight that changed both of their lives. The other dockworker died, drowned, and Theodore was charged with his death.

Walter argued it was self-defense when Theodore was arrested, only to be told to shut up or he'd be arrested, too. He hadn't been about to shut up, and went to the police station, still arguing, trying to prove Theodore's innocence. He was kicked out several times, and finally went to a lawyer, hoping for help.

Arthur Marlow hadn't been willing to take on the case, not at first, but Walter hadn't given up.

He and Theodore had been as close as brothers, and he'd had to help him. Had to. With no money to pay the attorney, Walter begged Marlow to let him work off the fees to represent Theodore. Arthur eventually agreed and Walter had thought everything would work out perfectly.

It hadn't.

The jangle of the phone pulled Walter out of the past. He entered his office and crossed the room.

Hope. That's what that girl from Nebraska said she had. He'd had that once, too. So had Theodore.

Picking up the phone, Walter held the receiver to his ear and the mouthpiece to his mouth. "Hello."

"Walter? Walter, that you?"

Instantly recognizing Sam Wharton's voice, Walter answered, "Yes, Sam, it's me. How are you this evening?"

"Good. Real good. I'm down at CB's, and Tony Ebbert and I need some legal advice. Can you drive over here?"

Sam had been a client for years; the money he'd paid for assistance on business deals had nearly paid for Walter's house.

Walter considered the request for a moment. Normally, he'd suggest a meeting in his office tomorrow, but an evening out could be exactly what he needed to get his mind off other things, including that girl from Nebraska, and on to things that mattered. "Sure, Sam. I'll be there shortly."

"Hee-haw!" Sam replied with his signature statement. "See you soon!"

Cartwright's Basement would never be his first choice to visit. Known as CB's, it was downtown, in the basement of the ten-story Cartwright building. The main level was a grocery store, the upper levels apartments, including a floor where the girls who worked at CB's lived and used for alternate activities.

There were too many speakeasies like CB's within the city to count and Walter had figured out long ago that some things a person just had to accept. Like them or not.

He grabbed his suitcoat, told Mrs. McCaffrey he was going out and walked out the back door and to the garage.

After opening the wide double doors, he climbed in the car and hit the ignition. The engine roared to life with so much power the seat shook. The car was a luxury. There hadn't been anything wrong with his old one, except that he'd wanted a new one, and getting it had been easy, unlike some of the other things he'd wanted. Still wanted but continued to tell himself that he didn't.

He backed the car out and onto the road, then grinned as he shifted into First and laid his foot on the gas pedal. The roadster was a dream to drive.

Morning, noon or night, traffic always rolled up and down the streets downtown, and Walter had to circle the block before he found a place to park. He climbed out, then took the sidewalk to the alley, where the entrance to CB's was located.

The joint might be in the basement, but their secret had long been released. Everyone, including the police, knew where it was located and what went on in there, as well as hundreds of other places. In fact, there were just as many laws on the city books to protect the speakeasy owners as there were against prohibition. Federal agents didn't have a hope in hell of upholding the laws Congress had passed.

Cigarette and cigar smoke swirled up the steps as he walked down them, and music echoed off the walls, as did joyous laughter and the murmur of conversations.

He entered the long and wide room full of tables and an elaborately carved wooden bar that ran the entire length of the back wall. A band played music at the far end, where people danced, and cigarette girls sashayed around the tables, wearing tight, short red dresses and carrying more than packs of cigarettes in the white wooden trays hooked around their necks with thick white straps.

Walter scanned the chairs, looking for Sam and Tony. He and Sam noticed each other at the same time. Sam stood, waved one of his long and gangly arms. Where he found shirts with sleeves that long had been the topic of more than one conversation.

Weaving his way toward Sam, Walter nodded and said hello to numerous people at various other tables. Some he knew well, others were mere acquaintances, and a few, he wouldn't mind never seeing again.

"Hey, Walter. I ordered you a drink," Sam said, his straw-colored hair sticking out from beneath the rim of his flat tweed hat. "The good stuff. Have a seat. You know Tony."

"Thanks." Walter took a seat and nodded at Tony. A redheaded heavyweight champion boxer who had a good chance at the world title this year. "Good seeing you, Tony. Congrats. Hear this could be your year."

"It sure could," Tony replied with a voice so low it had to come from the depths of his stomach.

The conversation bounced from boxing to cars, to the latest rumors, including who had financed the building of the new theater, and back to boxing. Walter had finished his drink during that time, and enjoying the camaraderie, he reached out to snag a cigarette girl so he could order another drink.

Catching one by the arm, he twisted to tell her, "I'd like another—"

The startled blue eyes looking down at him stopped his ability to speak. To think. Except for remembering her eyes looked exactly like they had when he'd rounded his car and saw her sitting on her butt on the pavement.

She tugged her arm out of his hold just like she had that day. "Another what?" she asked.

"Whatever you got on that tray, darling," Sam said.

She kept her eyes averted as she set three drinks on the table and then spun around.

Walter jumped to his feet and followed. She stopped at the bar to refill her tray, and he stepped up beside her.

"What are you doing here?" He kept his voice low to not draw attention.

"Getting more drinks." She set drinks of rotgut on her tray.

He firmly but gently turned her to face him. "I mean, what are you doing here? Working at CB's?"

Her eyes snapped as she stepped back. "We can't all start at the top, but we still gotta start or we won't get anywhere."

"What? This isn't a start. It's a dead end." He

meant that literally and pulled out his pocketbook. "If you need money for the train ride, I'll give it to you. Right now." He held out several bills. "Take it. Go back to Nebraska."

She glanced around as if making sure no one was looking. He hoped that meant she'd finally come to her senses.

Settling her gaze on him, she asked, "What's in that noggin' of yours? Nothing? I don't want your money, and I ain't—am not going back to Nebraska." She pulled several bills out from beneath an ashtray on her tray and handed them to the bartender.

Walter knew how these joints worked. The girls had to pay for the drinks on their trays, and then collect the money from the customers. Any spilled drinks or unpaid ones came out of their pockets, not the owners'. "You aren't going to make enough money here—"

"Beat it," she whispered fiercely. "And mind your own beeswax while you're at it!" She spun in the other direction and marched off.

With a cigarette hanging out of the corner of his mouth, the bartender leaned across the bar. "That dame's a closed bank, forget her. We got ones that are more…friendly. For a couple of clams, I'll send one to your table."

"No, thanks." Walter walked back to his table

and positioned his chair so he could keep an eye on the room. On her.

"You know that doll?" Sam asked, raising an eyebrow.

"Do you?" Walter asked instead of answering.

"Never saw her before." Sam looked at Tony. "You?"

Tony shook his head. "No, but Mel has a longer assembly line of girls than Ford does cars."

Which was exactly why *she* shouldn't be here. She couldn't possibly know the dangers of working here. Walter's back teeth clamped tight. If she was working here, she was living here. Upstairs. His blood ran cold at that thought.

Sam started explaining the reason he'd called. He and Tony wanted to put on a boxing exhibition show and needed advice on the legal side of things. Walter listened, and answered their questions, and kept one eye on the woman the entire time. He didn't even know her name, so in his mind, started calling her Blondie.

She was still working the room, serving drinks, when Sam and Tony must have had all the information they needed from him, and called it a night. He bade them goodbye and stayed at the table, still keeping an eye on Blondie. Other girls had brought their table the drinks Sam and Tony had consumed. He was still nursing the only one she'd brought him. The ice had long ago melted.

He didn't care. He wasn't drinking it. Just using the glass as something to twirl between his fingers.

There were no laws governing speakeasies; most were open twenty-four hours, and it was up to the owners what sort of hours the workers put in. Walter glanced at his wristwatch. Almost two-thirty in the morning. He hadn't stayed up this late in years, but would sit right here until her shift ended.

A large portion of the patrons had long ago left. Some with cigarette girls on their arms as they walked out the doors; a few left in stumbling, ossified stupors, and others, like Sam and Tony, left alone, had simply been there to enjoy the nightlife but had jobs to go to in the morning.

So did he. Had to be at the courthouse by eight.

The room was almost empty by the time she made her way toward the bar with a full tray of drinks still strapped around her neck. He knew how that would play out. That the drinks would be dumped, and she'd be out the money for them. He stood and sidestepped, cutting her off before she made it to the bar.

"I'll buy those." He laid a bill on her tray, one that would pay for twice that many drinks.

Exhaustion showed on her face. He could understand why. She'd not only delivered drinks all night, she'd spent a fair share of time declining offers of more. More than once he'd wanted to grab her and haul her out of the door. The only thing that had stopped him was her. She'd handled herself well. That left him in a quandary. If he did haul her out of here and she came back, she'd get the wrath of Mel, the owner. If he didn't, there would soon be a man she couldn't fend off. Or worse.

"No." She nodded toward his table. "You still have a drink, and I don't need you or anyone else doing me any favors."

"It's not a favor." He picked up a drink and downed it, nearly choking at the rotgut whiskey. If it hadn't been so watered down, he wouldn't have been able to swallow it. "I'm thirsty," he said despite his burning throat.

"You're…" She shook her head.

She thought he was crazy. He might be. "I'm Walter Russell," he said. "Who are you?"

She huffed out a tired-sounding sigh. "It doesn't matter. Take your money and leave."

He took another drink off her tray. "Not until you tell me your name."

She glanced around and then sidestepped to the table he'd sat at all night. There, she lifted the final four drinks off her tray and set them on the table. Tucking his bill beneath her ashtray, she nodded. "Enjoy your drinks, Mr. Russell."

Walter grasped her arm, but the bartender, with

yet another cigarette hanging out of his mouth, cleared his throat. The glare the man gave Walter said he'd be in charge of anything that happened from here on out.

That could include her leaving with him, for a price, Walter understood that. He also understood it wouldn't be her choice. But she'd be expected to do whatever he wanted or she'd lose her job.

She, however, probably did not understand that.

Walter let that settle for a moment before he set the drink in his hand on the table and then pulled a calling card out of his suit pocket and laid it on her tray. He gave her and the bartender a nod before he turned about and left.

Every step got harder and harder to take, and by the time he was at the door, he was ripped right down the middle. She wasn't his problem, but she had no idea what she'd gotten herself into.

He did, and would do something about it.

## Chapter Three

Shirley lay on the lumpy cot in the room she shared with six other cigarette girls and stared at the calling card. It was shiny, like the pages of a magazine, but harder, stiff and small, just a few inches long and a couple inches wide. And the writing on it was gold.

Gold.

She'd never seen a calling card before, but had heard about them. The other girls had said she better not let Mel learn about it. He was the owner of CB's and would be mad because when a man gives you a calling card, he wants to see you outside of the basement.

That wasn't going to happen. She didn't want to see Walter Russell again. Not inside or outside of the basement.

Under his name it said *The Russell Firm*. She wasn't sure what that meant, but there was also an address and a phone number on the card. A phone was very expensive. Not even the Swaggerts could afford one. They sure as heck didn't have calling cards, either.

One of the other girls, Alice, rolled over, and Shirley quickly tucked the card beneath the one and only cover on the bed, a scratchy wool blanket.

Alice didn't open her eyes, but she did pull her blanket over her head to block the light shining in through the window.

It was the middle of the night, but the city, so full of lights, was never dark. The building next door had a big cigarette billboard on top of it, and the lights on the billboard lit up the room all night as brightly as the sun did all day.

Alice had been tricked into working at Cartwright's, too; so had Rita and all the other girls sleeping on the cots.

Shirley pulled her arm out from under the blanket and stared at the calling card again. It was him. The same man who'd almost run her over. She'd felt as if he had run her over tonight when she'd recognized him sitting at the table with a man that was as skinny as a match. The second man at the table not only had hair the color of a carrot, but he looked like one, too. A big one. Wide at the top and skinny on the bottom.

Walter wasn't skinny or fat. Just somewhere right smack in the middle. He was nicer to look at than the other two, too. Actually, he was nicer to look at than any other man in the room. Any other man she'd met since arriving in California. Mayhap in her whole life.

His eyes. There was something about them that made it hard to look away from him. It was as if they were sad or lonely. No—lost. That's what they looked like. Like he was lost.

She felt that way herself. Lost. With nowhere to go. All the fancy talking Roy Harrison had done turned out to be nothing but baloney. He'd hoodwinked her, that's what he'd done. It hadn't taken long to figure that out, but it had been too late.

Oh, he'd gotten her an audition where she'd sung her heart out, and had jumped with joy when she'd been given the job. Roy had even given her a fancy dress to wear and had shown her an apartment. Not this one. That one had been a real apartment. With nice furniture and a bathroom complete with tub, right next to the kitchen with a stove and refrigerator. This one, the one she was staying in, only had two rooms, and both of those rooms had nothing but cots in them. This apartment dang near packed in as many people as the Swaggerts' bunkhouse had during harvest time.

After all that, him showing her that apartment, giving her that dress and then the audition where she'd sung her heart out, Roy had left. She'd spent that first night in that fancy apartment, dreaming about the days to come. Believing her dream had finally come true, until morning.

That's when she'd met Stella.

Stella took away the dress, gave her the skimpy red dress and hideous white tray, showed her this apartment and then led her downstairs to work.

Shirley wasn't about to schlep drinks, and had said so. Also said she was here to sing, and had headed for the door.

Stella said she could leave right after paying the breach of contract amount.

Shirley's stomach had sunk all over again. She had signed a contract, and evidently hadn't read it closely enough because she hadn't known about a breach of contract, nor had she known the amount of money that had been listed. That any amount had been listed. She'd had nowhere near that amount in her purse. Not then or now. Weeks later.

Her options had been to work it off or go to jail. Jail.

So here she was, working off a debt that grew rather than shrank each day.

Some of the other girls said she had a good chance of being discovered here. Rita claimed lots of famous people came to the basement. Stars and producers, radio jockeys and singers. She took that to heart the first night, but soon thereafter figured out no one visiting the basement was looking for a singer.

The only person who had discovered her was Walter Russell.

The one person she wished hadn't seen her. He'd been right about too many things, and she didn't want him to be right about one more. He'd told her to go home, but she didn't have a home to go to. Hadn't for years.

The wage she made schlepping drinks was less than the Swaggerts had paid her. It had taken her four years to save enough to leave there, and at the rate she was going right now, it was going to take that long to pay off CB's.

Not only did she owe for the dress and the night staying in that fancy apartment, with a real bed and sheets, she had to pay for her lodging in this room. And the meals they fed her. At first, she'd decided she just wouldn't eat, until she was told she had to pay for the food whether she ate it or not.

The air in her lungs grew so heavy she had to push it out, but she refused to let the sting in her eyes get to her. She would not cry. Would not. She'd told Walter that not everyone could start at the top, but that they had to start. That's what she'd told herself, too. She had managed to make it to California, and somehow, she would become a singer. Make a life for herself, one where she didn't have to answer to anyone.

It would just take a little longer than she'd first thought.

Nothing was going to change her mind about that.

She took a final look at the calling card and then tucked it beneath her pillow.

That was the good thing about dreams. No one could take them away. She'd lost everything else. Her family. Her home. But not her dream. Not her hope.

No one could take that away from her.


Shirley was at work by ten the next morning. Schlepping drinks. She figured that by working all day and night, she'd make money faster, pay off her debt and get out of Cartwright's.

The morning and afternoon crowds were nothing like the evening and night ones, but she worked them because every penny counted. Every single cent was one step closer to getting out of here. She hadn't felt this trapped at the Swaggerts'. She may have thought she'd waited on them hand and foot, but it hadn't been anything like this. Here, she didn't have any sort of a life of her own. At times, like now, when her feet were hurting and disgust rolled in her stomach, she felt her determination slipping, but that couldn't happen. She couldn't give up on herself. She was all she had. That had been easier to accept four years ago, because she'd had hope then. Now, she had to dig deep to find that. Partially because of the other girls—those who had been here for months. They were so downtrodden, so lifeless, as if they'd completely given up. Given in to Mel and his contracts.

She wouldn't do that. Give in.

If she'd been on the other side of this tray, the place might be considered fun. Besides the piano player, two men played trumpets, and another pounded a huge drum, filling the room with jazz music that had women in bright-colored dresses and men wearing striped shirts and bow ties dancing, laughing and carrying on. It was a sight to see. The feathered headbands, strings of pearls and fancy hats were like the ones she'd seen in magazines back in Nebraska. Like the ones she wanted to wear. She would. Someday. Although the people appeared friendly—it was only to each other. She'd quickly learned very few wanted to know anything more than what was on her tray, and the number of them that tried to stiff her for their drinks was more than not.

She wasn't about to take that. Not from anyone.

While things were slow during the late afternoon, she took her break, ate a bowl of chili that was sure to leave her with a good bout of heartburn and then hooked her tray over her neck and headed back into the main room of the speakeasy.

The crowd had grown in her absence, and she hurried to fill her tray with drinks and get them sold. It hadn't taken her long to figure out who bought the more expensive drinks, and though they cost her more, too, those buying the higher priced drinks didn't try to short her.

She was filling her tray for the third time in less than ten minutes when she saw him.

Him.

Walter Russell.

He was as pesky as a fly that kept landing on a person's nose in the middle of the night. She purposefully didn't stop by his table, but kept an eye on him. He may not look it, but he was slippery. Had to be up to no good. Why else would he be here? Watching her.

Was he another Roy Harrison? Or Olin Swaggert and his fast-talking lawyer? Or Mel Cartwright with his contract? Tricksters, liars and cheats. That's what they'd been. He could be, too. Most likely was. Two other men, not the same ones from last night, were at his table. All three of them laughing.

At what? Her?

That possibility nagged at her for the next few hours, and grated at her nerves like a squeaky hinge. Not even having people fill the joint wall to wall helped. She knew he was still here. Knew exactly where he was sitting.

The room was in full swing, people dancing, laughing, buying drinks and having the times of their lives. She wasn't. Her feet were aching from the shoes she had to wear. White, with tall heels, and at least one size too small. It would be hours before she could take them off, so she forced herself not to think about them and kept passing out drinks, all the while keeping an eye on Walter.

A pretty young woman with hair as red as her lipstick and wearing a white-and-red polka-dot dress had been talking with him a short time ago, but was nowhere in sight now.

Shirley scanned the room for the red-haired woman as she made her way toward the end of the long wooden bar to refill her tray when, suddenly, he was at her side.

Startled, she jolted sideways.

He grasped her waist and pulled her against his side. "Stay close to me."

His aftershave was like a breath of fresh air. For weeks all she'd smelled was cigarette smoke and whiskey. He smelled so fresh and clean all she wanted to do was close her eyes and breathe. Just breathe.

She stopped herself before that happened and twisted so her cheek was no longer up against his shoulder. "My tray is empty. I—"

"Doesn't matter." He started walking, forcing her to walk with him. "You're leaving."

"Leave? I can't—" Her words were cut short by a high-pitched siren. It was so loud she couldn't hear what he said.

He grabbed the strap of her tray and pulled it over her head.

She was reaching to grab it when pandemonium hit. Chairs toppled and people started running, pushing and shoving others in their way.

Shocked, frozen, Shirley didn't know what to do. Didn't know what was happening.

Walter pushed her out of the way as a table toppled in the wake of two huge men. She stumbled backward, up against the wall. Sirens still filled the air, along with screams and shouts. "What's happening?"

Walter grasped her face with both hands. His nose was inches from hers, the length of his body pressed tight against hers.

"I'll get you out of here, Blondie, don't worry."

She heard him, but didn't. Her heart was pounding too hard, echoing in her ears. The heat of his palms, the pressure of his body, his fresh, clean scent, had her mind swirling. She swallowed, tried to breathe, but couldn't. His lips were too close to hers. So close they were breathing the same air. A heavy, tingling warmth filled her as she reached up and wrapped her fingers around his arms.

He was so handsome, so—

The haze around her shattered. The roar of the panicking crowd once again filled her ears. Someone had bumped into them and fallen. Recognizing the black curls, Shirley grabbed the arm of the cigarette girl and helped Walter lift her off the floor before she got trampled.

"The bulls are outside!" Alice shouted.

"Bulls?" Shirley asked. "Cattle? A stampede?"

"No! Police!" Alice shouted. "We have to run or be arrested!"

Shirley's heart leaped into her throat. There were too many people to run. To get anywhere.

Alice grabbed her arm. "This way!"

Walter grabbed her other arm. "No! This way."

"Only the customers can go out through the kitchen," Alice said. "We have to go out through the back and get upstairs before the bulls see us."

"No," Walter said. "We have to go this way."

"No! The bulls gotta arrest someone!" Alice shouted. "That will be anyone dressed like us going that way!"

Shirley felt as if she was being torn in two with the way they each tugged on her arm.

"Trust me," Walter said. "This way."

Shirley couldn't say why, but she pulled her

arm out of Alice's hold and then grabbed the woman's hand. "This way!"

"Hurry," Walter said, pulling her forward.

"We are hurrying," she said, pulling Alice behind her. "We just ain't getting nowhere!"

"We will!"

She hoped he was right. For all their sakes.

The next thing she knew, they were in the men's restroom. Others were in there, too, rushing through another door on the far wall. Walter hurried them through that door, then up a flight of stairs that led outside. To the side of the building.

"Rosie!" he shouted. "Take these two with you!"

The woman in the red-and-white polka-dot dress was climbing in a car, and waved frantically at them. "Hurry! Hurry!"

Sirens filled the air. Walter pushed her forward. "Go. Run."

"What about you?"

"I'll be fine."

"Come on, Shirley! Run," Alice said, pulling her toward the car. "Run."

Shirley ran, and as she climbed in the car, she twisted, scanning the crowd. He was gone. Gone. She sat down, and was shutting the door, while still searching the crowd, when she noticed Rita, who was a foot taller than even some of the men, running out of the door along with others.

"Rita!" Shirley shouted out the window. "Here!"

As Rita elbowed her way through the crowd and ran toward them, Shirley told the redheaded woman, "We can't leave her behind. Just can't."

Rita climbed in the back seat with her and Alice and then the redheaded woman leaped in the front seat and closed the door. The driver, another woman, shouted, "Duck down. Don't let anyone see you. All of you!"

They all complied, bending over and putting their head between their knees. The sirens were louder and the shine of flashing red lights filled the car as they drove away.

Walter watched the car drive away. That hadn't been part of his plan. Running into Rosie, a waitress from Julia's café, had been pure luck, and something that had worked out perfectly.

He walked to his car and climbed in, waiting as the police barreled down on the Cartwright building. The raid wasn't for the speakeasy; it was for the secretive opium room on the third floor. He'd heard rumors about that room, and had spent some time investigating it this morning, learning they weren't just rumors. This afternoon, he'd contacted a city council member. One he knew disliked the drug dens as much as he did.

Busts of joints like that happened daily. Speakeasies were overlooked for the most part, unless someone got riled or annoyed, someone with power. But very few agreed with the operating of opium dens. Other than those who were operating them, and those they dragged down into the bowels of hell with them.

Anger filled him, came from nowhere, as it did sometimes. Lucy had been dragged down into that world. Where very little mattered other than the next high. It's what had killed her in the end.

He glanced at the building again, at the police cars with red lights flashing. Whether Blondie appreciated it or not, he wasn't going to let what happened to Lucy happen to her.

He'd investigated her, too, earlier, learned her name was Shirley, but he still thought of her as Blondie. His plan had been to be at CB's when the raid happened and pull her aside. Show her the dangers she was in by working in the basement and then convince her to get on the next train heading east.

That would happen—he'd get her on a train— but sending her home with Rosie was better than what he'd planned. Mainly because it meant he hadn't had to haul her out of the basement kicking and screaming. He'd have done that. Carried her out. Had considered it when the first siren went off, before they'd gotten shoved up against the wall.

Walter took a deep breath, a struggle because

his chest was growing tight again, like it had when he'd been pressed up against her. He hadn't been that close to a woman in a long time, hadn't wanted to kiss—

He spun around, gave his head a clearing, cleansing shake.

The crowd had dispersed; the customers who'd been at CB's had driven or walked away without so much as a glance from any of the officers. The police cars were still there, lights flashing. He doubted the real people behind the opium den on the third floor would be arrested. Those there, smoking, hooked on the euphoric effects that made them forget their real lives, would have their wrists slapped, and by this time next week, they'd have already found another place. He'd seen it often enough and wished it was different. Wished he could have done something, anything, that might have saved Lucy.

She hadn't wanted to be saved, just like she hadn't wanted him in her life. Blondie didn't, either, but this time he was going to fight harder. Maybe, just maybe, if he could save her, the demons of regret that lived inside him would go find someone else to haunt.

Demons. He had enough of them. Not only from Lucy, but from Theodore. There, too, he hadn't done enough. Hadn't acted quickly enough.

That wasn't going to happen this time.

He started his car and pulled into the street, wondering if he should drive out to Julia's Diner, make sure that was where Blondie was at, but instantly knew that would be a bad idea. He'd be better off going there tomorrow morning, after she'd had a chance to get to know a couple of good people. So far, she'd only met the bad Los Angeles had to offer. There were good folks here, too. Julia Shaw was one of them. She'd taken in plenty of women who had arrived in town with nothing more than the clothes on their backs and stars in their eyes. She'd fed them, clothed them, given them a job and a place to live, and then, once they'd gotten their heads on straight, she'd let them go back out into the world. No longer wearing rose-colored glasses.

Years ago, Julia had come to him, asked him to look into how the Broadbent brothers had paid little more than pennies on the dollar for her family's property. The transaction hadn't been illegal, so all he'd been able to do was secure the last twenty acres for her.

Julia had understood, and held on to her small chunk of land with an iron fist. She was making it pay off for her. Her café was one of the most popular places to eat in the north end of the city.

He drove home, and after parking the car in the garage and closing the door, he walked into the dark and quiet house.

Mrs. McCaffrey had long ago gone to bed.

Once again, his long-lost dream of having a family fill the house weighed heavy on his shoulders.

He was in the hallway when the phone rang. He picked up the pace, hurried into his office and answered it on the fourth ring. He hoped not, but there was a chance one of his clients had been at CB's and needed his services.

"Walter here," he said into the speaker while still lifting the earpiece to the side of his head.

"It's Dean Smith."

Walter sat down, ready to listen to whatever the city council member had to say.

"Mel Cartwright just called me," Dean said. "He wants me to investigate who called in the raid on his joint tonight."

Not surprised, Walter asked, "What did you tell him?"

"That I didn't know anything about a raid on his place, but that I'd look into it tomorrow morning. Mel claims he didn't know anything about a dope den upstairs, that he doesn't regulate his renters. He's also claiming that some waitress from Julia's Diner was seen making a phone call and he's pretty convinced she's the one who called in the bulls."

Walter's heart rate increased. The moment he'd recognized Rosie, he'd pulled her aside and told her that she didn't want to be at the basement tonight and to leave. Smart, Rosie had kept her nose clean since coming to town, knowing if she didn't, she'd never get ahead. He made a point to breathe normally while speaking into the phone, "Really?"

"Yes," Dean said. "Mel's also looking for three of his cigarette girls. The rest are accounted for. He's mad about those girls missing. He's already reopened the doors and needs them on the floor."

Walter's mind went down another route. "Where does Mel recruit those girls from?" His clients were of a more elite level than those Mel recruited so he truly had no idea how women got trapped into working at CB's.

"Scouts. He has men who watch for those new to town and offers them jobs, a place to live, clothes, all the things they need. There's nothing illegal about it."

Walter's hackles raised. "Other than they are being scammed. The wages Mel pays them isn't enough to pay the rent he charges for them to live there."

"I know, but if we start chasing down every cheat in the city, we won't have time to take care of any real business." Dean let out a sigh. "Would you mind following up on that waitress for me? Under the table?"

Nearly everything in Hollywood was under

the table, and Walter wondered if he was digging himself a hole by getting involved in all this. He *had* gotten himself involved—he'd actually initiated it, so he didn't have much choice. "Sure. I'll check into it. I'll call you tomorrow."

"You might want to check into it tonight," Dean said. "Mel asked me to call the precinct and send a car over to the café where that gal works. I'll try to hold that off until morning, but will have to send cars over then for sure."

"I'll go check." Walter stood. "Right now. There's no reason to involve anyone else."

"I agree, but I don't believe I'm the only person Mel has called tonight."

"I'll talk to you later," Walter said, already lowering the earpiece from the side of his face. Julia had a phone at the diner, so he jiggled the metal hanger until an operator picked up.

"Connect me to Julia's Diner, please."

He tapped a toe, and then paced the short distance the cord connected to the bottom of the tall mouthpiece would allow. *Come on. Answer.*

"No one is answering, sir," the operator said.

"All right. Thank you." He set the phone down and hung up the earpiece at the same time, then jogged out of the room. Once in the hallway, he ran. Not only could Julia and Rosie end up in trouble, Blondie would be taken back to CB's.

He kept an eye out for police cars as he drove

to the diner, half expecting them to fly by him at any time. They wouldn't really fly by the Packard. He had it rolling at top speed.

Julia's place was across the street from Star's Studio. Jack McCarney had been a client of his for years. The studio owner was also a good friend. A lot of the girls Julia took in had arrived at her diner looking for Jack, hoping he'd make a star out of them.

Walter pulled the roadster into the driveway to Julia's home, set back a short distance from the diner, and cut the engine.

Julia, a pretty black-haired woman, walked out of her front door while he was climbing out of his car. They met on the walkway to her house.

"Evening, Walter," she said. "Rosie said if it had been anyone but you who told her to leave, she would never have called me to come get her."

"I'm glad she listened," he said. "A drug den was busted in an apartment above CB's."

Julia nodded, and he also saw the one thing he didn't want to see. Sympathy. Though it had been four years ago, Lucy's death had been the talk of the town for months, and no one believed she'd died in the car where her body had been found. Halfway down a cliff.

"Are they here?" he asked. "Rosie and the other girls who got in your car?"

She glanced past him, toward the road on the

other side of the grove of trees that kept her house somewhat secluded. "Why?"

"Because Mel's looking for them."

"I figured as much. He guards those girls closer than prisoners in order to keep them working for him." Her dark eyes narrowed in question as she asked, "Why are you involved in this?"

It was out of the ordinary. After spending years dealing with Lucy and her addictions, he'd kept himself separated from any of the nightlife and underworld of Los Angeles. Keeping his reasons to himself, he shrugged. "Wrong place at the wrong time."

"Or the right place at the right time," Julia said. "You know how those raids go. They have to arrest someone. Find a patsy to take the blame. Pay the price. Rosie could be spending the night in the hoosegow rather than sleeping in her own bed tonight."

"That's why I'm here, Julia." He shook his head. "Someone saw Rosie call you, and they're saying she's the one that called the police."

Julia shook her head and then smiled. "And you're here to defend her. That's awfully kind of you, Walter. She'll appreciate that." Her brows tugged together in a frown. "I didn't think you took criminal cases. Thought you specialize in business deals."

A hint of guilt struck him because he hadn't

considered Rosie might need an attorney. But that gave him the perfect reason for being here. "I don't want to see anyone railroaded. I'll represent Rosie and all three of those other women." He looked at her house. "They are all here, aren't they?"

Julia never blinked an eye as she said, "No."

# Chapter Four

Shirley tugged the blanket tighter around her shoulders as she leaned back against the side of the cabin and watched the sun rise. It was almost as if she wasn't really watching it, but like someone else was, someone using her body. Someone who was so relieved to wake up this morning and not have to go downstairs and schlep drinks all day that they didn't really care what that truly meant.

Instead, they were focused on how orange the sky was, how the big yellow ball barely peeking up over the horizon made those tall palm trees look black. They were unique trees. Unlike any she'd ever seen. There were other trees around the small cabin. Pines and hardwoods that dried out once cut and split and made good, hot fires. Pine was better for starting fires. Everyone knew that.

There wasn't a cloud in that big orange sky and she wondered what that meant out here. A red sky in the morning back home meant a weather change. She wasn't sure if red and orange were interchangeable out here or not. Nothing she'd thought she'd known about California had been true as of yet.

She hadn't been here all that long, but had to admit, she was mighty disappointed by it so far.

Mighty disappointed.

That other person inside her, the one who'd been focused on watching the sun rise, slowly slipped away and Shirley let out a long sigh. The gal who had driven the car last night, Julia, had sent them all out here to this little cabin. Rita and Alice, as well as redheaded Rosie, were inside. Sleeping.

Julia had said they'd have to stay out here for a couple of days until things quieted down. Alice and Rita had readily agreed to stay right here, in this cabin, for as long as it took for Cartwright's to hire new girls and forget all about them.

She hadn't. That couldn't happen. She not only owed Cartwright's money, and therefore had to go back to work there as soon as possible, that was where her belongings were.

It wasn't much. A suitcase of clothes that could be replaced easily enough, and a pair of shoes that didn't hurt her feet, but they were hers. The picture of her mother was also in that suitcase as was her grandma's Bible. Those two things couldn't be replaced. It was all she had left of her family, besides her dream. Her mother's dream.

Working at CB's wasn't ideal, or what she wanted, but neither had working for Olin Swaggert been, but she'd done it and then moved on, having fulfilled her obligation. That's why Olin got the farm, because Pappy had owed him money. That wasn't going to happen to her; she wouldn't owe anyone for anything. Yet, she did. She owed Mel Cartwright, and now Julia, and, heaven forbid, Walter Russell for making sure she didn't get arrested last night.

The sun was completely up now and all that orange was giving way for a bright blue to take over. There still weren't any clouds, but those big awkward-looking palm trees no longer looked black. Their huge, oddly shaped leaves were green and the thin bark on the trunks was a gray-brown. The other trees were green; so was the grass and the vegetables growing in the big fenced-in garden. It was even bigger than the garden she'd taken care of back at the Swaggerts'.

She didn't think she'd ever miss weeding a garden, but gal-darn it, if there wasn't a yearning inside her to open the gate and start plucking out weeds.

Rising up, she folded the blanket and left it lying on the porch. Then, wearing the cigarette-girl getup and no shoes since hers were inside and she didn't want to wake anyone, she walked down the two short steps and made her way over to the garden.

She'd plucked every weed out of two rows when sirens echoed through the quiet of the morning. Her heart rose into her throat as a thousand thoughts fought to get her to concentrate on specific ones first. Everything from being arrested, to being taken back to CB's, to wondering how far she could run with no shoes, and if there were any sandburs that she'd later have to dig out of her feet.

It had been dark last night, so she wasn't certain how far they'd walked from Julia's house to this cabin in the woods. No more than half a mile, she'd guess. It wouldn't take the police long to get here. Letting out a heavy sigh, she walked back to the garden gate, made sure to secure the latch behind her and then made her way to the house to get her shoes. Too small or not, she needed them.

The other girls were still sleeping and she questioned whether she should wake them or not, but ultimately decided they'd get woken up soon enough. Quietly, she carried her shoes back outside to wait on the front porch.

At least an hour had to have passed while she sat there, wondering if she should make her way back to Julia's so the police didn't have to trek through the woods, or if she should finish weeding the garden while waiting on them. Walter kept filtering into her mind, too, especially how wonderful he had smelled last night, but she squelched those thoughts. She had enough to worry about.

She finally decided there was no sense putting off the inevitable and chose to trek through the woods. It wasn't that far, and if not for the stupid shoes on her feet, she would have made it in less time. Things always looked different in the daylight, and she took a moment to ponder the two-story house before she fully stepped out of the woods. Charming with its gray siding and yellow trim, it was the kind of house that would be nice to call home. Someday when her singing profited enough money, she might just have to buy a house like that.

Beyond a grove of trees, which to her way of thinking were more like bushes that nearly encircled the house, was the diner. A long building painted bright red with white trim. Folks out here must like red. The diner where she'd met Roy Harrison had been red and white, too.

She shifted her gaze. From where she stood, she couldn't see any police cars.

She'd heard sirens, that was for darn sure. Maybe they hadn't been coming for her. Either way, she had to figure out a way to get back to CB's. She didn't want to go back, but she had to. Whether she'd slept there or not, she'd be charged for lodging, just like the meals. Working there was her only choice. A person couldn't just run away from their debts. Life didn't work that way.

With her eyes peeled for any spot where someone might hide, in case those police were sneaky buzzards, she stepped out of the woods and slowly made her way to the house. No one popped out from behind the corners of the house or the bushes. That eased the way her nerves were making her want to jump right out of her skin, but it didn't do much for the way her stomach had sunk clear to her knees.

Her first weeks in California sure hadn't panned out to be what she'd imagined.

She climbed the steps to the house and knocked on the door. When no one answered, she turned the knob and stuck her head inside. "Hello? Any-one home?"

Silence was her answer. She closed the door, walked down the steps and took the well-worn pathway through the trees to the back side of the diner. The path ended at the back door. People were certainly inside. She could hear all sorts of chatter, so she knocked once, and then pushed open the door.

"Hello?"

Julia didn't look all that different this morning; she was wearing a bright pink dress covered with a white apron, and standing near the stove.

"Shirley, right?"

Shirley nodded.

"Good morning," Julia greeted. "I have to get these orders out, then I'll fill you in on what's happening. I'm sure you want to know."

"I sure do," Shirley answered, walking into the kitchen and closing the door behind her. The room was big, and unlike the kitchen at CB's, this one was neat and clean. Sparkling clean. "Anything I can do to help?"

"I'm a little shorthanded right now, with Rosie being out at the cabin." Julia flipped a big slice of ham onto a plate and then two eggs, one after the other, yolks still intact and bright yellow. "Greta's running off her feet, and the dishes are piling up."

Shirley headed toward the double sink where dirty dishes were indeed piling up. Washing a few dishes was the least she could do. "I'll get these washed up in no time."

Julia laughed, grabbing up another plate. "That's only half of them. Greta has several tables to clear off yet."

"I can do that, too," Shirley offered.

"Nope. Not dressed like that." Julia filled another plate with ham and eggs. "We don't want to set any tongues wagging." She carried three plates toward the door. One in each hand and one on her forearm. "If you don't mind doing a few dishes, I'd sincerely appreciate it. The breakfast rush will be over soon."

Like at CB's, the diner had hot water right at the sink. All she had to do was turn on the faucet. When she had time, she was going to check out how that happened. Right now, she had dishes to do. She poured in some soap flakes and then filled the sink with hot water.

The Swaggerts' house was the first place she'd seen a hot-water tank. She'd had to keep a small coal fire burning to keep it hot, and didn't see anything resembling that big old copper tank anywhere in this kitchen.

She did see where the dishes were to go once they were washed. Open shelves held plates, cups, bowls, glasses and big trays for all the silverware.

When Julia returned with her hands full of dirty dishes, she set them on the long counter next to the sink. "It'll slow down, I promise."

"I don't mind," Shirley said. "I've washed dishes my entire life."

"How long have you been in California?" Julia asked as she walked back to the stove.

"Not long," Shirley answered.

"Where you from?"

"Nebraska."

They talked as they worked. Julia cooking and carrying plates out the door, and Shirley washing and putting away dishes. Julia said she'd never been anywhere except California and Shirley explained that she came here to become a singer and how she'd got the job at CB's.

Another woman, Greta, who was a waitress, buzzed through the door with dirty dishes and back out with plates full of food at regular intervals. She was young, with dark brown hair, friendly green eyes and a giggle in her voice despite the pace at which she moved.

The pace at which they all worked slowly tapered until it nearly came to a stop. Shirley wiped down all the counters and washed out the sink while Julia scrubbed down the long flat grill on one side of the stove that also had six burners on the other side. On her last trip through the door, Greta had carried a broom and dustpan.

"You must have a lot of customers," Shirley said, hanging her wet dishcloth over the edge of the sink.

"We did today," Julia answered. "Some days are like that. Breakfast is usually our slowest meal."

"You'll do this all over again for lunch and supper?" Shirley asked. That's how it had been at the Swaggerts'. As soon as she'd finished cleaning up after one meal, it had been time to start the next one.

"Yes. We'll close for a few hours now and then again in the afternoon. If not, I'd have a room full of freeloaders sitting in the diner, doing nothing but staring across the street."

"Why? What's across the street?"

"Star's Studio." Julia opened one of the three refrigerators lined along the far wall. "I'll fry you some ham and eggs now. How do you want your eggs?"

"You just cleaned the stove," Shirley said, shaking her head. "I don't want you to get it dirty just for me."

"It'll get dirty soon enough, anyway. I'll have to make something to take up to the other girls." Julia grinned. "I told Rosie to keep all of you girls out there until I sent word that the coast was clear."

"I didn't know that," Shirley said. "The rest of them were still sleeping when I left."

"I figured as much, and needed the help, so didn't mind in the least." She slapped a slice of ham on the stove and cracked open an egg. "Over easy?"

Shirley's stomach had been growling for the last hour. The aromas had been the reason. That and she was hungry. "That will be fine. Thank you."

"Thank *you*," Julia said, cracking a second egg. "Greta and I were just about drowning when you opened the door."

"I'm glad I could help," Shirley said. Then,

because she truly wanted to know, she asked, "What's Star's Studio?"

Julia's dark brows tugged together. "It's a movie studio. Jack McCarney owns it and makes some of Hollywood's best movies over there."

"They make movies right in the middle of town?" Shirley wasn't sure where she'd expected movies to be made, but it wasn't in the middle of town. Then again, she'd never seen a movie, so knew very little about them.

"Yes, there are studios all over this part of the city." Julia flipped the ham and eggs onto a plate. "Let's go sit down."

The front room of the diner was long and narrow, with tables and chairs, and a long counter with stools. The entire room was red, black and white, including the checkered floor. They sat at a table, and Greta carried over three cups of coffee.

"So you worked at CB's," Greta said, sitting down at the table.

Shirley could only nod because she'd poked a fork full of food into her mouth. It tasted so good compared to what she ate at CB's.

"Roy Harrison con you into that?" Greta asked. "He tried that on me, but I'd heard to be wary of him and his two-bit contracts."

The food turned cold in Shirley's mouth, not so much at Greta's words, but with the disgust with which she said them.

"You don't have to worry about that any longer," Julia said. "Walter said those contracts are full of holes, as close to being illegal as they come, and that he'll be able to get you and Rita and Alice out of them."

One word stuck in Shirley's mind. "Walter?" Her mouth had gone dry. Like it or not, he was stuck in her head, and her heart fluttered at memories of last night, when she'd been pressed up against the wall, his face inches from hers.

Julia's smile grew. "Walter Russell. You should count yourself lucky he's offered to help. He's one of the best lawyers in California. If not *the* best."

This time it was Shirley's blood that went cold. "A lawyer?" His calling card, still tucked beneath her pillow at CB's, flashed in her head. "The Russell Firm is a law firm?"

Walter peeked through the window while walking toward the door of the diner. Blondie was sitting at a table with Julia and Greta. Rosie and the other two cigarette girls were nowhere in sight. He'd been here earlier this morning, convinced the police that Rosie had only called Julia for a ride last night, and that they had no legal reason to be looking for her. As far as the other girls, he'd said he was their lawyer, and that all questions toward them needed to come through him.

After the police left, he'd gone to his office,

created and made copies of three representation contracts, which were now in his satchel, and called Mel Cartwright to inform him that the three women were now ex-employees and all communications needed to go through him. Now he just needed their signatures to make it all legal.

He wasn't too concerned about Rita and Alice, but Blondie was a different story. She hadn't believed him about jaywalking or going home, so convincing her this was the only legal way to get out of the contract she'd signed with Cartwright's wasn't going to be quick or simple. He'd done his research last night. Not only had he discovered all of the women's full names, this morning he'd been able to obtain a copy of what Cartwright had coerced girls to sign. It was more in-depth than he'd imagined. Which also made them more binding. Hence the reason very few lawyers would even listen to girls that had come to them for help once they'd realized how trapped they'd accidently become.

That didn't faze him. He'd already discovered the loopholes he needed. A part of him wondered if he'd lost his senses. Gone over the deep end. He didn't know these women. In fact, if one of them had approached him, asked him to take on a case against CB's, he'd have referred them to someone else.

He provided pro bono services on a regular

basis, but they were usually for business deals, those starting up, just getting established, or for nonprofit groups. Contracts were his specialty. He thrived on getting the best deal possible for his clients.

It didn't make a lot of sense to become involved as deeply as he had already, but he was excited about it. Blondie was the reason. She was full of spunk, but that would only get her hurt here. He had to make her see that, and get her out before it was too late.

He tapped on the window of the diner's door. Julia rose from her chair to open the door, but it was Blondie's reaction that made him wonder all over again exactly what the hell he was doing. Her blue eyes shot daggers at him. He sucked in air. Helping someone who didn't want help was hell. Plain and simple. But he didn't need another Theodore or Lucy on his conscience.

"Hello, Walter," Julia greeted with a smile that didn't quite hide the apprehension in her eyes. She closed the door after he stepped into the diner. "The other girls are up at the cabin, but Shirley is here. The two of you can talk while Greta and I take some food to the others." She glanced between him and Shirley. "I told them to stay put until I come get them."

He caught the full understanding of that.

Blondie didn't listen to anyone. "All right," he said, walking toward the table where she sat.

Blondie shot to her feet. "No, it ain't all right. I ain't got noth—" She drew in a deep breath and huffed it out. "I don't have anything to say to you." She pointed at him and then herself. "We don't have anything to talk about."

It took effort to keep a grin at bay at how she corrected her speech. He waited as Julia and Greta cleared the dishes from the table and walked into the kitchen. "We don't?"

She crossed her arms, but bowed her head slightly. "Well, it was nice of you to keep us from getting arrested, so thank you."

He was a bit taken aback by her statement. Should be, because she was full of surprises. "I'm glad you appreciated that, Miss Burnette." He set his satchel on the table. "I believe it will behoove you to listen to what I have to say about that."

"*Be* what me?"

"It would be appropriate and to your benefit to listen to me." He pulled out a chair. "Please sit down."

"No, I don't need to sit down. I don't have time to see how many big words you can throw at me. I have a job I have to get back to."

Walter opened his satchel and chose his words carefully. "That's why I'm here. In your best interest, Miss Burnette. To assist you and the other girls in being released from your contract with Cartwright's."

Her lips were pursed, her eyes glaring straight at him, and once again, he found it difficult not to smile. She was a good-looking dame. Her short blond hair was a mass of curls this morning, and the flashy red dress, with layers of fringes from her shoulders to her knees, looked more fetching here than it had back at the speakeasy. Last night, while looking into those big blue eyes, while feeling the softness of her skin with his palms, he'd considered hauling her home, locking her up inside his house. That was also when he'd considered kissing her. Alice had gotten shoved up against him then, and it knocked some sense into him. Blondie's comment about cattle, a stampede, confirmed his initial thoughts—that she only knew enough about life off the farm to get hurt.

He hadn't gotten much sleep last night. It had been a long time since a woman, or a case, had kept him up until the wee hours of the morning.

She planted her hands on her hips. "I don't like lawyers."

He sat down. "You know many of them, do you?"

"No. I don't know any, personally, and I don't want to, either."

More than willing to hear her out, he leaned back and crossed his arms. "Why?"

A frown took over her entire face. "Why, what?"

"Why don't you like lawyers?"

Anger flashed in her eyes as her shoulders stiffened. "'Cause they're liars and cheats. Cheat people right out of their property. That's what they do. Without blinking an eye."

He was good at reading people, and knew exactly what had happened to her. "You lost your farm."

Her shoulders slumped and her face emitted a sadness that stabbed his chest like a knife. "Weren't mine. Was my grandpappy's." She plopped into the chair as if all the life had just leaked out of her. "He was barely cold when the Swaggerts rolled in, claiming it all. Their lawyer was with them. So was the sheriff."

Leaning forward, he set his hands on the table. This could be it. A way for him to get her back to Nebraska. "Would you like me to check into it for you? See if there is any way for you to get it back?"

She blinked several times and sniffed. "You can't do that. It was pert near five years ago."

"If there was something illegal about it, it won't matter if it was five years ago or yesterday." A sense of reason told him not to get her hopes up. "I can't practice law in Nebraska, but I can investigate the case, and hire a lawyer who could represent your case."

She sat quiet for so long he wondered what filled her thoughts, her mind. Going home? He should hope that was exactly what she was thinking about. And told himself exactly that.

"Why would you do that?" she asked. "I don't have any money to pay you. And I know lawyers cost lots of money. The sheriff told me so when the Swaggerts were boxing up anything worth a dime."

He shrugged, but then a desire to tell the absolute truth struck. A truth he'd nearly forgotten about. "I was cheated out of property, too. I was too young to do anything about it. Only ten. An early spring storm had hit, the river flooded. A flash flood. It hit so fast there wasn't anything we could do. Anything anyone could do. My parents drowned. So did my younger brother, Owen." It had been years since the images in his mind had been this clear. His bones even remembered how cold it had been. "I'd caught ahold of a tree. Climbed to the top and hung on. That's where they found me. Two days later."

"You stayed in a tree for two days?"

"Yes. And nights." An age-old anxiety, one he'd long ago buried, attempted to rise up. He fiddled with the clasp on his satchel to keep himself grounded. He'd learned how to do that, how to distract his thoughts from overtaking him at the orphanage. "There wasn't anyone left. Besides me. So I became a ward of the state. Sent to an orphanage, and the state got the farm."

"There wasn't anything you could do?"

"No, there wasn't."

She had both elbows on the table, and her chin rested on her clasped palms. "Is that why you became a lawyer? To get your land back?"

"No. It may have been the catalyst, though." He paused, then changed his word. "The basis of the reason, but I've never attempted to do anything about the past, about the farm." A part of him wanted to tell her about Theodore, and Arthur Marlow. He hadn't told anyone about that, about how and why he'd become a lawyer. Arthur had insisted they hadn't failed Theodore, but Walter still got a knot in his stomach when he thought about Theodore, and how that had ended.

"Why not?" she asked.

He countered by asking, "Why?" Then shrugged. "There's no reason. Whoever owns it now had nothing to do with it back then."

"Are you sure?"

"I've never checked to see who owns it." He released the clasp. "Never felt a need."

"Was your farm around here?"

Walter wasn't sure why, but he didn't want her

to know that had all happened in Nebraska. Her Nebraska. That was a connection he didn't need. "No. It was miles and miles from here." No one in California knew about his past. About the orphanage, about the farm. Arthur had, but he'd died several years ago, after mentoring him to become the lawyer he was today. He hadn't even told Lucy, and there had been no reason for him to tell Blondie. Yet, he had. However, there was no reason to continue talking about it. He pulled the papers out of his satchel. "I've drawn up some papers I'd like to go over with you."

She sat back in her chair and shook her head. "I don't want to know what's on your papers. I still don't like lawyers."

"You don't have to like lawyers." He separated the top two papers and pushed one to her side of the table. "Let me ask you this. Do you like working at Cartwright's? Want to continue working there, giving them every penny you make while increasing the debt you owe them?"

# Chapter Five

Shirley didn't like what was happening inside her mind. Doubt. She never doubted herself. Or her decisions. And shouldn't now. His suggestion of getting her farm back was impossible. There was nothing left of it. Besides, that wasn't her dream. It was to become a singer, and that's what she would do. Yet, that wasn't going to happen while she was stuck working at Cartwright's. It hadn't taken her but a few hours to figure that out. That's about how long it had taken her to figure out that she'd been duped, too.

That's where her doubt came in now. Wondering if Walter was lying to her. She'd only met that one lawyer in Nebraska but knew they cheated people. Not just Pappy. Lots of folks back home complained about lawyers. Pappy himself had. But Walter sure wasn't what she'd pictured a law- yer to look like. He didn't have squinty eyes, or talk in circles. He hadn't even used a bunch of big words, outside of that one about hooves.

They all had to be the same. Lawyers. Whether they looked alike or not. Maybe all lawyers in California looked like him. That's how they fooled people into trusting them. Some folks could think anyone as handsome as him wouldn't cheat them out of anything.

She'd already been cheated since arriving in California, and couldn't take the chance of that happening again. The only person she could trust was herself. No matter how good-looking some- one was, no matter how good they smelled.

Satisfied with that, she sat up straight. "It ain't—" She shook her head in a reminder to watch her words. He hadn't lied about that. Plenty of folks at Cartwright's had laughed at how she'd talked, and she'd put effort into that not happening again. "It's not so bad. Working at Cartwright's. Who knows, I might meet someone looking for a singer while working there."

"And then what? They can't hire you because of the contract you signed."

She shook her head. "As long as they pay me enough to pay off my debts, I can leave when- ever I want."

"How is anyone going to pay you for singing when you are working all the time?"

She wondered about that herself, and had asked

around. "They will give me an advance on my singing."

He nodded. "That could happen. I'd give it about a million to one odds."

"Oh, yeah? Well, you ain't heard me sing." She flinched inwardly. As flustered by herself as she was by him, she corrected, "Haven't. You haven't heard me sing."

"No, I haven't. And unfortunately, we don't have time to today, either." He laid a pen on top of the paper he'd slid to her side of the table. "I have a meeting at noon that I can't miss, and I need these papers signed before then."

"I'm not signing anything." She'd done that with Roy Harrison.

He sighed and then stuffed the papers in front of him back into his leather bag. "You can tell the others, then."

"What others?"

"Rita and Alice. My offer was to represent all three of you. Help you prove that Cartwright misrepresented what he had you sign, therefore making the contracts null and void."

She wasn't exactly sure what that all meant—her thoughts were more on Rita and Alice. They'd been at Cartwright's longer than her, and Alice had that downright worn-out look to her. "You can still help them."

He picked up the paper in front of her and put it

in his bag. "No. The deal is to represent all three of you, or none of you."

Flustered, she pointed out, "That's not very kind."

He stood. "I'm not in the business of being kind, Miss Burnette." He winked. "I'm a lawyer."

A thousand retorts flashed in her mind, of names she could call him, things she could say, but none came out. Not until he was almost at the door. She jumped to her feet. "Wait."

He turned. Looked at her expectantly.

Last night, while walking to the cabin, Alice had been so excited to be out of Cartwright's she'd cried. Had said that she would walk all the way back to Missouri before going back to that joint. "You have to help them," Shirley said.

He shook his head. "No, I don't. I don't have to do anything. I was offering my services, free of charge, but you chose not to take them."

"For myself. That doesn't have anything to do with them."

"All or none, Miss Burnette." He opened the door. "All or none."

She didn't like being pushed into a corner. Had said she'd never let it happen again. That's what had happened with the Swaggerts and at Cartwright's. That right there proved men couldn't be trusted. Not a single one of them.

He opened the door. She balled her hands into

fists, telling herself she couldn't stop him again. Couldn't trust him. Even if he had kept her from being arrested. His promises were just like the ones Roy Harrison had made. False. Empty.

A pang in her chest said some part of her didn't believe that he was anything like Roy Harrison. But he had to be. He was a lawyer. She couldn't trust a lawyer. Couldn't trust any man. Alice and Rita shouldn't, either. They'd been lied to, too, and like it or not, they were bound to CB's until they cleared their debts just like her.

She watched as he walked past the window. Debts didn't just go away. Not even a lawyer could make that happen. Someone always had to pay.

A sigh stuck in her chest. She could admire him, though. A little bit. For all he'd been through. That had taken strength and courage. Being only ten years old and stuck in a tree for two days. And nights. Then to have to go live at an orphanage. She'd heard stories about those places. Pappy used to threaten to send her to one when she misbehaved. He never would have, though. They'd both known that, but the threat alone had made her mind her p's and q's for a while.

She sure missed Pappy right now. Wondered what he'd think of Walter. What he'd think of the mess she was in.

*If a person don't like the lot they got, then they*

*gotta get about changing it. It's up to you, ain't no one gonna do it for you.*

That's what Pappy would have to say about her mess. That's what he'd always said. He'd have agreed with her about Walter, too. That she shouldn't trust a lawyer. Shouldn't trust anyone but herself. Shouldn't depend on anyone but herself.

Nothing in life was free.

Nothing.

She made her way into the kitchen, to the sink, and set about washing the dishes from her breakfast.

The back door flew open and Alice's heels nearly left skid marks on the floor as she slid to a stop. "Isn't he still here? Is it true? That Walter Russell is going to get us out of the contracts with Mel? That we won't have to schlep drinks for the rest of our lives?"

Rita flew in the door just as fast, but she didn't stop in the kitchen; her long brown hair flowed in her wake as she ran all the way to the door leading to the diner. "Where is he? Did he leave papers for us to sign? Julia said he had some. Glory be! I can't believe he's going to represent us. That's the only way we'll ever be free of Mel."

Shirley had never seen either one of them looking so happy. So excited.

"It's a miracle! That's what it is. A downright

miracle." Alice frowned as she looked through the open doorway into the empty diner. "Where is he?"

The taste of bile coated Shirley's tongue and her stomach weighed heavier than a sack of potatoes. "He had a meeting," she said, dunking the plate she'd just washed in rinse water.

"About us? When will he be back?" Rita asked. "Did he leave papers for us to sign? He's the best lawyer in all of California, you know. If he said he'd get us out of our contracts, he will. Free and clear."

Shirley wanted to tell them her thoughts on that, but it would be no use.

Alice's smile grew as she stepped closer. "He could very well get you a singing job, Shirley. He knows all the right people."

"He sure enough does," Rita answered. "He knows everyone, and everyone knows him. If anyone can give Mel Cartwright what he deserves, it's Walter Russell."

"We sure are lucky he was there last night," Alice said. "Downright lucky."

It wasn't luck. Not to her way of thinking. Holding her silence, Shirley carried the dishes to the shelves.

Julia and Greta entered the kitchen. Greta set a basket of dirty dishes on the counter, while Julia held the door open.

"You three head over to the house," Julia said. "Rosie's there, and she'll get you some clothes to wear. Make sure to bag up the ones you're wearing so Walter can give them back to Mel. I have jobs and a place for all three of you here at the diner until Walter gets everything settled, and afterward, until you find something else. No worries there."

"Thank you, Julia," Rita said, rushing for the door. "Thank you so much."

"Yes, Julia," Alice said, right behind Rita. "Thank you so much!"

Shirley reached for the basket, but Julia stopped her.

"I'll wash these. You go find something else to wear. I've acquired clothes and shoes of all sizes over the years." As she started unloading the basket, Julia asked, "Did Walter leave papers for the other girls?"

Shirley shook her head. "No."

"Did he say when he'd be back? They're anxious to get things rolling. As I imagine you are, too. I certainly was glad to see him this morning when the bulls were knocking on my front door, ready to arrest all of you. They'd probably have hauled me in, too, if not for Walter."

Shirley bit down on her bottom lip to stop it from trembling. Why couldn't any of them see it wasn't right? That debts couldn't just disappear?

"Go on," Julia said. "Get changed. I'll give Walter a call, ask when he'll be back. Once those papers are signed and he's officially representing you, there won't be any fear of being arrested or hauled back to CB's."

None of them would be happy to hear that she'd refused his offer. His all-or-nothing offer. Shirley huffed out a breath of air so thick it burned her throat. "He said he had a meeting at noon."

"I'll call him this afternoon, then." Julia frowned. "You look worried. Don't be. I've never heard of Walter going back on his word. Not even when he should have."

"When he should have?"

Julia shook her head. "I shouldn't have said that."

"Then why did you?"

Julia let out a sigh. "His wife, but she's been dead for years." She waved to the door. "Now scat. Get changed. I'm going to put you all to work before the lunch rush because you'll all have to stay scarce once customers arrive. At least until Walter has all those papers signed."

A wife? Shirley walked out the door and closed it behind her. She didn't want to know anything more about Walter Russell. Not that he had a wife, alive or dead, or that he'd sat in a tree or lived in an orphanage. If he was so wonderful, why had he made her out to be the bad one? Because he couldn't be trusted, that's why. If he was truly a miracle like Alice thought, he'd be helping them right now. But he wasn't. He'd left.

Left without even telling them he wasn't going to help them. She didn't want anything to do with him. Nothing. Couldn't make herself walk along the pathway to the house, either. Alice and Rita, even Julia and Rosie, were all on her shoulders. She felt like a scrawny old mule with a work-horse's harness buckled on her.

She turned in the opposite direction, walked around the diner. The only thing she could do was go back to CB's herself and tell Mel that she wasn't being represented by Walter, but that the others were. It would be a lie, but maybe Walter would change his mind. Help Rita and Alice. They sure were expecting him to. Maybe he knew another lawyer, one who would help them.

Although she'd had her head ducked between her legs for a portion of the ride here, she had a good sense of direction and surely would be able to find her way back to the Cartwright building. Maybe she should just tell Mel she didn't know where the others were, but that she was back to pay off her debt, like her contract stated.

A part of her would just like to give in, have Julia call Walter. Tell him that all three of them were ready to sign those papers. But she couldn't. She knew what it felt like to be cheated. If she backed out of the contract with CB's it would make her as much of a cheat as the lawyer who'd given Pappy's farm to the Swaggerts.

Furthermore, she didn't want his help. Didn't need it. Didn't want or need anyone to help her. That only meant she'd owe them. She was sick of owing people. She was sick of being disappointed, too. That's the other thing that happened when you trusted someone and they went back on their word.

With anger increasing her speed, she stepped onto the sidewalk and headed in the direction of the tall buildings downtown. They stretched so high in the sky it was impossible to not figure out which way to go. It was impossible to get Walter out of her mind, too.

That made her madder. Made her walk faster. She didn't want to think about him. Especially how last night, in the middle of a raid, she hadn't been scared because he'd been there. She been confused and startled, but the only time she'd been scared was when she'd been forced to leave him to run for the car.

She didn't want to think about how she'd been scared *for* him, and she didn't want to think about how that scared her right now. How she couldn't get him out of her mind.

It was impossible. As impossible as pretending her feet weren't killing her. She'd worn these shoes day and night for weeks, and thought blisters were no longer possible.

That wasn't true. She had a whole new set of blisters, and they'd already broken open. The Cartwright building was only a few blocks away, and she couldn't wait to sit down, get out of this heat. Even though she wasn't looking forward to what awaited her there.

Her mind circled its way back to Rita and Alice.

And Walter.

Boy-oh-howdy, he'd had a tough row to hoe. Orphaned and a dead wife. She couldn't help but wonder how much he'd loved his wife.

She'd loved Pappy, and the hurt when he'd died had been awful. She still felt it years later. It wasn't as powerful, as painful, but it was still there. An emptiness she knew would never be full again.

She didn't want it to be full again. Didn't want to love someone ever again. It hurt too much. Not that she had to worry about it. She was never going to fall in love. Not with a man. That's why her mother had quit singing, because she'd fallen in love. She could have been a real star if that hadn't happened. Pappy said that was for sure. That no one could sing as well as her momma had. Other than her. She had to believe that's why Momma had wanted her to become a singer, to fulfill the dream that had been cut short because she'd fallen in love and gave up singing to have a family.

Her mind shifted gears again as she turned down the alley that led to the back door of CB's. Every step closer to that red painted door made her stomach churn a bit more. She really didn't want to go back there. It wasn't the work. Working for the Swaggerts had been far more laborious, and the hours just as long.

It was the principle of the whole thing. She'd never gone back on her word, and wouldn't now. There were cheats out there, in all walks of life, she didn't doubt that. She just wouldn't be one.

She didn't want to disappoint Alice and Rita, or cause trouble for Rosie and Julia, but a person had to stick to their principles.

Her twisting and churning mind came to an abrupt halt as she noticed a stack next to the trash bins along the wall. Her suitcase and her purse, sitting right there for anyone walking along to snatch. She marched past the red door, went right to the pile.

Sure enough, it was her belongings, thrown out with the trash. She opened the suitcase and a mixture of relief and resentment washed over her at the sight of her mammy's Bible, with the picture of her mother still tucked between the pages. Closing the suitcase, she glanced at the other bags. They belonged to Alice and Rita.

"Of all the dirty rotten things to—" Her lips clamped shut as a car pulled up behind her.

"Those things belong to you?"

She hadn't turned around yet, and didn't need to now. That voice was familiar. In fact, it was becoming way too familiar. She sighed and twisted about. Just when she hadn't thought about him for a whole five minutes, he showed up. "Anyone ever tell you, you're like a bad penny?"

Walter shut off the car, relieved to have found her. The meeting he'd had at noon had only been across the street from the diner. With Jack Mc-Carney, who was busy filming his new movie. The meeting had been about the copyrights for the movie. After obtaining a copy of the script to file, Walter had walked back across the street to the diner.

As soon as Julia had told him Blondie was gone, he'd known where to find her. At CB's. She had to be the most stubborn woman ever born and he'd been afraid he might be too late. That she'd have already told Mel he wasn't representing her or the others.

"I've never quite figured that out," he said. "An old scratched-up penny spends like any other, so what makes it bad?"

Blondie's eyes narrowed at him before she turned back to the suitcases on the ground.

He opened his car door and climbed out. The roadster didn't have room to haul things, other than in the rumble seat, so he unhooked the latch and pulled open the heavy door to expose the seat. Then he walked over and picked up two of the suitcases. Blondie was digging through the contents of a small handbag.

"Those dirty rotten scoundrels," she hissed.

"Something missing?" He asked the obvious.

"Only every red cent I had."

He wasn't surprised. "Do you know how much you had?" he asked while setting the other suitcases on the rumble seat. "How much is missing?"

"Yes, twenty-two dollars and eighty-six cents." She shot to her feet.

Reading her mind, he reached out and snagged her arm before she reached the stoop of the door to CB's. "Hold up there, Blondie."

"They stole my money." She tried to break his hold. "Right out of my purse."

"I'm sure they did," he said, keeping a tight hold on her. "Is anything else missing?"

She shook her head. "No. Just the money."

"What about these bags?" He nodded toward the rumble seat. "Anything missing in them?"

"I don't know. They aren't mine."

"Rita's and Alice's?" he asked.

She nodded.

"All right." He nodded toward the car. "Let's go."

She refused to move. "I'm not going anywhere except inside this building to get my money back."

"Yes, you are." She was stubborn enough to do that, so he grabbed her around the waist with his other arm. "You are getting in this car and driving away with me."

"No, I'm not." She glared at him. "And you can't make me."

"Yes, I can." He didn't wait any longer to prove it. Just hoisted her up and, despite his car being brand-new, lifted her over the driver's door and plopped her in the seat. Before she had a chance to do much more than drop her feet onto the floor, he was in the driver's seat and had the car running.

He shifted into First.

"Wait! My suitcase and purse!"

He hit the brakes, and then leveled a stone-cold stare at her. "If you get out of this car, I will chase you down."

She glared at him, then leaned back against the seat and folded her arms over her chest.

He kept one eye on her as he climbed out, got her suitcase and handbag. After putting the suitcase in the rumble seat with the others, he handed her the purse while climbing back in the car. The blunt truth appeared to be the only way to get through to her.

"Do you know why the police were here last night?" he asked while driving down the alley.

"Yes. They raided the speakeasy."

"No." He checked for traffic, then pulled out of the alley. "They raided the den on the third floor."

"Den? You mean the smoking room?"

He turned the corner and headed out of downtown. As far away from CB's as he could get. "You know about that?"

"Only what I was told."

"What were you told?"

"That if anyone asked about the smoking room, I was to let the bartender know and he'd go talk to them. It seemed awfully silly. Nearly everyone in the joint was smoking right where they sat."

"The smoking room isn't for smoking cigarettes or cigars, it's where they smoke drugs. It's called opium. And it's deadly."

"Deadly? You mean they smoke so much they die?"

"Yes," he answered, a bit surprised that anger didn't attempt to overcome him. That usually happened when he thought about opium. About the lives it stole.

"I ai—haven't ever heard such a thing."

"It's the truth. Unlike speakeasies, the police don't cast blind eyes on drug dens." He glanced her way before looking back at the road. She was frowning, as if pondering what he'd said, so now was the time to give her more to think about. "I know you were only there a short time, but didn't you wonder why Mel had to coerce— trick girls into working for him?"

"I was there long enough to figure out that once he gets someone to sign his contract, he has as close to free labor as he could get."

She was a smart cookie, but he'd never questioned her intelligence. It was just her naivety that got her snagged into the worst of the worse. "There is that, but there's more. The girls he gets to work there often get caught up in other things, like the smoking room or the other activities that take place on the third floor."

The way she glanced out the side of the car let him know she was aware of those rooms, too.

"Sometimes they get so caught up in it they give up, and soon they just disappear," he said. It was an ugly truth, but a truth nonetheless.

"Disappear? Like in die?"

"Yes," he answered. "Not all. Some are taken to other places to work, just not as cigarette girls." He could explain how many were shanghaied, shipped to other cities and countries, but had already given her enough to think about. "Most are like you and Rita and Alice. New to Los Angeles, with no family to come looking for them.

Los Angeles has over a million people living here now, and more arrive every day. For those who own businesses like Mel Cartwright, it's a never-ending supply, so getting rid of the ones who don't work out are of no great concern to him."

"Do any ever get out?" she asked. "Ever make enough to pay him off?"

"I honestly don't know. I assume some might, but I don't patronize places like his enough to know." Cartwright wasn't the only one taking advantage of young, naive women.

"But you were there twice recently, so that tells me you do patronize it often."

"I was called to meet a client there the first night. Normally, I would have said no, and set up a meeting the following day. I'm not sure why I agreed to meet him there, but am now glad that I did. Because I saw you. That's why I came back last night."

"Because of me? Why?"

Walter couldn't answer that. He didn't know why he'd cared enough about her to go back or even why he didn't want to see her go down the same path as so many others. All he knew was that he couldn't get her out of his mind, and that was enough for him to dedicate whatever it took to get her out of her contract with CB's and put her on a train back to Nebraska. The crossroad ahead gave him the opportunity to change the subject. "Have you seen the ocean yet?"

"The ocean?"

"Yes." California wasn't all bad, and for whatever reason, he wanted her to know that. See that it had some wonderful, beautiful things before she left. "The Pacific Ocean."

"No. Not yet. I will, though."

"Yes, you will." He turned and headed west. "Today."

# Chapter Six

Shirley could barely breathe. The ocean was as big and blue as every picture she'd ever seen, and so immense it made her feel small. It was all so amazing. How those tall buildings were built right up to the sand, and that the sand was full of people. Some were sitting on the sand, under umbrellas; others were walking, and far too many to count were swimming. Swimming in the ocean.

The breath eased out of her lungs. Now this. This was the California she'd dreamed about. The California she'd wanted to see.

"Do you want to get out? Walk down there and step in the ocean?"

She spun to face Walter as excitement sent her heart racing. "Could we?"

"Sure."

He opened his door, and she looked down at the one next to her. The Swaggert boys had cars, so did Olin, but she'd only ridden in them a few times, and wasn't sure how to open the door on this one. This car was so nice, so pristine, she was afraid to touch anything. It only had the one seat, other than that little one he'd made pop up out of the back.

"I'll get the door for you," he said while walking around the front of the car.

As she climbed out of the door he'd opened, she asked, "Why doesn't your car have a top?"

"It does. Right here." He laid a hand on the thick white leather that was folded down along the back of the seat. "It's just folded down right now."

"What do you do when it rains?"

"Unfold it and hook it onto the windshield." He closed the car door. "I'll show you how it works someday." His grin grew and he nodded toward the water. "Right now, you are going to step in the ocean."

Her heart skipped a beat.

"Come on!" he said.

She followed, pinching her lips against the excitement rising inside her.

The car was parked on a large paved area, along with hundreds of others. Once they reached the sand, Walter sat down. "Time to take the shoes off. It's much easier to walk in the sand without them."

She sat down and pulled off both shoes. Then,

when he'd removed both shoes and his socks and rolled up his pants, they stood.

The sand was hot, but it still felt good. She couldn't help but giggle at the happiness bubbling up inside her as she shuffled her feet, burying her toes deep into the sand.

Walter tugged on her arm. "Come on. At the pace you're walking, we won't get to the water until dark."

She laughed. "The sand feels so good. I want to remember it forever."

"You'll remember it if we don't get our feet in water soon," he said. "They'll be blistered."

She already had blisters, but the sand had nothing to do with it. "No, they won't." Not wanting his feet to get too hot, and anxious to feel the water, she hurried beside him.

They dropped their shoes near the edge of the water, and the first few steps into the ocean was like heaven. It cooled her hot, aching feet like nothing ever had. Then, just as she was thoroughly enjoying the tiny waves splashing into her shins, she had to suck in air as her heels began to sting like no tomorrow.

"What's wrong?" he asked.

"I have a blister." She blew out her breath. "Blisters, actually."

"The salt has to make them burn. Let's get out of the water."

She grabbed his arm. "No, they'll stop sting-ing soon. The salt will be good for them, and the water feels so good."

"You're sure?"

His frown was so sincere she had to smile. Giggle actually. "Yes, I'm sure. This is heavenly. Absolutely heavenly." The sting had either ended, or she no longer cared if her heels were sting-ing or not because she did not want to step out of the water.

"Let's walk this way." He took her hand. "Along the edge."

She told herself the giddiness inside her had nothing to do with him or with holding his hand. It was all because of the ocean. Seeing it, breath-ing the salty air, was proof that dreams could come true. Little ones, and that meant big ones could, too.

"Keep an eye out for a seashell," he said.

"A seashell? Really?"

"Yes, really." He bent down and stuck his hand beneath the water.

Her heart nearly beat right out of her chest as she waited for him to rinse off whatever he'd pulled out, and then hold it out for her to see.

It was tiny, not much bigger than a penny, a golden-white color, and nearly see-through. "Oh, my. It's—it's a seashell. Isn't it?"

"Yes."

She took it from his hand and held it up to the sun. A rainbow of colors swirled through it. "It's gorgeous." She bit her lip for a second, but couldn't help but ask, "Can I keep it?"

He smiled. "Yes, but that's a little one. There are millions like it. We'll look for a large one."

She laid the shell in her palm and ran a finger over the smooth surface. "There's not a million like this one. This one is special. Will always be. It's my very first seashell." She grew a bit teary-eyed looking at the tiny shell. It was as if it was a sign of all the good things yet to come and she knew one thing for sure. "There will never be another one as beautiful as this."

"You might be right about that."

He sounded so odd she had to look up into eyes that were looking at her, not the shell. Something in his eyes made her heart skip a beat.

Blinking, he looked away. "Let's see if we can find a bigger seashell, one that you can hear the ocean in."

"Hear the ocean?"

"Yes, you can hold it up to your ear, and hear the ocean."

"You're lying."

"Maybe," he said, laughing. "But you can hear something when you hold them to your ears. I have one at my house that I found when I first came here."

"Can you still hear something when you hold it to your ear?"

"Yes."

"Well, I'll be."

He laughed. "Would you like me to put that shell in my pocket until we get back to the car so you don't lose it?"

She rubbed the shell again. It was so small she could easily drop it, and then it would be lost forever. But could she trust him not to lose it? A warmth curled inside her as she looked at him, at his smile, his eyes. They were bright and shimmering.

It wasn't just the ocean making her happy. He was. Because he was happy, too. Despite everything he'd lived through, he was still able to be happy.

"I won't lose it," he said. "I promise."

It was hard trusting someone she thought she shouldn't, but something deep inside her said she could. Said he wouldn't lose the shell. "Yes, please. If you don't mind."

"Not in the least." He pulled a neatly pressed handkerchief out of his pocket and had her lay the shell inside it, then folded the material around the shell and tucked it in his pocket. "There. Safe and sound."

"Thank you."

He nodded and took her hand again. "This way,

up near those rocks we might find some bigger shells."

As his fingers closed around her hand this time, tingles filled her palm, then spread up her arm and kept going, gently flooding through her entire body. She'd never felt anything like that before. Like this. Holding his hand and walking in the ocean. It was magical. Dreamlike.

They found several shells, and he saved each one for her. Some were as large as her palm, but not the kind he said they needed to find in order to hear the ocean.

"How are your feet doing?" he asked after both of his pants pockets had to be full of shells.

The sand had changed to pebbles as they got closer to the rocks, but they were smooth pebbles. If there were any jagged edges, she certainly didn't feel them. "Fine? Why? Are yours hurting?"

"No. But let's sit down on the rocks over there anyway."

A large cluster of rocks stuck halfway out of the water a short distance ahead of them. "All right."

The rocks were slippery, but they climbed up on them and sat there, looking out at the ocean. Shirley sighed at the sense of contentment that filled her. "Do you come here often?"

"No. I haven't been down here in years."

Flabbergasted, she asked, "You haven't?" She would come here every chance she got. "Why not?"

"Work. Life. I don't even remember it's here most of the time."

"I'll never forget that it's here." She wouldn't. Not ever.

"I hope you don't."

There was sadness in his tone. She looked at him, wondering why.

He sighed. "I left the papers with Julia for Rita and Alice to sign. I left yours there, too." He turned, looked directly at her. "Tell me what I can say to convince you to sign them."

Shirley hadn't changed her mind about that, nor had thoughts along those lines entered her head, but she wasn't feeling as adamant about returning to Cartwright's. It could have been because someone at CB's had stolen all the money out of her purse, or it could have been because of this—an extremely handsome man making a sliver of her dream come true. She wouldn't be able to come here to see the ocean while working at CB's. Stuck in a basement, surrounded by cigarette smoke and pungent whiskey, she wouldn't even know if the sun was shining. She looked out over the water. Would she forget the ocean was here? Like him? That made her sad. So very sad.

She didn't want that. Not for herself, or for

him, and she wanted more than a sliver of her dream. More than a glimpse of what life could be like. "You said you came back to CB's last night because of me, but you never answered why. What had I done to make you come back?"

"You hadn't done anything. I just didn't want you to end up like so many others."

"In the den, or those other rooms?"

"Yes."

No one had cared what happened to her for a long time, and it made her a bit uncomfortable that he did. If he cared about her, she might have to care about him. "Why? Why me?"

"I don't know. Maybe because I'd almost hit you with my car so I felt as if I knew you. Knew the trouble you'd eventually face while working there."

That made sense. She sort of felt as if she knew him, too. Knew. Not cared about. "What would it mean for you to represent me? Us. Me and Rita and Alice? What would we have to do?"

"You wouldn't have to do anything, really. Unless the case would go to court, then you'd have to tell the judge your version of what happened."

"My version? It's not a version. It's the truth."

"Yes, it is, but I say version because Mel's version could be very different." He twisted so they faced each other. "I highly doubt it will go to court. Mel doesn't want that sort of publicity. I believe it's only going to take a meeting with me, and he'll release you all from your contracts with no further obligations."

That all sounded fine, except nothing had happened for Mel to just release any of them from their contracts. "Why would he do that? I mean, nothing's changed since we signed them."

"No, but he made you sign those contracts under false pretenses."

"What do you mean?"

"What he verbally promised you wasn't in the contract."

That was true. Sort of. "Mel never promised me anything. Roy Harrison did. It wasn't until after I signed everything that I met Mel. Well, Stella first. That's when I learned what was expected of me."

"Mel could claim Roy Harrison lied, that he didn't know anything about it. However, no judge would believe the exact same thing happened to all three of you and that Mel didn't know anything about it." He shrugged. "Roy's name isn't on the contract. Only Mel's."

"How do you know that?"

"I was able to obtain a contract Mel's used in the past, and I'm sure it's identical to the one you signed." He frowned slightly. "Do you have a copy of yours?"

"No. Roy took it as soon as I signed it. How did you ob-obtain one?"

"I can't reveal my sources, but don't worry, it was legal."

A hint of disappointment washed over her. Figuring she knew why, she said, "I still don't like lawyers."

He grinned. "That's all right. I'm not going to force you to like anyone."

That's good, because liking him scared her. She turned away and stared out over the water again. This sure was nice. Sitting here with him. But it wouldn't feed her. Or clothe her. Or put a roof over her head. Or make her a singer.

"I know you feel as if your grandfather was cheated out of his property," he said quietly. "He may very well have been. I can't say one way or the other without fully researching what happened. However, I know many lawyers, and most of them are honest, hardworking men who do not go around cheating people out of anything. Lawyers are people who have studied the law for several years—all laws—and use those laws to protect their clients' rights and privileges to the best of their abilities. Without them, people could interpret laws any way they deemed fit, and laws would then no longer be worthy of being written."

She pondered that for a moment. It sounded confusing, but made sense at the same time. Except for one thing. "We don't have any money. Rita, Alice or me. So, if we sign your contract, we'll owe you just like we do Mel." She hadn't signed a contract before coming to California, but they sure seemed to be everywhere out here.

"No, you won't. My services will be pro bono."

She'd been able to figure out what most of the words he used meant, even had made a mental note to use some of them. In all honesty, changing the way she spoke around him was easy. All she had to do was listen, but for the life of her, she couldn't figure out the word he'd just used. "What's *pro bono*?"

"It means for free. That I will donate my services to you and Alice and Rita."

"Nothing in life is free."

He nodded. "Normally, I'd agree with you, but not in this situation. Lawyers have a responsibility to see that justice is equally accessible to all people, including those unable to pay. I provide pro bono work whenever I can."

"For other girls like us?"

"No, I've never offered my services in a situation like this before."

Just when she thought she'd understood things, he confused her all over again.

Walter wasn't sure what more he could say or do, so he slid off the rock, stood in the water and held a hand out to her. "You can think about it on our way to Julia's."

She looked at his hand and back at his face. "I've never heard of a lawyer being free before."

"Lawyers, just like every other profession, are people. Just like other professions, other jobs, some may not strive to do their best. I do. I take the oath that I made very seriously."

He always had taken the opportunity he'd been given seriously, but had never wanted someone to believe him the way he wanted her to believe him.

She looked at him for a length of time. He never broke eye contact, but didn't say more, either. Trust didn't come easy to her, and he could see why.

With a nod, she took ahold of his hand, slid off the rock and then let go.

He accepted that. Holding her hand earlier had cracked a part of him that had been closed off for a long time, and he wasn't prepared or willing to let his inner self become fully open. Not ever again. He was as serious about that as he was about being a lawyer.

They walked along the water's edge, where the waves barely washed over their feet all the way back to their shoes. Neither of them said a word, and still didn't as they picked up their shoes and walked across the hot sand toward the roadster.

He stopped her from stepping on the pavement.

"We'll put our shoes on here. The pavement is hotter than the sand."

As if testing that he was telling the truth, she stepped one bare foot onto the pavement, but quickly pulled it off. "You're right. It is."

He grinned, but didn't reply as he sat down and put on his socks and shoes. He took note of her feet while she put on her shoes. Dainty, like the rest of her, and cute; her feet also had several blisters. On the toes, sides and heels.

"You need bigger shoes."

"These were the closest to my size that CB's had."

There wasn't animosity in her voice. He gave her credit for that. With blisters like that, he'd never have been able to wait tables the way she had. Or walk all the way downtown from Julia's Diner.

Once at the car, and she was settled in the passenger seat, he dug into his pockets. "Hold out your hands."

"Wait a minute," she said, picking her handbag off the floorboard. She opened the clasp and held the top of the bag wide open. "Ready."

He dropped handfuls of shells into her bag until his pockets were empty, then handed her the handkerchief. "You can keep the hanky, so your first one won't get mixed up with the others."

"Thank you. I will wash it and see that you get it back."

He walked around the car, climbed in and started it before saying, "I meant you can keep it. Keep the shell in it so it doesn't get mixed up with all the others."

"Forever?"

She sounded dumbfounded. Like no one had ever given her something before. He leaned over, took the handkerchief and lowered it into her purse. Their faces were as close as last night, when the thought of kissing her had struck. Just like then, her lips looked so soft, so kissable, he couldn't take his eyes off them. All he'd have to do— He stopped the thought right there and sat up straight. "Yes, forever."

"Oh, well, thank you." She set her purse on the floorboard. "And thank you for bringing me to see the ocean today."

He took a breath and focused on starting the car rather than how breathless she sounded. "You're welcome. I'm glad you enjoyed it."

"I did. Very much. But I still need to think about signing your contract."

He shifted the Packard into Reverse. "All right. Just let me know any questions you might have." Deciding to give her time to let a few things mull, he shifted into First, pulled out of the parking lot and then turned to take the road that ran along the coast.

"This isn't the same way we came," she said almost instantly.

"No, it's not. This way we don't have to go back through downtown." He chose not explain it was also longer. Time didn't really matter, as long as he had those papers signed sometime today, so the date coincided with what he'd told Mel Cartwright. He needed to get this case going and settled.

She leaned her head back and closed her eyes as the wind of driving with the top down blew her curls about. It took a concentrated effort to keep his eyes on the road.

"Will everyone know?"

Walter guessed what she was referring to. "Know you signed a contract with me?" he asked, assuming that had to be it.

"Yes. Will they know that I backed out of the contract with Mel? That could put a mark against my name. Folks back home gossiped about things like that to no end."

"No one will gossip. In fact, if anyone does learn that you'd worked at CB's and found a legal way out, they'll praise you for it."

"Why? That don't—doesn't seem right."

She was really working on her language. An underlying edge of guilt crept into his gut. He should never have pointed that out to her on their first meeting. He liked her accent, Midwestern words and all. It reflected an innocence that didn't exist out here. If it did, he sure hadn't seen it. Not in a very long time. He didn't want to see her lose that, either.

"Because," he said slowly, choosing his own words carefully, "Mel's contracts are bad, and the way he uses them are morally wrong. You are not the one in the wrong, he is. People know that he stalks unsuspecting newcomers and cons them into working for him."

"Then why don't the police do something about it?" she asked.

He took a chance and glanced at her. She was still sitting back, but her eyes were open and gazing out over the seashore that ran along the road. It was a moment before he could turn his eyes back on the road. "Because Mel's not the only one who makes employees sign a contract, or makes them believe it's legal."

"But it's not legal, right?"

"No contract is legal if it's signed under duress. Mel knows that."

She let out a long sigh. "What made you want to become a lawyer?"

Her question took him off guard. He shrugged and answered honestly. "I can't say I ever wanted to become one."

"Then why did you?"

He could avoid answering, but chose not to. "When I came to California many years ago, a friend was with me. Theodore. We got jobs at the docks, and a short time later, Theodore got in a fight with another worker. During the scuffle, the other man fell in the water and drowned. Theodore was charged with murder."

"How old were you?" she asked. "How old was Theodore?"

"Sixteen. We were both sixteen."

"What happened to him? Where is he now?"

Walter kept his eyes on the road. "He was arrested, jailed. I convinced a lawyer, Arthur Marlow, to take on Theodore's case and to let me work for him in exchange for his fees."

"Did he win? This lawyer."

His stomach clenched. This was the first time he'd spoken about Theodore's case with anyone other than Arthur. "Yes, but it was too late."

"Too late? What do you mean?"

In an odd way, he felt a sense of relief telling someone about what had happened. "Theodore had been at the orphanage with me, and while awaiting his trial, he was incarcerated. Jailed." Walter squeezed the steering wheel harder. "He said he couldn't take it. That it reminded him too much of the orphanage. That he had to get out. I told him to wait. That Arthur would get him out.

But the confinement got to him. He attempted to escape the night before his trial and was shot. He died two days later. After his trial, where the other man's death was ruled an accident."

She touched his arm. "That's sad. I'm terribly sorry."

He shook his head. "There's nothing for you to be sorry about."

"Yes, there is. I'm sorry that your friend died."

He nodded, and offered her a smile. "Thank you. I'm sorry he died, too."

"Is that why you became a lawyer?"

He shrugged. "I didn't have a choice. I owed Arthur for his services. He took me on as a full-time apprentice, and then a partner. When he passed away six years ago, I took over his practice." Theodore's case was the reason he'd stuck to contract work and not trials. Defending lives.

Until now. Her life needed to be defended, and he was the person who could do that. He specialized in writing contracts, not getting people out of them, but knew the fine details better than anyone else.

He glanced her way.

The gaze she returned was thoughtful.

He tore his gaze away and focused on the road again.

"All right," she said.

He waited a moment, hoping she had just

agreed, before asking, "All right you'll sign the papers?"

She nodded. "Yes. I'll sign."

There was no money involved, not a single cent, so why did he feel like he'd just gotten the go-ahead for the biggest contract of his life?

# Chapter Seven

It was such a simple thing, signing her name, yet it had felt like it was so much more. Why? She'd done it before. Signed her name. Too many times to count. It wasn't as if she'd signed her life away. In fact, from all Walter had said, as well as Julia, and Rita, and Alice and Rosie, by signing that contract, she was getting her life back.

Why, then, did it feel different?

Perhaps because it *was* different. Once Walter settled everything with Mel, she'd be able to pursue her singing career. That's what people called it out here. A career.

Julia had said she could stay here with her and work at the diner while pursuing a singing career. Just not at the diner. She didn't allow anyone working for her to bother the customers by requesting auditions or even talking about them.

Shirley could understand that. CB's had the

same rule. Furthermore, people weren't interested in listening.

She rolled over and glanced up out the window beside the bed. Rita and Alice chose to stay at Julia's house. It was a bit peculiar, considering how badly she'd wanted to get here to the big city, but she'd chosen to stay out here, in the cabin. After those nights of sleeping in the apartment, with little more than a few inches of her own space, the cabin seemed like a luxury. She'd never have imagined that. Just like she'd never have imagined she'd miss a garden, but when given the choice, she'd said she'd stay out here and look after the big garden out front of the cabin, where Julia grew vegetables for the diner.

Shirley stared up at the stars for a time, comforted by the silence after all the noise that used to filter in through the open windows at the Cartwright building downtown.

Maybe she'd been wrong. That could be why signing Walter's papers had made her stomach jittery. Maybe life in the big city wasn't for her and by signing those papers it was now going to be whether it was what she truly wanted or not.

She pushed out the sigh weighing down her chest until her lungs were completely empty. So empty they burned. Then she drew in a breath and her mind shifted. All on its own, as if the fresh air she drew in gave her fresh thoughts.

Or fresh memories. That's what formed in her mind. A memory. Of the ocean. It had been so big, so blue, so, well, timeless. People had stared out over that ocean long before she came around. Years and years and years before. They'd looked at the same sky as she had, the same water; some had probably sat on the same rocks.

Yet, somehow, sitting there on those rocks with Walter, it all had seemed like she was the only one who had ever done that. She had no idea what all that meant, except that it did mean something. Deep inside, in a hidden part of her that she'd never really noticed before, a little tickle had appeared. A hint of things yet to come.

It scared her a bit. That was as peculiar as everything else, because she didn't scare easy.

Certainly hadn't in the past. So why now? Because she'd put her trust in Walter? He hadn't lost her seashell. Just like he'd promised. He'd also said she didn't have to like him, but at some point today, she'd discovered she did like him. Maybe that's what scared her.

She'd met a lot of people since leaving Nebraska, more than she'd known her entire life. Not one of them could compare to Walter.

He was different. When she was around him, she felt safe. And, good heavens, was he handsome! Especially when he smiled and laughed. A wave of warmth filled her. His eyes had lit up as bright as that sky over the sea when he laughed. It was a sight to see.

He was honest, too. He didn't have to tell her about his friend, about how he'd become a lawyer, but he had, and something about that touched her deep inside.

Maybe that's the reason signing his paper had affected her so oddly. Because once everything was settled with Mel, there'd be no reason for her to ever see Walter again. To ever go to the seashore with him again.

Shirley closed her eyes and let out another sigh. She was tired. That's what was wrong right now. Whenever she got tired, her mind started spinning about, roaming down roads that led nowhere, except to other roads that went nowhere. A good solid night of sleep was what she needed, and then, tomorrow, she'd figure out a way to get back on track for making her dream come true.

Of becoming a singer.

"If you're serious about becoming a singer, you have to learn some new songs."

The mop in Shirley's hand stopped midswipe as quickly as the words she'd been singing stopped on her tongue midnote. "What do you mean?" she asked Rosie. The diner had closed an hour ago and they were completing the last of the evening cleaning.

Rosie continued wiping down the counter. "All I've heard you sing are hymns. They're nice, but no one is going to pay you to sing them outside of a church."

Shirley began mopping again. Hymns were all she knew, other than silly songs she and Pappy had made up. He used to play his fiddle and she'd sing, making up words as they went along. She'd tried, many times, but couldn't remember any of the songs her mother used to sing to her. In fact, she only knew that had happened because Pappy told her about it. "What kind of songs will people pay for?"

"Fun ones." Rosie walked around the counter and then leaned against it. "Didn't you hear any at CB's?"

"No," Shirley answered. "They had a band playing every night, but no one ever sang."

"I always heard that place was dull."

Shirley gave the final corner a swipe with the mop and then carried it over to the bucket. "Heard? You were there." It had been six days since the raid, five since she'd seen Walter. Not that she was counting. Just curious if he was getting everything settled or not.

"Only because I'd never been there before and wanted to see what the place looked like." Rosie shrugged. "I'd barely set foot in the door when

Walter told me to leave. If it had been anyone else, I wouldn't have listened."

Shirley had heard about that. How Walter had warned Rosie to leave. Julia said it made sense, that being a lawyer, he could easily have heard a raid was going to happen. Still, Shirley had to wonder why he would have put himself in the middle of a raid. It couldn't have been just to save her.

Rosie pushed off the counter. "Come on. Let's put that mop away and I'll show you what kind of songs I'm talking about."

Shirley picked up the bucket and carried it and the mop toward the kitchen. "Where?"

"There's a joint only a few blocks from here," Rosie said, holding open the kitchen door. "We'll ask the others if they want to go with us."

"Just like that?" Shirley asked. "We're gonna go to a joint?"

Rosie shrugged. "Sure. Why not? It's Saturday night. The diner is closed tomorrow. Why can't we go out and have some fun?"

Shirley had to think for a moment. It was a bit hard to get used to, not asking someone for permission to go someplace. First it had been Pappy, then the Swaggerts, then at CB's; she hadn't had a choice, but she did now. A wave of something she couldn't quite describe washed over her. "Why not indeed," she agreed with a nod.

Within no time she and Rosie, along with Rita and Alice, were walking up the street, giggling. Shirley was more than a bit giddy. Julia had loaned her clothes, including shoes that didn't hurt her feet. Rosie showed her how to use a hot rod on her hair, to tame down some of the curls, and she was wearing a headband with a feather on it. A blue one that matched the dress she wore. It was bright blue, sleeveless and had an uneven hem with points that swished around her calves as she walked. The white beads around her neck shimmered like her seashell did, and for the first time in her life, she was wearing lipstick. It tasted funny, and had made her lips stick together at first, but she'd gotten used to it, or simply didn't care. She was on her way to seeing a singer. A real singer.

She'd seen one before. Pappy had taken her to town to see a troupe that had played in the town square. He'd said the troupe was like the one her mother had sung with. Small, but good. The woman singing that evening had been as beautiful as her voice, and Shirley had pretended that the singer had been her mother. Afterward, she'd asked Pappy if her mother had really wanted her to be a singer, too. Just like she'd been. He'd said that she had. That from the moment she'd been born, her mother had said that she'd grow up to be an even better singer. Be a real star. That had sealed her fate. Her dream. From that day on, she'd known she'd become a singer when she grew up and she'd started singing all day long, every day.

Pappy liked that. Liked to hear her sing, and told her, if she wanted to be a singer, then a singer she would be.

"Where are we going?" Alice asked.

"Right up there," Rosie responded.

Shirley frowned and glanced at Rosie to make sure she was looking at the same building Rosie was pointing to. "The butcher shop?"

"By day," Rosie said. "By night it's known as the Pig's Tail. A real hopping joint." Increasing her speed, Rosie added, "You'll see!"

Much like CB's, they walked around the back of the building, but here they didn't go down into the basement—instead they took a set of outdoor wooden stairs to the second floor of the butcher shop. Music wafted out of the open windows, so did laughter.

Rosie was the first one through the door.

Shirley the last, and the moment she stepped into the room, her eyes went to the stage in the corner, where a woman stood, singing. It was a lively tune, one that made her foot tap the floor. Her heart started pounding and excitement filled her.

She stood right there, listening, until the song

ended and the room filled with applause. The singer dipped into a curtsy, then stepped off the stage and walked to a table.

The room was only half the size of CB's, but packed wall to wall with people—men and women. Very few women had patronized CB's. The other thing that was different here was that there were no cigarette girls. Customers had to walk up to the bar and get their own drinks.

Shirley made her way through the crowd, making a beeline for the singer sitting at the table with others. Two men and one woman. The singer was beautiful. With coal-black hair cut short so it bobbed around her chin, and sparkling dark eyes. Shirley had no idea what she'd say to the singer, but had to talk to her. Just had to.

Walter hung up the phone and leaned back in his chair, closing his eyes for a moment. He should have known what he'd gotten himself into, and thought about it before taking the steps he had. It was too late now. The phone hadn't stopped ringing all week. Word had spread about him representing girls from CB's, and now every woman working in every speakeasy in the state wanted representation. Mel Cartwright hadn't been paying Shirley and the others a minimum wage, and had forced them to work much more than the recommended eight-hour shift. That wasn't the case with every establishment. He'd had to explain that several times the past few days.

If things continued this way, he'd have to hire another law clerk. One just to answer the phone and turn women down. Not every one of them had a viable suit. The others working at Mel's did, and by default, he'd had to agree to represent them. Judge ordered.

He hadn't believed it would have gone this far. But it had. Mel had thought he'd been bluffing, and rather than taking the easy way out, he'd called the bluff. Except it hadn't been a bluff. The judge pointed that out, and ruled if there were three women working at CB's under an unlawful contract, there were more, and he wanted them all represented.

Walter understood what was happening. The judge was making an example out of this case, with the hope that other places would fall in line on their own. It had turned into a class action suit, and he was now representing twelve girls in total, which meant it was all going to take much longer than he'd first expected.

He knew where the judge was coming from. There had been too much public disapproval of certain things lately.

Not speakeasies, or even alcohol, despite it being illegal. The disapproval came from the overall low wages and work environments. Henry

Ford's announcement last year that all of his employees would maintain no more than a forty-hour workweek, eight hours a day, five days a week, had created a wave of protests for better work environments. Ford had touted the importance of leisure time, and that it was not a privilege of only the upper class. Those words had taken the nation by storm.

Congress hadn't made it a law, might never, but cities and states were taking his lead in ruling against unfair work conditions.

The phone rang again, and Walter leaned forward. Little had he known the can of worms he'd opened by bringing this case before a judge.

"Walter Russell here," he said into the speaker.

"It's Mel Cartwright."

Walter held back his grunt of surprise.

"We need to talk," Cartwright said in his raspy voice. "Put an end to this shenanigan."

Walter lifted up the standing mouthpiece so he could lean back in his chair. "I offered you the chance to discuss things, you chose not to. Now, the only advice I can give you is to hire a lawyer."

"That wouldn't do me a lick of good," Cartwright said. "There's not one in the state that will win against you."

No pride filled Walter. He'd never claimed to be one of the best lawyers in the state, especially when it came to lawsuits. His specialty was contracts, and that's the way it was going to stay. As soon as this case was over. "That's the only advice I can offer you."

"I don't need advice." Anger laced Cartwright's words. "I want a deal. What do I have to do to end this case?"

"Well, in the beginning, it was simply releasing those women from their contracts, and repaying them any money or possessions missing from their belongings. Now's a different story. The judge will decide." Walter let a half grin form. "There could be back wages you need to pay out, or—"

"We don't need this going to a judge. It's hurting my business. Don't have but a couple girls left working for me." Cartwright paused for a moment, then said, "You have to talk to the judge. Put an end to this now."

There was nothing more that Walter would like than to put an end to this. Now. It was taking up far too much of his time. He hadn't even had a chance to complete the paperwork to file the copyright for Jack McCarney's latest movie or get the paperwork drawn up for Sam Wharton's boxing exhibition.

"What's it going to take, Russell?"

Walter shook his head at the bribe Cartwright was offering; however, he was willing to get this over with as soon as possible. "I'll see if I can get an appointment with the judge, and let you know what he says."

"Tomorrow?"

"Tomorrow is Sunday," Walter pointed out.

"So?"

The ignorance of some people never failed to astonish him. "I'll call you after I talk to the judge." Walter sat forward and hung up the earpiece while setting the base of the phone on his desk.

He glanced toward the window, and as he had most every free moment for the last week, he wondered what Shirley was doing. The diner would be closed by now. Would she be at the cabin? The fact she'd chosen to stay there instead of at Julia's house intrigued him. He hoped it was because she missed the solitude and quiet of the country. That perhaps she was indeed thinking of returning to Nebraska.

That was his hope. The reason he was doing all of this. So she would return home. So he would have saved her from going down the same trail that Lucy had.

He looked away from the window and gave his head a clearing shake. There was no sense pulling up ghosts, or in making new ones. That's what all his thinking about Shirley was doing. He'd purposefully stayed away from the diner this week. There wasn't any news to share with the women, and keeping his distance from Shirley was his only protection. She did things to him.

To his insides.

He wasn't about to walk down that lane again. Not ever.

Less than an hour later, he found himself storming up the stairs at the Pig's Tail. Thankfully, Julia had had a good idea of where they'd gone. He hadn't rescued Blondie from one speakeasy just so she could go and get a job at another one. Talk about no sense. Not a single ounce of—

His thought was cut short as he opened the door and caught sight of the women on the stage. Two of them. Shirley and some other dame.

The dame was singing. So was Shirley.

Singing backup, repeating the words the other dame sang, but singing she was.

She was good, too. The tune was fast, but she didn't miss a word. Or a move. She had those, too. In perfect sync with the music, her hips swished, her toes tapped and her shoulders twisted as she swung the bottom half of the beads around her neck in a circle with one hand. And her smile. Wow. It shone. Lit up the entire stage. She was beautiful. So was her voice. It put the other singer to shame. *She* put the other singer to shame. He wasn't the only one to think so. The crowd was cheering, clapping, encouraging her to keep on

singing, keep on swirling the end of those beads.
Every man in the room probably thought—

Damn it!

With no regard to who might care, he elbowed
his way to the stage. It was only a foot above the
floor, making him eye to eye with Shirley. "What
the hell are you doing?" He didn't wait for her response, just grabbed her arm, pulled her off the
stage and started for the door.

She resisted, dug her heels into the floor.

He twisted and lifted her off the floor. Catching her beneath the knees with his other arm, he
continued to the door.

The crowd separated, giving him room. She
yelled in his ear, insisting he put her down. He
ignored her, all the way out the door and down
the stairs.

There he dropped her feet to the ground. "What
are you doing?"

"Me? What are *you* doing?" she shouted in
return.

The flare of anger that had struck upon seeing her onstage was still full-blown inside him.
"I'll tell you what I'm not doing! I'm not working
day and night to get you out of one two-bit joint
just to find you immersed in another! Do you not
have any sense?"

"Sense? I have plenty of sense!" She pushed

against his chest with both hands. "You're the one who doesn't have any sense!"

"Yes, I do!" He wanted to shake her or kiss her. He wasn't sure which. That wasn't true. He knew. But he wouldn't kiss her, or shake her. "I have sense enough to stay away from places like this!"

She lifted her chin, bringing their faces closer. "You're here now!"

Anger still boiling, he squeezed her shoulders. "Only because I heard this is where you were."

Her fingers curled around the lapels of his jacket as she stretched onto her toes. "Where I am should not matter to you!"

It shouldn't, but it did, and that irritated him even more. Her lips being so close to his was driving him crazy, too. "It does while I'm representing you."

She stretched even higher, brought her lips closer and screamed louder, "Then stop representing me! I came here to become a singer and that's what I'm going to do!"

"I can't just stop representing you." The tip of his nose touched hers, and the connection was like a spark of static electricity. It may have been static electricity because she snapped backward just like he did. Taking a step back, he released her shoulders at the same time she let go of his lapels. He could release her as a client, too, but wasn't about to. "It's too late. The case has already gone to a judge."

She had the tip of one finger on her nose, and her hand slowly fell as she said, "I thought you said that wouldn't happen."

He'd thought a lot of things couldn't happen. Especially inside him. "I thought it wouldn't. But Mel felt he had a case and wanted to fight our claims."

She folded her arms across her chest, as if stifling a shiver. "Does he? Does he have a case?"

Flustered in so many ways, Walter sighed. "He's changing his mind now that others have joined in—more girls that had worked for him—but it's too late for a simple agreement. I'll talk to the judge this week, see if we can come to an agreement of sorts, but I can't say for sure what will happen."

"What does that mean?" she asked solemnly.

A wave of guilt at how he'd reacted to seeing her onstage made his stomach churn. Still, she had to understand the dangers of her actions. At least the potential dangers. "It means that until I know more, you should refrain from visiting any businesses remotely close to CB's."

"Why?"

"Because it'll be more difficult for me to prove you didn't want to be working at CB's if you are continuously visiting other joints."

"Visiting one isn't the same as working at one."

She was right, it was different, but not everyone would see it that way. "No, it's not the same, but it could appear similar to a judge."

She took a few steps away and leaned against the front bumper of a Ford while glancing up at the doorway of the Pig's Tail. "Are you going to go carry the others out, as well?"

"No."

"Why not?"

"Because I highly doubt they're onstage singing." He shook his head. "That is what makes it appear as if you want to work at these places. Right now, appearances matter. A lot."

Her chest heaved beneath the shimmering blue dress she wore. "I suspect you're right on that account."

"Suspect?"

She shrugged. "Fine. You are right." Pushing off the Ford, she walked past him.

"Where are you going?"

"Back to Julia's." She stopped, looked at him with eyes that once again flashed anger. "Or can't I work there, either?"

The guilt inside him doubled. "Working there is fine."

"So it's *fun* that's not fine."

"You can have fun," he said.

"Doing what? Washing dishes? I've done that my entire life, and I can tell you, it's not fun."

An indescribable impulse had him holding out his hand. "There are a lot of ways to have fun besides going to joints. I'll show you."

She frowned and shook her head, but didn't pull away when he took ahold of her arm.

Impulsiveness wasn't one of his strong points, and he searched his mind for something *fun* to do while they walked to his car. It struck him then that they were in Hollywood, the film capital of the world. A motion picture was fun.

"Where are we going?" she asked once they were both in the car.

He grinned. "To have some fun."

# Chapter Eight

A little voice inside Shirley's head told her she should still be mad at him for dragging her off the stage and carrying her out of the joint. She had been mad then, even during the car ride downtown, but now was in too much awe to let a little bit of anger overtake her joy. The movie theater was amazing. Beautiful. Like a castle with all the velvet-covered seats and curtains and the shimmering chandeliers overhead.

She'd never seen anything like it. She'd never seen a motion picture, either. A man dressed in a red suit and sitting inside a brick box with curtains on the windows had sold Walter two tickets and said the first feature was almost over, but that it would cost the same, twenty-five cents each, to see just the second movie.

Walter had said that was fine and paid the price. He'd also asked her if she'd wanted some popcorn, peanuts or candy from one of the many vendors on the sidewalk in front of the theater. She'd declined, already in awe of the building. It was as elaborate on the outside as on the inside.

The carpet beneath her feet was so thick and soft she wanted to take her shoes and socks off and dig her toes into it. She refrained, but couldn't stop herself from pressing her feet hard against that gold carpet, and watching how the toes of her shoes sank deep into the softness. The curtains on the high stage were gold and made of velvet just like the seat cushions they sat on.

They had stood outside a massive set of doors until the first movie had ended. That had nearly killed her. She'd wanted to peek inside the door so badly her insides had been jumping around like she'd swallowed a bowlful of grasshoppers.

Walter had said there was no use disturbing others by trying to find seats while the first movie was ending.

She'd accepted that, but the moment he'd opened the door, she'd shot inside, and had never seen so many seats all in one place in her life. They'd walked all the way to the front and sat down in the center of the front row.

"This is where you wanted to sit, isn't it?" Walter asked.

"Yes." She was barely able to answer, so awestruck over the surroundings. "It's like nothing I've ever seen before."

"Wait until the new theater is done," Walter said. "The State. It's being built a few blocks from here and, from what I've heard, will put this place to shame."

"I can't imagine that," Shirley answered before pointing toward a U-shaped wall in front of the stage. "What's that?"

"That's called the pit. After the intermission, the musicians will return."

"Musicians?"

"Yes, they'll play music during the movie." He nodded as several men entered the room from a door next to the stage. "Here they come now. They'll do a short performance before the movie starts."

The men were all dressed in black suits and wearing white shirts. "I had no idea."

"Sit back and relax," Walter said. "I think you'll enjoy this."

Shirley sat back, but was too eager to stay there. It was simply too exciting. Bounding forward, she asked, "Do you come here often?"

"No, not overly often." He let out a long sigh. "But I have seen a large number of movies."

Shirley sensed there was something more behind his heavy sigh. "But not here?"

"Some have been here, some at other theaters. I have a lot of clients in the movie industry."

He had leaned back in his seat and seemed at

ease, yet she didn't quite believe he was at ease. "You don't enjoy movies?"

"I enjoy them."

She eyed him critically for a silent moment, then shook her head. She'd tried, but couldn't quite believe him. "You're lying."

He shook his head as a tiny grin formed. "I'm not lying. I do enjoy movies. I just haven't been to many lately."

"Why not?" she asked.

They stared at each other for several moments. Shirley could almost see his mind working, and wondered what he was thinking so hard about.

He looked away before saying, "Because my wife had been an actress."

An odd sensation struck her square in the chest. He'd had more people die in his life than she had. "In movies?"

"Yes. In movies."

Shirley wasn't sure what to say next, but ultimately couldn't stop herself from asking, "How did she die?"

"A car accident." He nodded toward the stage. "They'll be turning out the lights now."

That was exactly what happened; the entire room went dark except for lights shining up out of the area he'd called a pit.

Shirley leaned back, but then tilted toward Walter. "We can leave if you want to."

"No. I don't want to."

She didn't want to, either, but if coming to a movie made him sad, made him think about the death of his wife, she would leave. "I won't mind."

"I will," he whispered. "We aren't leaving."

The music that blasted up out of that pit sent her back in her seat like the booming voice of a preacher proclaiming some pews had been empty for too many Sundays. She remembered that happening often enough, and how those preachers used to stare straight at her and Pappy on those Sundays when they'd finally made it into town in time for church.

The music softened a lot quicker than those preachers ever had, and when a man started singing in a low baritone voice about traveling on the ocean blue, she softened, too. The song sucked her in—the words, the melody, the singer's deep voice. She closed her eyes and could almost see a big ship floating over the waves. When the music boomed again, she could see lightning and rain, the storm the singer described tossing a ship about.

The song continued—so did the music—and in the end, as the final notes faded away, she saw the ship safely arrive in harbor.

"Open your eyes," Walter whispered. "The movie is starting."

Shirley opened her eyes and pinched her lips

together at the shiver of delight his whisper sent down her neck. She'd been fighting hard to focus on anything, everything, except him since he'd lifted her off that stage. He was tall and broad shouldered, but she hadn't realized how strong he was, how hard and firm his muscles were. She shouldn't have noticed such a thing, should have been too mad, but she had noticed, and sitting this close to him, her body was tingling like her nose had when his had bumped it. Every part of her was fully aware of how close they sat. How dark and intimate the theater was. That wasn't like her. Not like her at all.

"The curtains are separating," he whispered.

Swallowing, she nodded and stared straight ahead, watched as the gold velvet curtains were pulled apart and a screen appeared. She read every word that appeared about the gold rush in Alaska, about the men and women who traveled there and about the gold they'd found.

She barely blinked as the words left the screen and pictures appeared. Moving pictures. Of people walking, and horses and wagons. It was fascinating and bit unbelievable for someone who had never seen anything like it. So was the awareness of his closeness. It was like listening for a sound, but not knowing what she'd do when she heard it. Nothing she'd ever experienced was like this. Then again, no one she'd ever met was like him.

Gently, softly, his hand wrapped around hers. "Don't think," he whispered. "Just watch the movie. You'll like it. I promise."

The warmth of his palm settled the jumpiness inside her, and within minutes, her entire body was so relaxed, so at ease, she was able to become engrossed by the action on the screen.

The movie was about a prospector in Alaska, dreaming of finding a motherlode of gold. There were some funny scenes when the prospector wound up in the cabin with another, much larger man. They were both hungry and the large man kept envisioning the smaller prospector as a chicken. Imagining that's what the other man was thinking, the smaller man boiled his shoe and fed it to the bigger one.

Laughter abounded all around her. Shirley laughed, too. Until a bear broke down the door and the men had to shoot it. They then had a real feast.

The poor prospector didn't find gold, and soon was forced to leave the cabin and go back to town, where he saw a dance hall girl he fell in love with, but another man was already in love with her.

Eyes glued to the screen, Shirley read the words explaining what was happening, or about to happen. At times, she held her breath in anticipation and, at others, sighed with relief, right up until the end. Then, when the prospector, who had eventually struck it rich, and was now engaged to the dance hall girl, sailed away from Alaska, Shirley wanted to jump to her feet in excitement for the prospector and the girl.

No one else had jumped to their feet, or even clapped, so she had to settle for pressing both hands against her heart.

"Did you like it?" Walter asked as the lights came on.

"Oh, yes, very much. It was amazing. And so real. I didn't know…" She paused, not exactly sure what she hadn't known. She shrugged. "I simply didn't know."

Walter chuckled. "Charlie's films are some of the best. This one especially."

"Charlie who?"

He frowned. "Charlie Chaplin."

"Oh. Was he the prospector?"

"Yes. Well, the actor who portrayed the prospector." Walter's frown deepened. "You don't recognize his name?"

Shirley shook her head. "No. Should I?"

"He's about the best-known movie actor there is. Worldwide." Still holding her hand, Walter stood.

She stood and curled her fingers into her palm when he let go of her hand. "I don't know much about movies. The closest theater was in Lincoln." Shirley stopped before saying that the only reason she'd ever gone to Lincoln was to sing for funerals. That used to seem important, but it no longer did.

Walter took ahold of her elbow as they walked up the aisle. "Well, I'm glad you enjoyed your first movie, and now you can say you've been to a movie theater."

"Yes, I did and I can. It won't be the last time, either. I'm going to come here every chance I get."

They had to wait in line to exit the building, and once outside, Walter asked, "What about an ice cream soda? Have you ever had one of those?"

"Can't say as I have," she admitted. "I did have ice cream once. On the Fourth of July."

"There's a parlor right next door," Walter said. "Let's go have one."

Shirley wasn't sure if she was shocked or confused. "At this time of the night? It's been dark for hours. The diner's been closed for hours."

"The ice cream parlor does most of its business after the theater lets out," Walter said, weaving their way through the crowd of people streaming out of the movie theater.

A store that sells nothing but ice cream. Pappy would never believe it.

She and Walter were lucky. They found a table with two seats to sit at. Others stood along the wall, drinking their sodas and talking about the movie. She couldn't help but notice how many couples there were, and wondered if they were on dates. This was the closest thing she'd ever had to a date, yet it wasn't. She couldn't pretend it was, but had to wonder if this was what it would be like.

The waitress arrived, and because she didn't know what flavor to choose, she copied what Walter ordered. It turned out to be cherry, and so pretty she hated to ruin it by taking a taste. Two large scoops of ice cream were in a tall fluted glass, surrounded by pink juice, with a straw and a spoon sticking out of the top.

Following Walter's actions and his encouragement to taste it, she used the straw and took a small sip. It was so delightfully delicious she had to contain herself from gobbling it down as fast as the first pig to the trough in the morning.

While they sipped the delightful cherry juice and ate the creamy ice cream, they talked about the movie, different flavors of sodas and other things that were of little matter until their glasses were empty.

Once again, she told herself this wasn't a date, because dates were for people who liked each other, who were falling in love. That would never be her. No matter how much fun she'd had tonight.

The crowd had diminished, leaving only a few others sitting at the tables. Walter pushed their empty glasses aside. "I'm sorry I pulled you out of the Pig's Tail the way I did."

Shirley wasn't sure she wanted to talk about that. The time since then had been so wonderful she didn't want the fun to end. She leaned closer to the table to make sure no one else would hear. "If I remember correctly, you pulled me off the stage, and then *carried* me out of the joint like a sack of feed."

Walter grinned and nodded slightly. "Yes, that's how I remember it, too."

An inkling of fear tickled her spine at something he'd said back at the Pig's Tail. "Can the judge make me go back to CB's?"

"No," Walter said. "But as your lawyer, I need to advise you that we don't want to give him the wrong impression. We don't want to give Mel any ammunition, either. For the time being, it would be in your best interest to stay clear of speakeasies."

A heavy sigh seeped out of her lungs. As her lawyer. How had she forgotten that? That's why signing his paper had made her stomach sink. Pro bono or not, she owed him. Had to listen to what he told her. Do what he told her.

"For appearance's sake," he said. "You understand?"

She nodded. "Yes, I hadn't thought of that. Rosie had said if I want to be a singer, that I needed to learn more songs, so we went to the Pig's Tail."

She couldn't tell him, but the moment she'd stepped on that stage, it was like, well, like she was exactly where she belonged. Onstage. Like her mother had been. It had been so exciting, so wonderful. She hadn't even known the words, yet they'd come to her as if she had sung them a million times before. It had all been so much more than she'd ever expected.

"They gave you a singing job that quickly?" he asked.

"No." Shirley shook her head. How she'd ended up on the stage was sort of a blur, because it had happened so quickly. "They didn't give me a job. I'd just introduced myself to Eva, the singer I was onstage with, and told her I was a singer, too. Then a man at the table said something about competition, and the next thing I knew, Eva pulled me on the stage and told me to repeat whatever she sang." It all had happened fast, and now that she thought about it, she wondered why Eva had done that—pulled her on the stage and told her to sing. It was like when she'd learned to swim. "I think it was a test."

"A test?" Walter asked. "You mean an audition?"

"No, it wasn't an audition. I think Eva thought I'd fail. That I wouldn't be able to sing. But I did.

The people clapped. Then she told me to sing another song with her. The same way. Repeating after her. I'd sang four songs when you arrived." The oddity of how it all had happened was rolling faster in her mind. "Why do you think she did that?"

"I don't know," Walter said.

"I don't, either." The more she thought about it, the more she was convinced it was a test. Before pulling her on the stage, Eva had laughed, and said every girl thought she was a singer, but few actually were. Eva had seemed angry, too, after that first song, and angrier with each one thereafter.

"Maybe she was afraid," Walter said.

"Of what? I just wanted to meet her."

He grinned. "I'd say competition, because that's what you gave her. More than she wanted."

Shirley thought about that. Competition. That's what the man at the table had said, but that was silly. Singers should like each other, want to know others who sang, too. She certainly did.

"It's a dog-eat-dog world here," Walter said. "People will do anything to get to the top and stay there."

She wanted to ask what he meant, but needed to think about things first. Not only how Eva had acted and how wonderful it had been to be on that stage singing, but about what he said about staying away from speakeasies.

"Shall we go?" Walter asked.

Shirley nodded and stood up at the same time he did.

He grinned and leaned closer. "A lady should always stay seated and wait for the man to help her out of her chair."

She looked at him skeptically. "Why?"

His eyes twinkled. "Manners."

She glanced around the room. Just then, a man at a table on the other side of the room stood. The woman stayed in her chair until he walked around the table and pulled back her chair. She then laid her hand in the man's before she rose to her feet. Shirley figured she'd probably seen that all happen before, but had never thought much about it. Now she would. Just like she'd thought so hard about never saying *ain't* again. Her mind was going to be plumb worn-out by the time she fell asleep tonight.

"When in Rome, do as the Romans do."

She peered up at Walter. "What's that supposed to mean?"

"It's an old saying referring to how to behave like others in certain situations."

"Oh." She let that sink in as they walked to their car. Once seated, she asked, "So you weren't trying to be mean when you told me I should have stayed sitting down?"

He started the car. "No, I wasn't trying to be mean. I know you want to fit in, so I thought I would point that out."

Once again, she mulled that over. Telling herself she truly had no reason to distrust him. In fact, she probably had more reason to trust him than anyone else. Especially that Eva singer. The more she thought about that, the more irritated she became that she hadn't realized that Eva was trying to make her fail right from the start. The way she kept singing faster and faster with each song. By the time Walter had arrived, she'd dang near sounded like an auctioneer with a pen full of swine to get rid of. That was just mean of that woman, and a part of her took delight in the fact that Walter had hauled her out of there before Eva had done something else.

Turning her thoughts back to him, she said, "Thank you. Will you point other things out to me? Things I should know, but don't?"

"I suppose I could, but…"

She waited for about a minute for him to say more, but couldn't wait any longer. "But what?"

If he could have, Walter would already have kicked himself. More than once. He hadn't enjoyed an evening this much in a very long time.

And it was because of her. She was special. Unique. In ways he'd totally forgotten about. Watching her at the movie theater, and again tasting an ice cream soda for the first time, had reminded him that there was still innocence in this world. Pure, unadulterated innocence.

"Well," he finally said, "don't worry about the things you don't know because there is nothing wrong with being an ordinary person."

"An ordinary person?"

"Yes. Everyone is unique in their own right, and that's special."

"So am I ordinary or am I unique?" she asked.

He chuckled. "You are as unique as they come, Shirley Burnette from Nebraska. Don't ever doubt that." She was, and for some reason, he wasn't ready for tonight to be over. He turned left at the next corner and headed for the highway that led out of town.

"Where are we going now?"

She had a good sense of direction. Knew he wasn't headed back toward Julia's place. "I want to show you one more thing." He glanced her way. "If you don't mind?"

"No, I don't mind."

"Good. I think you'll like it."

"You were right, you know," she said.

"About what?"

"Having fun in many different ways."

"You liked the movie?" he asked.

"Yes. And the ice cream soda, and this. Just driving. It's fun."

"It is." He turned onto the highway. "What did you do back in Nebraska for fun?"

"Not much." She sighed. "But when Pappy was alive, I had fun. Lots of it. We were always laughing. And singing. We would make up songs about what we were doing and sing them, adding silly made-up words when nothing else would rhyme."

Her giggle was delightful. "That does sound fun."

"It was. Right up until he got sick and died and the Swaggerts got the farm."

"With their lawyer," he pointed out, clearly remembering when she'd told him that.

"Yes. With their lawyer."

"Where did you go then?"

"To the Swaggerts' house. They offered me a job, cooking and cleaning, and whatever else they needed done. Mary Swaggert had died a few years before then and Olin was raising his six sons on his own. They raised hogs. Lots and lots of hogs."

"You lived with a man and his six sons?"

"Yes, for over four years."

He wasn't impressed with what he was hearing at all. "How old were his sons?"

"The oldest is twenty-six, and the youngest is eighteen now."

His concern rose up another notch. "Are any of them married?"

She laughed. "If you think I don't have any manners, you should meet the Swaggerts. They have less the manners of the hogs they raise."

"I never said you didn't have manners." Searching for a way to keep from sinking due to his earlier statement, he said, "You've just never been around men who do have manners."

"I'll agree with you there," she said. "Oh, and I'll pay you what I owe you once we get to Julia's. Alice put everyone's money in her purse so we wouldn't all have to carry our own purses. They can get bothersome at times."

He knew how bothersome purses could be. He'd ended up carrying Lucy's purses more than she ever had. That hadn't bothered him at first, but along with so many other things, as time went on, that, too, had been something that had irritated him to no end. Letting that go, he said, "You don't owe me any money."

"Yes, I do. Twenty-five cents for the movie and ten cents for the ice cream soda."

"I don't expect you to pay for those things."

"Why not? I've always paid my own way, and will continue to do so. I don't like owing anyone for anything."

He bit the end of his tongue to keep him from saying anything more than "It was my treat."

Her silence said she was pondering that. She did that a lot. Thought long and hard.

She was stubborn, and probably wouldn't let it go, so he said, "I'll let you treat me next time."

"Oh," she said, as if surprised. "That will work. So, where are we going now?"

"We're almost there." He'd already turned off the highway and was taking the winding road up to the top of the bluff that overlooked the city. She'd like this. He was sure of it.

At the top, he pulled the car as close to the edge of the bluff as possible.

She was already stretching her neck to see over the top of the windshield. "What is that? All of California?"

"No. That is Los Angeles."

She slapped the seat. "Baloney!"

"No, that is LA." He opened his door and grinned at her when she grabbed the door handle. "A lady should wait for a man to open her car door."

She let go of the handle. "Well, don't dilly-dally, then."

He laughed and jogged around the front of the car. She jumped out as soon as he opened her door. "Be careful. It's a long way down over the edge of that cliff."

"I will be," she said, walking toward the edge.

He'd left on the headlights so they could see where the ground ended. Which was exactly where she stopped.

"I feel like I did when you showed me the ocean," she whispered. "Small. Like an ant."

He looked over the miles and miles of city lights down below them. It did make a person feel small. He'd never thought of it that way.

She let out a low whistle. "That's just Los Angeles?"

"Yes," he replied. "Five years ago, it was only half this size, and half that size five years before then."

"I had no idea it was this big."

"It is, and growing every day."

"A person could get lost down there, and no one would ever find them."

"Yes, they could."

"They do, don't they?" she asked, looking up at him. "Those girls you told me about, the ones that work at places like CB's."

It was as if his arm had a mind of its own, because before he realized what was happening, it had settled around her shoulders. Since it was there, he rubbed her shoulder as he said, "Yes, they do."

She turned back to the lights of the city and stared at them for a few quiet moments before saying, "I owe you another thank-you, Walter. I truly do."

He tightened his hold around her, tugged her against him. She leaned her head against his shoulder and sighed softly. He told himself he would not kiss her. Would not let the pull of desire inside him win.

She lifted her head and looked up at him. The draw inside him became so strong he bit the inside of his cheek. She was so pretty, her eyes so enchanting, he couldn't look away. Not even as she stretched onto her toes and pressed her lips against his cheek. They were so soft, so tender, his muscles tensed as he fought against a commanding desire to reciprocate.

# Chapter Nine

In bed that night, the movie she'd seen played in Shirley's mind all over again. It had been amazing. So had the ice cream soda and looking at all those lights from that bluff. It seemed that everything worth seeing that she'd seen since arriving in California had been because of Walter. She wouldn't have seen any of those things if not for him.

Actually, if not for him, she'd be at CB's, working until the wee hours of the morning rather than lying in bed here in Julia's cabin. Her debts to him sure were adding up.

That was as sobering as the buckets of cold water she used to toss on the Swaggert boys on Saturday mornings. Olin had never minded the boys going to town on Friday night, but he'd been madder than a cornered coyote when they didn't get up come Saturday morn.

She'd only had to witness that once before she

started throwing cold water on the boys. They'd all spit and spat, but they'd been at the breakfast table when Olin walked in the room. Not a one of them had ever been mad at her about that. Not a one of them learned, either, and for a moment, she wondered how things were going for all of them.

It hadn't been what she'd wanted to be doing, working for the Swaggerts, but it hadn't been all that bad. Not when compared to CB's.

Like it or not, she owed Walter for getting her out of there. She owed him for tonight, too.

She had been spitting mad when he'd pulled her off that stage, but not now. Not after seeing the movie, and eating that ice cream soda, looking at all those lights and, well, pointing out that there were things she needed to know.

Like other things, he was right about that.

California was a lot different from Nebraska.

Walter was a lot different from anyone she'd ever known, too.

It was remarkable, how in a city this big she'd run into him her first day. And kept running into him.

She closed her eyes. He was remarkably handsome. So handsome it made her heart feel funny. Other parts of her, too. Sometimes when he looked at her, it was impossible to breathe. That had happened the strongest on top of that cliff tonight. When she'd told him that she owed him another thank-you.

Something else had happened right then. She'd had the strangest desire to have him kiss her. On the lips. She'd wanted that so badly she'd kissed him. On the cheek, and that—how amazing it had been for her lips to touch his skin—had scared the dickens out of her. She'd run. Straight to his car, opened the door and jumped inside.

She regretted that now. Her heart started pounding again as she remembered it, and she wondered, seriously wondered, what might have happened if she hadn't gotten scared. Or if she'd fought that fear, and had stood right where she'd been.

She'd never know, and that saddened her.

It worried her, too, because she'd never wanted a man to kiss her before, had never kissed a man before and didn't know why she had.

All of that was still on her mind the next morning as she tugged a few weeds out of the garden, then, because there were no more weeds and the diner was closed today, she went inside to give the cabin a thorough cleaning. Thoughts of Walter hung with her there, too.

Now she wondered what he was doing today.

Rita, Alice and Rosie arrived midmorning, wondering what had happened to her last night.

Julia's house had been dark when Walter had brought her home. He'd insisted upon walking her all the way to the cabin. And had. Then left, after lighting the lamp for her.

She told the others what Walter had said, about how they should stay away from speakeasies until their case was settled, but didn't tell them about the movie, or the ice cream soda, or the lights or several other things, just like she hadn't told anyone about the ocean.

Those events were like her mother's picture and Mammy's Bible. She just wanted to keep them tucked away. Safe.

Rosie plopped down in one of the two chairs sitting near the table. "Stay away? That's impossible. Especially for you."

"Why?" Shirley asked, glancing at all three of them. "Why is it impossible?"

"Eric Johansson," Rosie said.

The name meant nothing to Shirley. "Who?"

"He owns the Pig's Tail, and after Walter carried you out the door, Eric found out you'd come with us, and asked us about you. About your singing."

Shirley's heart skipped a beat. "He did?"

"Yes. Eva was furious that you're a better singer than her," Alice said, sitting down on the cot. "She stormed out not long after you did, telling Eric that she quit."

"She did?" Shirley asked. "Why? I'm not a better singer than her. I was only copying her."

"No," Rosie said. "You are much better than her. I don't think anyone realized how bad she was until they heard you."

"It's true," Rita said, sitting down in the other chair. "After Walter carried you out the door, and only Eva was singing, people started shouting to bring that blonde girl back onstage." Rita pointed at Alice and Rosie. "We went looking for you and saw you and Walter drive away."

Shirley bit her lip, trying to disguise the desire to know more, but it was to no avail. "What happened then?"

"Like Alice said, Eva quit." Rosie's grin grew. "And we told Eric that we know you, and that you're looking for a singing job."

"He wants you to go see him today," Alice said, her grin going from one pierced ear to the other. "This afternoon at the Pig's Tail. Before the joint gets busy so he can audition you himself."

"Oh, dear." Shirley pressed a hand to the frantic beat of her heart at the idea of her dream coming true. Her stomach sank then. "I can't go see him. Walter said our case has gone before a judge, and until it's settled, we don't want to give Mel any reason to win the case. Working at a speakeasy could do that."

"Even singing?" Alice asked.

Completely deflated, Shirley sat down on the cot beside Alice. "Yes. Even singing."

"Oh, that's really too bad," Alice said.

"Are you sure?" Rosie asked.

"I'm sure," Shirley said, huffing out a breath.

"Singing at the Pig's Tail isn't anything like being a cigarette girl at CB's," Rita said.

"Maybe not to us," Shirley answered. "Because we know the difference." Then, mimicking what Walter had said last night, she added, "Others don't know the difference, and appearances matter right now. A lot." She shook her head. "None of us want to go back to CB's, and that's what could happen if I go talk to this Eric person."

"There has to be something we can do," Rita said.

"I know!" Rosie leaped to her feet. "We can disguise you. No one will know it's you."

Shirley shook her head. "Eric already saw me."

"We'll say we couldn't find you, but say you're your sister." Rosie rubbed her chin. "That could work. With some hair dye and a pair of scissors, and…"

Shirley stopped listening. Had to, because if she didn't, she might go along with the idea. That couldn't happen. If anything went wrong, they'd all be back at CB's or worse. She didn't know what or where, but knew from what Walter had said about those girls coming up missing that there were worse things than working as a cigarette girl.

Truth was, she was afraid of going back to CB's knowing what she did now. After all that had happened, none of them would be safe there. Not at all.

Rosie grabbed her arm. "Come on. This is going to work. I know it will, but we can't tell anyone. Not even Julia."

Shirley shook her head, in disagreement and to clear her mind. "What? No? No. It won't work. I can't go there. None of us can."

"You came here to be a singer, and a singer you will be," Rosie insisted.

"No," Shirley argued, even as Pappy's words repeated in her head. "Not right now. I'll have to wait."

"You can't wait. Eric will find someone else. It's now or never, Shirley." Rosie let go of her arm. "Which is it going to be?"

A shiver rippled over Shirley. What if this was like last night, when she got scared and ran for the car? She'd never know what might have happened if she'd stood there, waited just a bit longer, and now, she'd never know if she didn't take this chance. If she ran scared again.

Walter took his time walking into his office, even though he'd heard the phone ringing from the kitchen. It was Mrs. McCaffrey's day off. She'd left early this morning to attend church with some of her lady friends, and would then spend the afternoon with one or more of them.

He rounded his desk before picking up the earpiece with one hand and the mouth stand with the other. "Hello."

"Russell, it's Mel Cartwright."

Walter sighed. "I told you that I'll speak—"

"The deal's off."

A shiver tickled his spine. "What do you mean?"

"I have on very good authority that the little blonde you are representing was singing over at Eric Johansson's place last night," Mel said. "And I know she left with you."

*Damn it.* Walter sat down and took his time coming up with a response.

"The judge is going to hear about that, too," Mel said.

Walter had no doubt about that. "She hasn't broken any law by singing at the Pig's Tail. That has no bearing on the case." It did, but he didn't want Mel to have any ammunition. "What this case pertains to is the false pretenses upon which you hired those women, and how you didn't pay them a fair wage."

"Eric doesn't pay any better than I do."

"She doesn't work for Eric. She was merely

singing a song with one of Eric's singers," Walter said, forcing his tone to stay even.

"Then why did you pull her off the stage and carry her out of the building?"

Walter closed his eyes. Word traveled fast in this town. Always had and always would.

"Or is there more to you and her than you're letting on? Maybe the judge needs to know that, too," Mel said.

Walter sucked in air through his nose. "I am her attorney, nothing more. But as her attorney, I have the right to advise her of what might and might not be within her best interests. That's all that took place last night."

"The deal is still off," Mel said.

The line went dead before Walter could respond. He hung up the phone and set it down on the desk so hard it jingled. This can of worms just kept getting bigger. He normally wouldn't take advantage of the reputation he'd built for himself in such a manner, but right now, he didn't have much choice.

He opened his desk drawer and pulled out a long list of phone numbers. Locating Judge Wallis's home number, he picked up the earpiece and clicked the hanger until an operator answered and then gave her the exchange.

To his relief, Wallis welcomed him to drive

over so they could speak in private. Walter didn't waste a second. He ran to his car and jumped in.

The judge's house was on the other end of town, and traffic caused the drive to take more than an hour.

Much less time than the actual meeting took.

Wallis appeared empathetic, and admitted that this case had caught more attention than he'd wanted, which also made it imperative that everything about it was by the book—no plea deals whatsoever—so that no one could come back later and use it against any of those involved, including both of them.

Walter agreed. Prohibition agents had pretty much thrown up their hands at trying to control the federal law the Volstead Act had laid down, and that meant the underground world of Los Angeles had flourished and spread crime-wise. It now festered like fruit rotting on the ground, and the newspapers sensationalized each and every bit they got their teeth into. The courts could use this as a good piece of public service, show how they were fighting back against a portion of the seedy grime that was growing exponentially, but only if it was on the level. He also promised that Shirley wouldn't be singing in any speakeasies until all was settled.

He left then and, while driving home, accepted

it now was completely on his shoulders to make sure that promise was fulfilled.

There was only one thing he could do. Head over to Julia's. The good thing was that, after last night, Blondie seemed to understand the complexity that had taken over this case. He wasn't too worried about any of the others. None of them appeared to be as determined to become a singer, or anything else that concerned him. He'd never had to counsel clients to this level before, and didn't plan on ever doing it again.

In some ways, this all reminded him too much of Theodore. Of how he hadn't listened.

Traffic filled the roadways and the trip back across town was slow-going. By the time he arrived at Julia's, the day was more than half-over.

The diner was closed so he drove past it and into Julia's yard. Last night he'd taken the trail behind the house that led to the cabin in the woods where Shirley was staying. He'd insisted upon walking her all the way to the cabin, despite his own better judgment. He'd felt things last night that he hadn't felt in a long time, and had he not been careful, something might have happened.

If things were different—if he was different— he might have kissed Shirley last night. When they'd been standing on the bluff and again when he'd delivered her to her door.

Luckily, his failed marriage had left him with a

healthy amount of restraint. Failed because that's what it had been. Long before Lucy's death, their marriage had fallen apart. So had his love for her. He'd just been too stubborn to let her go. For her own good.

And his.

He'd been smitten with Lucy. The beautiful, bright, glamorous star who'd entered his office, seeking advice on her acting contract. Their relationship had been a whirlwind and short-lived. Four weeks after meeting each other, they'd gotten married, and four months later, they'd hated each other.

If he'd been smart, he'd have let her go, but he hadn't been smart. He'd been determined not to fail. The entire city had proclaimed him the luckiest man on earth to have caught the eye of Lucy Marshall. She'd made a name for herself as an actress in her first picture, and men had clamored for her attention. He'd been filled with pride to be that man. To have won her love.

Trouble was, he hadn't won her love. He'd won her business. Nothing more. She'd wanted him to oversee her contracts, make sure no one could take anything away from her, even while she and a male costar maintained an affair that had started long before she'd walked into his office that first time.

Walter had come to understand that Lucy

didn't love Karl VanBuren any more than she'd loved him; however, she had loved what Karl had continued to provide to her. Opium. Seeking it out on her own would have been too risky. Especially if one of the magazines got wind of it.

Toward the end, that hadn't even mattered to her.

He'd known all that, but had thought he could change her. Make her see what a wonderful life they could have had together. The family they could have had together. But now, he realized that had been his dream, not hers.

"You certainly are becoming a regular around here."

Walter shook the ghostly memories aside and turned to Julia. He hadn't heard her approach, but she had, and now stood next to his driver's door.

"How are you today?" he asked, lifting the latch on his door.

Julia laid a hand on his shoulder. "I'm fine, but there's no sense getting out. I'm assuming you're here to see the girls. They aren't here."

"All of them?"

She nodded. "Yes, all of them."

He let go of the door handle. "I need to talk with them. Do you know where they are?"

"No. They left here together, though, all four of them."

A chill made the hair on the back of his neck stand up. "Where do you think they went?"

She let out a sigh and shook her head. "I discovered a long time ago that we have to let people make their own mistakes and learn from them. It's hard sometimes, because we think we know better." She shrugged. "But maybe we don't because not everyone wants the same things that we do."

He wasn't in the mood for advice, direct or indirect, because he suddenly knew exactly where he'd find Shirley. He muffled a curse, started the roadster's engine and shifted into Reverse.

The Pig's Tail was only a few blocks away, and considering it was Sunday afternoon, there were only a couple of cars in the parking lot. Anger burned hotter inside him than it had last night. He had half a mind to quit. Void out the contracts he'd signed with these women and get back to his other clients. The ones who actually paid him and didn't have him running around the city on a Sunday morning, making promises to judges that he may not be able to keep.

Walter glanced up at the two-story white-washed building. He couldn't quit. There was too much at stake.

He killed the car engine and climbed out. In the light of day, there was nothing ritzy or glamorous about this place. It looked like any other butcher shop, complete with a small barn out back for unsuspecting animals. Then again, folks didn't come here for glitz and glamour. They went to the clubs downtown for that. Not CB's, but the ones that catered to the rich and famous. The ones he and Lucy used to visit. He still attended parties once in a great while, for special events pertaining to some of his clients.

The stair steps creaked as he walked up them. Storage was painted in large black letters on the dirty white door, and he shook his head while reaching for the handle. Why couldn't Shirley see places like this weren't going to get her anywhere in life?

Walter frowned when the knob wouldn't turn. He jiggled it and tried turning it again. He was sure this was where he'd find the women, and the locked door caused concern to rise up in him. He'd never heard anything bad about the joint, or the owner, but that didn't mean it didn't exist.

He knocked on the door. Hard.

A moment later, a click sounded inside the lock and the door opened a crack. Music filled his ears.

"Sorry, we're closed until five," a man said, barely peeking through the crack.

"I'm not here to drink," Walter said, giving the door a hearty shove.

The man, a short gray-haired man, tried to bar the door, but Walter gave it a second shove and stepped inside as the other man stumbled backward.

Like last night, Walter's gaze went directly to the stage. She was there again. Singing again. She stopped abruptly as their eyes met. The piano music stopped, too, and everyone sitting at the two tables in front of the stage looked over their shoulders.

A big, burly man leaped to his feet. "Woodrow!"

"I told him we were closed, Mr. Johansson," the older gray man said, closing the door. "He barged in anyway."

"I'm not here to drink," Walter repeated, this time directing his statement at Eric Johansson.

With black hair and a barrel chest, the man looked like a butcher. Big enough to toss a full-grown cow around like others would a chicken.

"Then what do you want?" Johansson asked.

"Her," Walter said, pointing at Shirley, who had stepped off the stage. Realizing that could be perceived wrongly, he added, "And the others."

"Why?" Johansson asked.

"I'm an attorney and am representing them in an employment dispute," Walter answered.

Johansson's jaw, which was about the size of a kettle, dropped as his eyes grew wide. "Against Mel Cartwright? I've heard about that. About you."

Walter didn't need to respond.

Johansson had already spun around. "Out!" he shouted. "All of you, out!"

"Mr. Johansson—"

"I don't want to hear it!" He interrupted whatever Shirley had been about to say. "I won't get mixed up in that shenanigan! Out, I say, all of you! I don't ever want to see any of you in my joint ever again!"

The others had already started for the door. True to form, Shirley was the only one holding back. "Please, if you'll just let me explain."

"There's nothing to explain," Johansson said. "Woodrow, open that door!"

Turning her gaze from the butcher to him, Shirley marched forward. "I hope you're happy," she snapped while stomping past.

Walter bit back a retort about saving her hind end yet again as he nodded to Johansson. "Sorry to have disturbed you."

"I sure don't envy you," Johansson said. "It's too bad, though. She's one hell of a singer." His bushy brows tugged downward as he glanced toward Shirley. "Once this court case is over, could I hire her?"

His first instinct was to say no, but Walter stopped himself from saying that. Instead, he shrugged. "I won't know if the judge will order any stipulations until he rules on the case."

Johansson nodded. "It's just as well. She wouldn't stay here long. Someone always lures away the good ones." He held out his hand. "I owe you thanks for showing up when you did. I was ready to hire her. Put her to work singing tonight."

Walter shook the man's hand, even as anger rolled in his stomach. So much for thinking she understood the complexities of this case. "I'm glad I arrived before that happened, too."

Johansson's grasp tightened slightly and he stepped closer. "No one needs to know about what happened here, do they?"

"They won't hear it from me," Walter said, tightening his hold on the man's hand. "And I hope they won't hear it from you. That could be detrimental to your business. Both of them."

Dropping his hand to his side, Johansson shook his head. "No one will hear it from me or those who work for me." He nodded toward the piano player and the man named Woodrow, who stood at the door, holding it open. "I guarantee it."

"Good enough," Walter said. He crossed the room and nodded at Woodrow while walking out.

The other girls were walking down the road, but Shirley was standing beside his car with her hands on her hips and fury in her eyes. He was furious, too. But was also humored. By her. Her attitude and how cute she looked glaring at him.

Like all this was his fault. Damn her. She was affecting him in too many ways.

He took his time walking down the steps, but never took his eyes off her. Something churned inside him, low and deep. He wanted to think it was anger. Or at least righteousness, but knew it wasn't either. He was attracted to her. Had been since their first meeting, and that was hitting too dangerously close to home.

# Chapter Ten

Shirley's chest heaved as she watched Walter walk down the steps. It was the silly grin on his face that really had her steaming. It would be better if he was as steaming mad as she was at this moment. How? How on earth did he know where she was *all* the time? And show up at precisely the *wrong* moment?

She waited until he stopped right in front of her before saying, "I sure am getting tired of you showing up out of the blue like you do."

His smile increased slightly. "I could say the same. That I'm tired of it." He laid a hand on the hood of his car. "I thought we'd come to an agreement."

The way he leaned closer made her heart flip.

"Was I wrong or were you playing me for a sap?" he asked.

"A what?"

"A sap. It means a fool." He planted his other hand on the hood, on her other side.

She was trapped between his arms with the car up against her back and him in front of her. Her heart threatened to beat its way right out of her chest. Not because she was scared. She was thinking about kissing him again.

"Well, I'm not a fool, so you can quit playing me for one."

She swallowed and shook her head. "I'm not playing at anything. And I don't think you're a fool."

"Then what the hell were you doing here? Onstage? Singing?"

Guilt bubbled in her stomach. So did frustration.

"Did you not hear what I said last night?"

"Yes, I heard you." She had to stop thinking about kissing him. That's not what this was about. It was about her. Her dream. She couldn't let anyone take that away from her. She'd be empty then. Truly have nothing. "I just… I just had to know."

"Know what?"

"If I really could get a job as a singer. I just wanted to know if he would hire me, then I was going to tell him that I couldn't come work for him until after you get things settled with CB's."

He shook his head, and she swore she saw disappointment in his eyes, which made sadness well up inside her along with everything else.

"What did you expect him to say to that? To do?"

"I hoped he'd be all right with it." She bit her bottom lip, knowing that would have been unusual. To ask for a job, but then say you couldn't actually go to work, not for a while. "You said it won't be that long."

He sighed. "It wouldn't have been before last night. Mel got word that you and the others were here last night, and is no longer willing to negotiate."

"He did? How?"

"I don't know."

She glanced over her shoulder. Rita, Alice and Rosie were nowhere in sight, had already turned the corner on their way back to Julia's. "What does that mean? That he's no longer willing to negotiate?"

"That the outcome will be completely up for the judge to decide."

She closed her eyes as an entirely new wave washed over her. This time it was laced with dread. And fear of being ordered to go back to CB's.

"I told you the importance of staying away from joints," he said.

"I know. And I was going to."

"Right after getting a job at one?"

"Yes. No." She opened her eyes. "I told the others that I couldn't go to work here because you'd said we needed to stay clear, but they said that Mr. Johansson wanted me to come audition with him today. That I wouldn't get a second chance. Rosie offered to dye my hair so no one would recognize me, but I said I wouldn't do that. That I'd just find out if he would hire me, and then tell him I'll come to work for him later."

"Do you have any idea how that little scheme right there could have gotten you blackballed from working anywhere?"

Another word she didn't understand. "Blackballed?"

"Yes. Word spreads fast around here. Just like Eric Johansson had heard about your case against Mel Cartwright, others would hear about you accepting a job, but then stipulating that you wouldn't go to work until you're ready. Others will hear about that and share the word that you aren't worth hiring."

Her heart sank. "They would?" Being on that stage again, even though it had only been for half a song, had been as amazing as last night. She hated this. Being so close, yet so far away. She hated having him so angry with her, too.

"Yes, they would," he said.

She slumped against the car. "Oh, horse feathers."

"Luckily, Mr. Johansson has agreed not to tell anyone about your little stint today," Walter said. "For his own sake as much as yours."

That should have been a relief; instead, it made her feel worse. It seemed everything she'd done since leaving Nebraska had been wrong. So wrong. Hanging her head, she whispered, "I should never have come here. I should have stayed with the Swaggerts. Cooking. Washing dishes. Slopping hogs and—"

"No." Walter's hand cupped her chin and he forced her to look up. "You shouldn't have stayed with the Swaggerts." He grinned slightly. "But you shouldn't have come here to the Pig's Tail."

She sighed. "I know."

He closed his eyes for a moment, and when they opened, there was a sadness in them. "I told you about my friend, Theodore, and how he hadn't listened to me, to his lawyer, and what happened."

A lump formed in Shirley's throat.

"This is as serious as that," he said, dropping his hand on the car again. "You have to promise me you won't come here again. I'm not trying to be mean. I'm just trying to keep you safe."

At that moment, she hated herself for what

she'd done. For betraying him by coming here. He made her feel safe, had since the raid. "I won't."

"You promise?"

She wanted to hug him, kiss him, take away the sadness in his eyes. It was still there. In his eyes. She couldn't help but see it. His hands were either side of her on the hood of the car again. The backs of her thighs were pressed up against the metal.

He had her trapped. She couldn't run if she wanted to… She didn't want to run. Not this time.

Slowly, and hoping he wouldn't move, wouldn't run, she lifted her hands to his face. As her palms cupped his jaw, she eased forward, brought her lips closer to his. Licking them as they tingled with anticipation and holding her breath at the idea of kissing him. On the lips this time.

Her heart fluttered as she felt the warmth of his breath on her lips. She inched closer, but as her lips touched his—a mere, soft tap—she paused, not knowing what to do.

He grasped her shoulders and pulled her forward, up against him as his lips did more than tap hers. They pressed against her mouth, gently, but with enough pressure her entire body tingled from the heat of his lips.

An instinct she didn't know she possessed took over. Her entire body arched upward, toward him, and her hands tightened their hold on his face.

But suddenly, his lips were gone.

The kiss was over.

She felt deprived. As if he'd stolen something from her and pulled her eyes open.

Had he stolen her kiss? Was that even possible?

He still had ahold of her shoulders, and was looking at her. Directly at her. She met his gaze and her lips quivered, as if they knew what she saw even before she did. His eyes. There was no pain in them. They were sparkling.

The thrill that shot through her was indescribable. As was the sensation that rippled over her as his lips met hers again. They were still gentle, but there was purpose in the way they moved. They glided over hers several times. The pressure grew, the intensity increased with each amazing stroke.

Her hands slid off his face and around his neck, giving her something solid to hold on to as his lips taught hers how to move, how to meet his and then how to part so she breathed his air.

It was amazing, sharing air, but not as amazing as what happened next. His tongue slipped past her teeth, into her mouth. She held on tighter, surprised and delighted by how amazingly wonderful kissing him proved to be. She was so glad she hadn't run this time.

So very glad.

They were both breathing hard and smiling when they parted.

His eyes were still sparkling, too. "So you promise to not come back here?"

"Yes, I promise." Then, because she was full of silly happiness, she added, "I can't. Mr. Johansson said he didn't want to see any of us in his joint ever again."

Walter chuckled. "Yes, he did say that."

He may no longer be mad, but she still owed him an apology. "I truly am sorry, Walter. I didn't think... Well, I guess I just didn't think."

He let go of her shoulders and touched the tip of her nose with one finger. "Then it's a good thing you have a lawyer who is thinking." He took a step back. "I spent the morning at Judge Wallis's home, promising him you wouldn't be singing in any joints until this case is ruled upon."

The air seeped out of her lungs. "You did? Why?"

"Yes. After Cartwright heard about you singing here last night, he withdrew any negotiations, and I had to make sure that Judge Wallis knew the truth about what happened."

She'd never even talked to a judge, but knew she'd have been scared out of her wits to have to go see one, especially on a Sunday. "Do you do that often? Go to a judge's house?"

"No. I've never done it before, and I don't want to have to do it again." He nodded toward his car. "Let's go."

She didn't move. Couldn't. She was too busy realizing something. Now that she'd kissed him, she wanted to do it again. She'd thought once it happened, the desire would end. But it didn't, and now she had to wonder what that meant.

He took her arm and led her around the car. "I'll give you a ride to Julia's. We have to let the others know how important it is for them to stay clear of joints."

He opened her door. She climbed in and then watched him walk around the car and climb in. Not sure she wanted to go Julia's yet, she said, "I already told them."

"And just like you, they came here anyway." He started the car. "I'll tell them and make them understand the importance of that by letting them know what could happen if any of you try a stunt like this again."

"They know. We'll all end up at CB's again."

He put the car in gear and drove around the parking lot toward the road. "It's not that simple."

Her insides quivered. She knew he was referring to what had happened to his friend again and pulled her eyes off him. If she'd known how complicated life would be out here, she would have stayed in Nebraska.

No, she determined a moment later, she wouldn't have. She'd just have to figure out a way to make everything work out right. And a way to not worry him again. He truly was worried about her, worried that she'd end up like his friend. Her dream was to become a singer, not be dead. Then she'd really be singing like an angel.

This was all so hard. Being so close to her dream, but not being able to get it because of past mistakes. That would have to stop right now. Mistakes. She'd made enough. Her dream was out there. That was for sure. It would just take longer than she'd expected. Saving the money to get here had taken longer, too, but she'd made it happen. Nothing worth having is easy. Pappy told her that long ago and he'd been right.

With a new outlook on things, she gave herself a nod, and then turned to Walter. "I truly am sorry. And do appreciate all you are doing for me. I'm glad you're my lawyer. Glad I met you."

He glanced her way and she had to smile at the half grin on his face.

"I am," she said. "Really."

He chuckled. "I'm glad, too."

She drew in a deep breath and marveled at the jolt of happiness that sprang forth inside her. She was glad she'd met him. He truly was handsome, and always looked so spiffy. His white shirts were always crisply ironed and his suitcoats spotless.

A question formed as all that settled. Who made sure his clothes were so perfect? It had to be a woman. Unable to shake that thought, she asked, "When did your wife die?"

He was looking straight ahead at the road. "Four years ago."

A number of other questions formed about his wife, things she did now want to know. Shirley waited until he turned the corner before asking, "Were you with her in the car accident?"

"No. She was alone."

"Alone? She knew how to drive?"

"Yes. That surprises you?"

It did. At this moment, she couldn't remember if she knew a woman that knew how to drive.

"Julia drives. She picked you up at CB's that night," he said.

He was right. Julia had picked them up that night and drove her car regularly. That hadn't seemed odd. Probably because she hadn't thought about it up until now. However, prior to arriving in California, she hadn't seen a woman drive. Truth was, she hadn't seen that many cars.

"You should learn," he said. "It's not hard."

"I think I will," she answered.

He turned off the road, onto the driveway that led to Julia's house. The others were just arriving, still walking along the pathway from the back side of the diner, the same shortcut they'd taken when they'd walked to the Pig's Tail earlier. She felt bad about what had happened, but was glad they'd left. Otherwise they might have seen her and Walter kiss. She didn't want anyone to know about that. Mainly because she wasn't sure what it meant.

Julia stepped out of the house as Walter shut off the car. "Come inside," she said. "Out of the heat. I have a fresh pitcher of lemonade."

Rosie, Rita and Alice looked at the car as they walked past. Shirley offered what she hoped was a reassuring smile. Walter wasn't like other men. He wasn't going to bash or berate them, but they had to be prepared for his disappointment, and in some ways, that was worse. He was trying to help them and what they'd done could have hindered the case.

Her heart sank again. They'd done what they had because of her. For her.

Walter opened her door, and Shirley climbed out. "None of this is their fault," she said. "They went to the Pig's Tail because of me."

"I'm aware of that," he said, closing the car door. "However, they need to understand the importance of following whatever guidelines I lay down. It's in their best interests. In all of your best interests."

Shirley understood all of that and found no reason to answer with more than a nod. Later, while they all sat at Julia's kitchen table, drinking lemonade, she remained silent as Walter told the others what he'd already told her. About Mel, her singing, the judge, how things could look to others. He answered questions, too, especially about not knowing how long it would take, and said they weren't the only ones who wanted it all over as soon as possible.

He left after everyone agreed to stay away from joints, including Rosie, even though she wasn't involved in the case. Shirley stayed at the house the rest of the afternoon. Julia assured all of them that they had jobs with her as long as they needed them, and a place to stay. Shirley appreciated Julia's kindness, but couldn't shake the notion that she hadn't come to California to wash dishes. Not after singing on that stage. She felt bad about it, but only because of Walter. Everything else about it, she'd loved. And she wanted to do it again.

"You can use this time to practice your singing," Rosie said as if reading her mind. "Learn all sorts of new songs so that the next time you get an audition, you'll get the gig."

"We'll help you practice," Alice said. "If not for you, we'd still be working at CB's."

"No," Shirley pointed out. "If not for Walter."

"Walter is only helping Alice and me because of you," Rita said with a saucy look. "He likes you."

Shirley tried to deny that, but the others wouldn't

let her. She gave in quickly, because she wanted to believe that Walter did like her. It made her feel happy. As happy as singing on that stage had.

"It's about time he finds some happiness."

Shirley's ears perked up, and she looked at Julia, waiting for her to say more.

"He's a very successful lawyer, despite what his wife did to him. A scandal like that would have soured most men," Julia added.

"What scandal?" Shirley asked.

The room went extremely quiet as the other women looked at each other.

"What scandal?" she repeated.

Julia shook her head. "There's no raising the dead here. The newspapers do enough of that all on their own." Then with a nod, she said, "If Walter wants you to know, he'll tell you."

Heavens, that only made Shirley want to know more, but she tried to pretend it didn't. "Well, it's really none of my business."

The look the others shared said they saw through her pretense, but she chose to ignore that.

She tried to ignore the plethora of questions that constantly plagued her the next several days, too. Especially when there was no word from Walter. Was he soured? Didn't want nothing to do with women? Including her? Did he regret kissing her?

Julia had taken on the role of making sure they

all followed Walter's orders. None of them went anywhere without her permission.

Not that it mattered. Shirley was too busy to want to go anywhere. She and the others had fun, too. Julia had a radio that they listened to every evening, and she also had several packets of music. Songs of all sorts, even some that were on the radio. They would all join in with the singers coming through the speaker.

To say it was fun was an understatement. Singing along with the radio was the closest thing she had to being onstage, and she looked forward to it every day.

Rita knew a lot about music, and taught the rest of them how to read notes. Alice sang, too, but she did so while sewing. She could sew like no other and had made each of them a new dress. They were all looking forward to a time they'd be able to wear them.

Shirley had never had friends before, and had discovered how wonderful it was to have some now. Even Walter, although she hadn't seen him for several days. Not since the day they'd kissed. Memories of that day made her smile. Of her first stolen kiss, and her first very real one.

Walter's restraint had been pushed to the limit all week. He had no viable reason to contact Shirley. Judge Wallis was still considering if the case should be taken to court and Julia was fulfilling her promise of making sure none of the women went anywhere without her knowledge and approval. He hadn't asked her to do that; she'd volunteered and called him with regular updates.

That wasn't his issue. His lay deep within him. He wanted to see Shirley. Like a kid who wanted a bike. She had been on his mind since they'd met, but after kissing her... That was all he could think about. How perfect that first little stolen kiss had been.

It had been perfect, but kissing her, holding her, had opened up old wounds.

Lucy.

He couldn't go down that road again. It had been hell. Loving someone who hadn't loved him back. It had turned him into a different person. A person he hadn't wanted to be and, in some ways, still was. For it had changed him and he was still working on putting it all behind him.

It had been four years. Five since he'd first met Lucy. Since kissing Shirley, thoughts about how wrong things had gone started haunting him like it had all happened yesterday rather than years ago.

He'd thought his life had reached perfection those first few weeks with Lucy. Fortune, fame, a beautiful woman on his arm. Everything had seemed to just fall into place. The fast rise of the movie industry had given him a clear and clean route to fortune. Arthur had thought it was a crazy idea to put such focus on contract litigation, but Walter hadn't. It had taken hard work and long hours, but his dedication had paid off. He'd become *the* lawyer everyone in Hollywood wanted as movie studios had sprouted up throughout the city. His name had gained clout for months on end. Earned clout. And his bank account had reflected that. Still did.

He hadn't been surprised when Lucy had contacted him, but he had been surprised by her *affection* for him. He'd still thought of himself as an outsider, an orphan from Nebraska. Yes, he was a success, but as a lawyer. Not as a man. Lucy had changed that. She'd made him become an integral part of the glitz and glam of Hollywood.

It had been flattering at first. Lucy had been an actress and had played her part to perfection. Had sucked him in just like she had moviegoers to her films.

The phone on his desk rang, and for a moment, Walter considered not answering it. There were a limited number of people who had his phone number, and few of them would call on a Saturday. He stared at the phone as it rang again. Council Member Dean Smith and Mel Cartwright both called him here rather than at his office.

Julia called him here, too, which was why he answered the phone.

"It's Mel," the caller said as soon as Walter lifted the earpiece.

Walter held in a sigh. "I've told you before, I'm not your attorney, therefore can only offer you the advice to seek your own counsel."

"You could have heard a pin drop in my joint last night," Cartwright said. "You need to put a stop to this right now, or you'll wish you had."

A mixture of disbelief and anger rolled inside Walter. "Are you threatening me, Mel?" he asked. "Because if you are, I'm only going to warn you once." Making sure Cartwright knew who he was up against, Walter continued. "Right now, this is a labor dispute. You do anything stupid and it will become far more. The raid on your dope den will be a drop in the bucket compared to what happens when federal agents get involved. They're itching for action. Not only will you go down, all of your suppliers will, too, and we both know they won't like that."

It was no secret that the mob was embedded deep in LA, and that they were controlling every ounce of liquor. "Think about that, Mel. You won't even get your chance to have your day in court."

The line was silent.

"You understand what I'm saying, don't you, Mel?" Walter asked.

"Yes." The line went dead.

Walter hung up the phone. One more reason he stuck to contracts.

Mel's threat didn't unnerve him, but the fact the man thought he could intimidate him caused enough concern that he considered calling Julia. Then decided a visit was more in order.

On his way through the kitchen, he told Mrs. McCaffrey not to worry about the evening meal for him, that he didn't know how long he'd be gone. Once in the garage, he used the cuff of his sleeve to wipe a speck of dust off the driver's door of the roadster before climbing in.

He wasn't overly sure why he'd told Mrs. McCaffrey he didn't know when he'd be back, but the idea was settling deeper in his mind. Last Saturday night he'd taken Shirley to a picture show, and it had been fun. Of course, he'd first pulled her off the stage at the Pig's Tail, and again the following day, but that was all the more reason to consider taking her out to do something again this evening. Keep her from getting restless.

All in the line of duty. As her attorney. Until the judge made a ruling, she couldn't go out and about on her own.

Seeing a group of boys playing in the park as he drove to the diner added to his reasonings.

She'd wanted to see the angels in Los Angeles, well, he'd show her them.

A bout of happiness filled him as he parked on the street outside the diner. The closed sign hung on the door, but he could see people inside. Especially one blonde woman.

He'd missed her, and should take that as a warning, but a stronger part of him didn't want to. "Hello, ladies," he said, opening the door.

"Mr. Russell, has the judge made a ruling?" Rita asked.

She was one of the tallest women he'd ever seen, with brown hair that hung to her waist. He'd asked Rita and Alice how they'd gotten wound up with Mel Cartwright. Their situations were similar: new to town, low on money. Much like Blondie, who was standing behind the counter and gnawing on her bottom lip.

"No," he said. "I haven't heard from the judge. I just wanted to stop in and check on all of you."

"We're doing fine," Rosie answered, dropping the mop back into the bucket. "Just working our fingers to the bone and twiddling our thumbs."

"Yep, that's all we've been doing," Alice responded, tucking her fuzzy black curls behind her ears while elbowing the woman standing next to her. "Isn't it, Shirley?"

"I wouldn't say we've been working our fingers to the bone," Shirley replied. "There weren't but—there were only a few customers here all day so far."

"Saturdays are slow," Julia said, walking out of the kitchen. "We make up for it during the week."

Walter had only been thinking of Shirley, but as he looked at the other women and contemplated their situation, he included them in on his plan. "Well, good thing I stopped by, then. The Angels are playing this afternoon, and I was wondering if any of you would care to attend the game?"

"That's a fine idea," Julia said, beaming. "The fastest way to lose good employees is to never give them time off."

Walter got a feeling that something else was underlying here, but couldn't put his finger on what, or if Julia just needed a break from keeping an eye on them all.

Rosie leaned against her mop handle. "If you've seen one baseball game, you've seen them all, but thank you for the offer."

Alice grabbed the mop out from under Rosie's arm. "You're only saying that because you have a date."

The room took on a stunned silence as every eye in the room settled on him.

"Yes, she does," Julia said, "and I approved it because he's one of Jack McCarney's set builders. They are going to a movie this evening. I was sure you wouldn't mind, Walter."

"I don't mind." He wasn't about to step into that territory. Keeping Shirley from singing at a joint was one thing; approving who the others went out with was not within the realm of being their attorney. Using the moment to put things in perspective, he continued. "As long as it doesn't involve anything illegal, or singing at a speakeasy, which, despite public opinion, are illegal, you ladies are free to do as you choose."

The shine that appeared in Shirley's eyes made him wonder if he should retract that statement.

"I'd love to see a baseball game," Alice said. "Back home, my brothers played baseball all the time."

"Will we be back in time for the evening shift?" Rita asked.

"Don't worry about that," Julia answered. "Greta and Rosie will be here. We'll get along just fine without you three. Go, enjoy yourself. But—" She turned to him. "You'll want to take my car. All of you won't fit in your roadster. You can pull yours up next to the house. No one will lay a finger on it, I promise."

"Thanks." While Walter moved his car, the women ran to the house to get ready. When they returned to the diner, he bit the inside of his cheek at the familiar draw of desire. Shirley looked adorable in a purple dress with white fringe that showed off her sleek legs, and the purple feather tucked behind one ear fit her sass perfectly. The stadium had opened a couple of years ago and was proclaimed to be one of the grandest in the nation. It hosted minor league games year-round, and he was sure she'd enjoy watching one.

"Have you ever been to a baseball game?" he asked while holding the front door open for her.

"No, but the Swaggerts played ball in the field once in a while, and I'd watch them on occasion."

"The city has several ball teams, and the Angels are one of the better ones, for being in the minor league," he said. "I think you'll like it."

"I'm going to love it," Alice said. "I've wanted to see a game since arriving. Thank you for inviting us to join you."

Walter closed Shirley's door, then the two back doors while walking around to the driver's door. Once they were on the road that would take them to the south part of town, he said, "The judge doesn't want you girls to do anything that could jeopardize the case, but that doesn't mean you can't go out and have fun. He wants this case to set a precedent for others to follow."

"You mean make an example for others not to follow," Rita said. "If I'd known then what I know now, I'd never have let Roy Harrison baffle me into going to CB's. I hope the newspapers write about it so others will know."

"When it's over, you can contact a reporter

and ask him to print your side of the story," Walter said.

"I could?" Rita asked.

"Me, too?" Alice chimed in.

"Yes," Walter answered, glancing at Shirley.

She smiled at him, but didn't say anything. There was a thoughtfulness in her gaze that made him wonder exactly what she was thinking. He had a feeling it wasn't about newspaper reporters or telling her story.

# *Chapter Eleven*

The game had already started, but there was a line of spectators outside of the stadium buying tickets. Walter herded the trio of women into one of the lines and pulled out his billfold to purchase their tickets. This wasn't what he'd imagined while driving to the diner, taking them all to a game, but he truly didn't mind. They were all so excited. If Rosie hadn't had a date, he'd have four women with him.

Shirley's feather fluttered in the wind as she glanced around and smiled at Rita and Alice chirping like a couple of magpies.

They finally made their way to the ticket booth, and just as he was handed four tickets, someone clasped his shoulder and said, "Give that man back his money!"

Walter turned and grinned at the man. "Wilson. How are you?" Being a contract lawyer meant he covered all sorts of contracts, including baseball ones for Wilson Graham, one of the owners of the Angels.

"Your money is no good here, my friend. You'll have the best seats in the stadium on the house. Come with me," Wilson said. "It's good to see you. So good. You haven't been to a game since we opened."

"Been busy," Walter said, his usual excuse for becoming a recluse the past few years. "I have some friends with me."

Wilson didn't bat an eye at the three women. "Ducky! The more, the merrier!" He led them past the gate that most people were entering to a door marked Private. "Got a double header happening today, and you ladies are going to love these seats. They are right behind the bull pen."

Wilson held open the door for them all to enter the long and narrow corridor made of solid concrete.

"What's a bull pen?" Rita asked.

Wilson, taller than Rita by a foot and with a head of floppy black hair that went in all directions, stepped in behind her and closed the door. "Only the best thing about baseball. It's where the pitchers warm up before hitting the field. And anything you ladies want to eat or drink today is on the house, too. I wouldn't have this stadium if it wasn't for Walter—neither would Los Angeles." Wilson's laugh echoed against the walls. "I'd still be in Chicago, freezing my butt off if not for him. Best lawyer in the country. That's what he is."

"He's our lawyer, too," Alice said.

Wilson's eyebrows rose as he glanced from girl to girl. "Are you the gals in that suit against Mel Cartwright?"

"Yes, we are," Rita answered.

"Well, this here is a real special occasion, then," Wilson said. "You won the case, I take it."

"No," Walter replied. "It's still in the courts."

"Well, you'll win." Wilson winked. "Have no doubts about that, ladies." He then instructed them to turn left and led them to a row of reserved seats that overlooked the bull pen, but also gave a clear view of the entire field.

"You two sit in the front row," Wilson told Walter while pointing at him and Shirley. "I'll sit right behind you with these two lovely ladies."

"You're going to join us?" Rita asked.

"You bet I am." Wilson gestured for Rita and Alice to sit on each side of him. "You aren't going to get rid of me until both games are over. I've been mailing Walter free tickets for two years. It's an honor to have him here. A real honor."

"You should be in the movies, Wilson," Walter said while waiting for Shirley to sit in one of the two seats that made up the front row of the private area. "Your acting is almost believable."

"Acting! I'm just telling the truth about you,

my friend." Wilson waved to a man carrying a neck tray full of goodies. "What do you ladies want? Hot dogs? Peanuts?"

Once they all had more food than they'd be able to eat, Wilson said, "Now, let me explain the fundamentals of baseball to all of you."

Shirley had remained quiet during all this time; however, after listening intently to every word Wilson said about the game, she became enthralled with the action happening on the field. She clapped, cheered and booed along with the hundreds of other spectators in the stadium.

So did Alice and Rita, but Walter didn't have his eyes on them. Pulling his attention off Shirley was nearly impossible. Especially when she jumped to her feet in excitement or threw herself against the back of the seat in disappointment.

"That wasn't a ball!" she said to him. "It was within the strike zone."

She'd taken in every word Wilson had said, and had fully understood. "Perhaps it looks different when you're behind the plate," Walter said.

"It couldn't look that different," she said with disgust. "We're down by two and it's the bottom of the last inning." She cupped her hands around her lips and shouted, "Go Angels!"

The smack of the bat hitting the ball echoed over the stadium, and Walter grinned again as Shirley shot to her feet.

"Run!" she shouted at the batter. "Run!"

Walter stood up, along with everyone else in the stadium, clapping. Leaning closer to her, he said, "It's a home run! Over the fence! The Angels just won!"

"We won?"

"Yes!"

Jumping up and down, she wrapped her arms around his neck. "We won!"

He grasped her waist and hugged her back. The desire to kiss her struck so hard and fast he couldn't have stopped himself if he'd have wanted to. However, the moment his lips met hers, a bolt of comprehension hit like lightning. He pulled his lips off hers and tore his eyes away from her startled gaze.

"We won!" he said, trying to cover up his actions. He gave her another hug, hoping that made it seem as if he was simply excited over the game.

He had no way of knowing if it did or not.

"We sure did!" Wilson said. "Come on! I'll get you all some autographs before the next game starts!"

Shirley's knees were trembling, her hands shaking and her mind spinning. Walter had kissed her again. Sort of. Her lips tingled from the brief encounter with his and her heart pounded so hard it was nearly impossible to catch her breath.

With her senses reeling, she couldn't do anything except walk beside Walter, who had ahold of her arm as they followed Wilson, Rita and Alice back down to the long concrete hallway they'd walked in before.

The baseball game had been fun to watch, far more fun than watching the Swaggert brothers hit the ball and run from rock to rock. With them, the games hadn't lasted long because a fistfight usually ensued shortly after the game had started.

Dressed in their red-and-white-striped uniforms, baseball players started filling the area. Wilson shouted for someone to bring him some baseballs, and then he instructed the players to sign them.

Rita and Alice collected several balls, filling their purses, but Shirley was satisfied with just one, and thanked Walter when he offered to put it in his pocket for her. She hadn't brought along a purse. There had been no reason. Alice had again offered to carry whatever she needed in her purse.

Next, Wilson showed them to the powder room, where Alice and Rita gushed over how much fun they were having. Shirley agreed, for it *was* fun, and the more she thought about it, the more she was convinced Walter had kissed her again—just because of the excitement of the moment, but he had kissed her.

A sigh escaped her, but then caught before her

lungs emptied. Maybe he hadn't meant to kiss her. Maybe he didn't want to kiss her ever again.

"This is the most fun I've ever had in my life," Rita said, looking in the mirror while reapplying her lipstick. "Wilson Graham is so funny, and so generous."

"Yes, he is," Alice said, fluffing her black curls. "I've always liked baseball, but have never been to a real game."

Not wanting the others to know she was thinking more about Walter than baseball, Shirley said, "I do hope we win the next game."

"We will," Rita said. "With us rooting for them, the Angels can't help but win." With a smug grin, she added, "That's what Wilson said."

"Yes, he did," Alice said, giving her hair a final fluff.

They left the room together and found the men waiting for them. Wilson instantly held out both elbows. "Ladies," he said to Rita and Alice, who each hooked an arm though one of his elbows.

Walter held out his arm, and Shirley gently hooked her hand around it, testing to see if that, too, would send her heart racing.

It did.

"Enjoying yourself?" he asked.

"Yes. Are you?" She looked up at him, at his eyes, and bit her lip at how they twinkled.

"I am," he answered.

"Why haven't you come to a ball game for so long?"

"Been too busy."

She pondered that for only a moment. "That's what you said about the ocean and the movie. I know you're busy with this case against Cartwright's, but you're here and you took me to the ocean and the movie. Why?"

He nodded. Then slowed his steps until they were several feet behind the others. "Do you want to know the truth?"

"Yes, I wouldn't have asked if I'd wanted you to lie to me."

Stopping, he looked her straight in the eye. "Because there wasn't anyone I wanted to show those things to. Until now."

Her heart nearly pressed its way right out of her chest at the well of happiness that filled it. A man who looks you straight in the eye can't be lying. That's what Pappy always said.

"Come on, the second game is about to start."

She wanted to ask why her, but was afraid of what his answer might be. "They all have been fun," she said instead. "The ocean, the movie, the baseball game."

"There's more."

Excitement flared inside her. "Like what?"

"You'll have to wait and see," he said with a wink. "Wait and see."

The second game was as exciting as the first one had been. At one point, when a batter hit the ball, it flew in the wrong direction. She was so engrossed in watching how it spun in the air, it would have landed on her head if Walter hadn't stuck his arm over her and caught it.

He tossed the ball to the men in the bull pen, and she grabbed his arm afterward. "Are you all right? Did that hurt?"

"Catching the ball?"

"Yes," she said.

"No, it didn't hurt, and I'm all right."

He patted her hand wrapped around his arm, and then left his hand atop hers. She didn't mind. She liked touching him. Liked him touching her. There were times that she had to let go in order to jump to her feet, clap or to yell at the umpire for not seeing the ball correctly, but when she sat down, she wrapped her hand back around his arm. He didn't seem to mind that at all, and laughed when she told him that the umpire should look into getting a pair of glasses.

That umpire should. He had her holding her breath with every pitch thrown.

The game ended with the Angels winning again. She once more jumped to her feet, clapping and cheering, but she made sure not to throw her arms around Walter's neck again. Which made her somewhat sad. She was sad that the game was over because that meant their time together was coming to an end.

That made her realize it wasn't the things she did with him, it was him that was fun.

"I am taking you all out for dinner in celebration," Wilson said.

Walter looked at her, and it was as if she could read his mind. It was up to her. If she said no, he'd take them home; if she said yes, they'd all go to dinner with Wilson. She couldn't disappoint Alice or Rita, so smiled and nodded.

"All right," Walter said. "Where at? We'll meet you there."

Wilson shook his head. "These two ladies can ride with me, and you two can follow in your car."

"Will three of you fit in your roadster?" Walter asked.

Wilson looked at Rita and Alice. Shirley held her breath, wondering which one would be asked to ride with her and Walter. Either one of them would be sorely disappointed.

"You two don't mind sharing a seat, do you?" Wilson asked.

"Not at all," Rita answered.

"No," Alice said at the exact same time.

"Then let's go!" Wilson said.

They left the stadium via the same corridor they'd entered, and a car much like Walter's was parked right outside the door. But it was blue, and not nearly as shiny as Walter's red one.

While Wilson, Rita and Alice climbed in the blue car, she and Walter walked toward Julia's car, which was parked on the other side of the lot.

"Meet you near the road!" Wilson shouted.

Walter waved a hand. "We best hurry," he said, "or we'll get stuck in traffic."

"All right." Shirley had no sooner said that when Walter started to jog, pulling her along behind him.

Soon she was racing along beside him, gleefully laughing as they darted around cars, making others stop as they shot directly in front of them.

"Thank you!" Walter shouted at a driver who honked a horn at them.

Shirley laughed harder as the man in the driver's seat raised a fist in the air.

"You're going to get us run over!" she shouted as they dashed past another row of cars.

"I know a good lawyer if that happens!" he shouted in return.

Wilson's blue roadster zoomed past them, its horn letting out a long and ear-piercing honk. All three occupants laughed and waved.

"Hurry! If we go out the other way, we can beat them! There aren't as many cars going out that way!" Walter shouted.

"Beat them?" she asked, still jogging beside him. "I thought we were following them!"

"We will, once we are on the highway, but we can beat them to it!"

A heightened excitement overtook her and she passed him in the final dash to the car. She jumped in the passenger side while he ran around to the driver's door. "Hurry!"

Walter jumped in, and a moment later, the tires squealed as he pulled out of the parking space, in the opposite direction to the way Wilson had been driving. She saw the road they'd used to enter the lot. "You're right. No one is going in this direction."

"Because they haven't gotten to their cars yet," he said. "They're walking. Not running."

She laughed. It was silly, but so enjoyable.

The tires squealed again as he pulled out onto the road and headed in the direction of the line of cars that Wilson and the girls were in. It was a long line, with horns honking. This time, she and Walter waved as they sped past the line of cars still in the parking lot, waiting to pull out onto the road. The blue roadster hadn't yet made it to the exit.

She was leaning across Walter, waving out his window and laughing. When she could no longer see the roadster, she leaned back in her seat with happiness still bubbling inside her. "Now what?"

"Hold on," he said.

She grabbed the side of the door with one hand, and the seat near her knee with the other. "Why?"

"They're going to gain on us quick," he said, zooming past a long row of cars in the lane beside them.

She hadn't ridden in cars very often, but knew a few things. "Aren't we on the wrong side of the road?"

"It's a passing lane right now, and will be until we see a car coming at us." He winked at her.

She probably should be a little bit concerned, both at his speed and driving on the wrong side of the road, but wasn't. When a honk sounded, she twisted and looked out the back window.

"It's them! They are right behind us!"

"I know!"

She grabbed his shoulder. "Go faster!"

"I would if I could!"

"Oh, I wish we were in your car. We'd beat them for sure then."

"Yes, we would."

They both laughed, and did so again when Walter honked the horn in response to Wilson honking the roadster's horn behind them. They'd passed all the other cars, and Walter was now driving down the center of the road, swerving once in a while so Wilson couldn't pass them.

"Hold on, here's our corner," he said.

She still had ahold of the door, and her other hand was on his shoulder, and she tightened both grips as the car careened around the corner. Walter didn't slow his speed as they pulled onto the highway. The wider pavement gave room for Wilson to pull up beside them.

"Where's your Packard?" Wilson shouted.

"I had to borrow this one so we'd all fit!" Walter shouted in return.

"Poor sap!" Wilson shouted, and then sped in front of them.

"Aw, shucks!" Shirley said, slapping the door. "Next time, we're bringing your car! Rita and Alice will just have to find another ride."

Walter laughed. "Are you going to tell them that?"

"Yes." A twinge of guilt struck her, but not even that changed her mind. "Yes. I will."

"Well, this old girl of Julia's has more get-up-and-go than I'd thought. She actually gave Wilson a good run."

"Is it fun, driving?"

"Yes, it's fun." He glanced her way. "Want me to teach you?"

She might truly have a heart attack before this day was over with the way her heart kept leaping inside her chest. "Would you?"

"Sure. We can start tomorrow." He glanced at her again. "If you want."

"I want," she answered, thoroughly thrilled.

She was thoroughly thrilled a short time later, too, when they parked behind Wilson's roadster downtown. They all five laughed about the car race and carried on like kids on a playground, including Walter and Wilson, who slapped each other on the shoulders while joking about who was the better driver.

But then, when Wilson gestured for them to enter a tall building, Shirley's heart sank to her knees. She grabbed ahold of Walter's arm. "We can't go in there."

"Why not? You look fine."

She bit her bottom lip as her heart sank a bit deeper. She didn't want him to know that Alice had sewn the dress for when she finally got a singing job, or that Rosie had made that comment about working their fingers to the bone and twiddling their thumbs, so he wouldn't know she'd been practicing by singing along with the radio every night. She would tell him all that, someday, after the case was over.

However, right now, that wasn't what she was worried about. "The judge," she whispered. "None of us can be in a place like this."

# Chapter Twelve

"This isn't a speakeasy," Walter said, taking ahold of her hand. "It's Manchester's, the finest restaurant in Los Angeles. You'll see."

Excitement flared inside her. "Really?"

"Yes, really," he said.

Fully trusting him, she stepped through the tall wooden and stained-glass double doors. She'd thought the movie theater had been amazing, but this put all that glitz and glamour to shame. This truly was a palace, complete with a huge crystal chandelier that made everything in the room sparkle. She grinned at Walter as he squeezed her hand.

"Ah, Mr. Graham." A man dressed in a shimmering black suit walked toward them. "I thought you might be on our guest list tonight. I saved your table."

"Mr. Manchester, you know me so well." Wilson shook the man's hand. "My guests and I are eager to sample your fine cuisine."

"Congratulations on a double win," Mr. Manchester said with a smile so big it looked as if even his mustache was curled up at the edges.

"Word travels fast," Wilson said.

"I had bets on the game," Mr. Manchester said with a wink.

"Go Angels," Wilson said before nodding toward Walter. "You remember Walter Russell, don't you?"

"Of course, I do." Mr. Manchester shook Walter's hand. "It's been far too long, Mr. Russell. I was afraid you had received bad service or something."

"No, nothing like that," Walter said. "I just don't get downtown as often as I used to."

Shirley's insides jittered as Mr. Manchester smiled at her.

"I can see why," he said. "With this lovely lady at your side." He bowed slightly at her. "I do hope you'll enjoy your time with us this evening. We are so pleased to have all of you here."

"Thank you," Shirley said, feeling as if she needed to say something.

"Right this way. I will seat you and then Charles will be right over to serve you." Mr. Manchester led them through a massive archway and then snapped his fingers at a man wearing black pants, a white shirt and gold vest.

"Charles," Wilson greeted with a wave and smile.

"Good evening, Mr. Graham, Mr. Russell," Charles replied. "I'll be right with you."

"Bring some celebration when you come," Wilson said.

Shirley had no idea what celebration meant, but Charles must have because he instantly replied, "Of course, sir."

Mr. Manchester led them to the far corner of a room that had more chandeliers hanging from the ceiling and too many tables to count covered with white tablecloths. The table he stopped at had a long, curved booth seat that took up the entire corner.

One by one, Rita and Alice slid into the booth. Shirley followed, rubbing the smooth, sparkling white leather covering the seat and the backrest. It was as soft as kid leather.

Walter sat down next to her, and Wilson sat across the table, on the other edge of the booth. A tall, narrow vase holding a single red rose was positioned in the middle of the table. Shirley wondered if she should pinch herself. She'd never seen such luxury.

Charles arrived within seconds, holding a tray in one hand and had a white towel draped over his forearm. As he set down stemmed glasses before each of them, he said, "A little celebration for the magnificent win today."

Alice, who was sitting next to her, leaned closer. "Why is the water bubbling?"

Shirley looked closer at the glasses. There were bubbles in the liquid.

"Because it's not water," Rita whispered, who was sitting on the other side of Alice. "It's champagne. The real stuff, not the fake concoction CB's had."

"Oh," Alice said, placing a hand to her lips.

"May I order for all of us?" Wilson asked.

Once again, Walter looked at her. Shirley nodded and shrugged. She'd have no idea what to order.

"Of course," Walter said.

"Perfect." Wilson turned to Charles. "We'll start with the clam chowder, then shrimp cocktails, followed by lobsters and T-bone steaks, and we'll end with rum cakes, served warm."

"Excellent choices, sir, all of them," Charles said.

After the hot dog and peanuts she'd eaten at the baseball game, Shirley wasn't sure she'd be able to finish a bowl of soup, let alone all the other things Wilson had said.

"Just eat what you want," Walter whispered in her ear. "But I do believe you'll like it all."

"And, of course, more celebration as needed," Wilson said.

"Of course, sir," Charles said with a bow. "I'll be back momentarily with your soup."

As the waiter walked away, Wilson picked up his glass. "A toast."

Everyone else picked up their glass and held it in the air, so Shirley followed suit.

"To Walter, a friend I've missed dearly the past few years," Wilson said.

Walter shook his head. "Enough already. To the Angels and games well played."

"I'll drink to that, too," Wilson said, laughing.

They all clinked their glasses together over the single rose.

Then, once again following suit, Shirley took a test sip from her glass. Once she got past the bubbles popping in her nose, the sweetness won her over, and she took a full drink, relishing in the fruity flavor.

"I have missed you, though," Wilson said, setting down his glass. "The fun we used to have. Remember when we raced those Model Ts up the old bridge road?"

Walter chuckled. "Yes, and you blew out three of your four tires."

Laughing, Wilson said, "That's the only reason you beat me."

Shirley didn't believe she'd ever seen someone

look as happy as Walter did at this moment. She laid a hand on his arm. "So today wasn't the first time you two have raced?"

"Lord, no," Wilson said.

"But," Walter said firmly, "the only reason he beat us today is because we weren't driving my roadster."

"You think so?" Wilson asked.

"I know so," Walter answered.

"So do I," Shirley said, taking another sip of the bubbling wonderfulness in her glass.

"I sense a challenge," Wilson said. "You're on. Next Saturday, after the game. A race, all the way to here." He held up his glass again. "Winner buys."

Walter looked at her.

She nodded and picked up her glass.

He picked up his and held it out. "You're on!"

Rita and Alice joined in, and once again they all clinked glasses over the rose. The laughter around the table barely died down when Charles brought over five bowls of soup. It was so delicious Shirley wanted to lick the bowl, but didn't.

The men conversed about a variety of subjects, and made a point to include her and Alice and Rita in the conversations as they ate the soup, and then the shrimp. It had been ice-cold and resting in a spicy red sauce, but turned out to be delicious. As with the champagne, she'd been nervous to try the shrimp, having never seen anything like it before, but when the lobster arrived, she stared at it for a good length of time. Picking up a fork, she tapped the red shell. It was whole. An entire, red, clawed creature, and hard as a rock.

Slowly, hoping no one would notice, she peered up at Walter.

He grinned. "Here, let me show you. It gets messy, but it's worth it." Using both hands, he snapped off the claws and then broke them open. "Use your fork to dig out the meat. You'll like it."

She glanced at Rita and Alice, who were digging into the claws on their plates with their forks.

"Dip it in this." Walter pointed at a small bowl. "It's melted butter."

Cautiously, because she'd never eaten a creature like this before, she poked her fork in and tugged out a small piece of white meat.

"Now dip it," Walter said. Then after a moment's hesitation, she did, and ate it.

She put the fork in her mouth, certain it was going to taste awful. It didn't. In fact, it nearly melted in her mouth.

"Told you." He winked and then picked up the creature again. This time he pulled off the end. "The tail is the best meat." Someone had already cut open the hard shell, and he used his knife to widen the opening before setting it back down on her plate. "Try it."

She did, and then had to press a finger to her lips while savoring the rich flavor. "It's delicious," she said after swallowing.

Walter was fully enchanted by her. Couldn't help but be. It was as if he was reliving his life over, experiencing first things in ways he never had before. This time around, everything was better, brighter, bigger, more exciting. All because of her. What he'd told her back at the ball game was true. He had gotten so caught up in all the bad he'd forgotten the good. Forgotten how good it felt to laugh, to be happy.

He'd missed Wilson, too. They'd been good friends, but Wilson hadn't been a part of Lucy's crowd, so other than via work, she hadn't wanted him to see Wilson. Or several other people who had been his friends. He'd chosen her over them. He'd chosen what she'd wanted over so many other things, until he'd got sick of it. Got tired of every party they'd attended ending up with her in a back room, doped. There had been nothing more important to her than that. Not even him. No, especially not him. Except for the fact that he'd been her cover. She knew, legally, he'd get her out of any trouble she got herself into.

He had, too. Until that, too, got old.

"Don't you like lobster?" Shirley asked.

Reaching down, he pulled a claw off his lobster. "Yes, I do," he answered, letting his focus return to the here and now. Then he dug out some meat, dipped it in butter and forked it into his mouth. He savored the flavor, as Blondie had, really tasting it as if it was the first time he'd ever eaten it.

It was delicious, and he was never going to forget that again.

Actually, he was never going to forget how adorable she'd looked when she'd peered up at him beneath those long, curled-up lashes. Her friends were on the other side of her, yet it had been him she'd looked to for help. He liked that. He liked her.

He liked life again.

Picking up his glass, he held it over the table. "One more toast." He waited until the others picked up their glasses. "To us, and the mighty fine day we've had."

"Hear, hear!" Wilson said as their glasses clinked. "A mighty fine day."

"It certainly has been the best day of my life," Rita said.

Alice nodded. "Mine, too."

He glanced at Shirley, who laughed. "Mine, too."

They all clinked their glasses again, and afterward, Walter reached beneath the table and gently patted her knee, simply because he had to touch her. Had to.

She grinned at him and then forked another chunk of butter-dipped lobster into her mouth.

Charles arrived as they finished their lobsters and passed out warm, damp cloths for everyone to wipe their fingers as he took away the lobster plates. Upon returning, he set down plates loaded with steaks and potatoes fried with onions.

Walter chuckled at the little moan Shirley let out, then leaned his head next to hers. "You don't have to eat it all."

"But I would feel guilty letting it go to waste," she whispered in return.

"There's nothing to feel guilty about. You didn't order it, you didn't cook it and I know you didn't kill it." He grinned at the way she shook her head. "And you'll want to save some room for the rum cake. It's divine."

"Divine?"

He nodded.

She shook her head and cut off a slice of steak. Her expression said it tasted as good as the lobster had.

It did.

A quartet of men arrived at the table while they were eating the steaks. "Would you enjoy some entertainment?" one asked.

"Certainly," Wilson said.

The men began their song with a simultaneous and pitch-perfect hum, then broke into a ballad that soon had Shirley setting her fork down. He knew about her dream of becoming a singer, but until this moment, hadn't realized how much music moved her. She wasn't merely listening, she was fully captivated, right up until the final note.

Walter was prepared and slipped the men some cash, even though he knew Wilson was doing the same thing on the other side of the table.

He'd seen her eyes sparkle several times, but as the men walked away, and her gaze followed them, he saw a shine like he'd never seen before.

Charles arrived before anyone had spoken. "I do hope you have saved room for dessert." He collected their plates before setting the rum cakes before each of them. "Warm, as requested."

"Your service has been as excellent as ever, Charles," Wilson said.

Charles bowed slightly. "Thank you, sir, it has been my pleasure. I do hope to see you all again soon."

"You will," Walter said. "Next Saturday. Wilson will once again be picking up the tab."

Wilson laughed. "We'll see about who pays, Charles, but we all shall be here again. Save our seats."

"Mr. Manchester will be delighted to hear

that." Charles bowed again before taking his leave.

"What do you say we head up the street for a bit of dancing and fun before we call it a night?" Wilson asked while digging into his rum cake.

As much as Walter would enjoy dancing with Shirley, he knew that wasn't an option. "Not tonight, Wilson," he said. "Regrettably."

Rita, who was sitting next to Wilson and had been whispering with him occasionally, said something beneath her breath.

"I see," Wilson said. "Well, perhaps all will be settled by next Saturday night, and since Walter will be buying then, dancing afterward will be even more fun." He took a drink, and then added, "Walter, if you need a character witness for any of these fine ladies, you know where to find me." His grin grew. "Judge Wallis rarely misses an Angels game."

Having never resorted to such antics as Wilson was implying, Walter was ready to decline the offer, but stopped himself. In this instance, making sure Shirley and the others walked away free and clear from Cartwright, he nodded. "Thank you, my friend, I will keep that in mind."

He glanced at Shirley, who briefly met his gaze before looking at the half-eaten dessert before her.

"Delicious, isn't it?"

"Oh, dear," she said with a heavy sigh. "I have

never eaten so many wonderful things in my entire life, and I know nothing will ever compare to this. It's...divine." With a smile that lit up her eyes, she elbowed him. "And there's no need to say you told me so, I already know that."

They all laughed, and were still laughing when they walked out to the cars parked along the curb.

"See you all next Saturday," Wilson said, holding the back door of Julia's car open for Alice and Rita to climb in. "Make sure to bring plenty of clams, Walter!"

"You'll be the one needing the clams," he said while holding the door for Shirley.

"Horse feathers!" Wilson said as he shut the door. "Don't take any wooden nickels, my friend."

Walter closed Shirley's door. "You neither," he said, shaking Wilson's hand.

Wilson walked to his roadster while Walter walked around Julia's car and climbed in. Alice and Rita chatted about how the entire day had been the bee's knees. Walter agreed silently and kept glancing at Shirley, who remained relatively quiet the entire way home.

At Julia's, Alice and Rita rushed for the house while Shirley hung back after climbing out of the car. "Thank you for taking us all to the ball game, and then to dinner."

"You're welcome." He took ahold of her elbow. "I'll walk you to the cabin."

She shook her head. "No, I will go inside the house for a while. I was just wondering what time I should be ready tomorrow."

He hadn't forgotten the driving lessons, was looking forward to spending another day with her. "How about ten o'clock?"

"That would be wonderful." She pinched her lips as if trying to quell some of her glee. "Unless you've changed your mind."

The desire to kiss her, really kiss her again, was so strong he had a hard time keeping it at bay. Which meant it was time to leave. He released her elbow. "I haven't changed my mind. Have you?"

"No."

"All right, then." He pointed toward the porch. "I'll walk you in."

"That's not—"

"Yes, it is." He took her elbow again. "I want to thank Julia for loaning us her car."

He walked her to the door and spent a few minutes visiting with Julia before leaving. His house didn't seem as lonely that night, mainly because of his excitement about the following morning.

Shirley, wearing a blue dress with a matching scarf tied over her hair, ran down the steps as he drove into the driveway at precisely ten o'clock. Oddly, the sight of her made him nervous. Their other excursions had been impromptu. This one, being planned, seemed as if it was on a different level than the others.

She opened the passenger door as soon as he brought the car to a stop. Climbing in, she asked, "Will it be all right if I watch you drive first, really pay attention before I try it?"

He grinned at the caution in her voice. "That's exactly what I was going to suggest." He waited until she closed the door and then shifted into Reverse. "I thought we'd drive up into Hollywood-land. There won't be any traffic up there."

"Rosie says the houses up there are mansions." Excitement now laced her tone.

"They are. Ones only the big eggs can afford, but there aren't many up there, and the roads are wide, so it'll be the perfect place for you to practice." He'd thought about that last night while lying in bed. Where to take her. How to go about teaching her the fundamentals of driving. He'd learned by trial and error.

"Did you teach your wife how to drive?" she asked as they pulled out of Julia's drive.

"No." Up until lately, when someone had mentioned Lucy, he'd clammed up, but he didn't mind answering her questions.

"Who did?"

"I don't know. She knew how to drive when we met. Had her own car."

She nodded. "Julia says it's not hard, and that I'll get the hang of it in no time."

"I'm sure you will. Let's start with the fundamentals. There are three pedals on the floor. The gas, the brake and the clutch…"

She listened intently. He knew that by the questions she asked, and how she responded with additional questions upon his answers as they drove up the somewhat winding road into Hollywoodland.

Not even the elaborate homes pulled her attention away from his instructions. His attention wasn't as focused. His mind kept wandering off in a direction that didn't have anything to do with driving. He'd barely slept a wink last night, thinking about the day they'd had. The kiss they'd almost shared.

He regretted pulling away when he had, and wondered if the opportunity to kiss her would arise again.

Chasing away that thought, he pulled the car over to the side of the road. "Are you ready to try?"

She glanced around, swallowed and grimaced. "Already?"

He opened his door. "Yes, already. You'll do fine." Climbing out, he patted the leather seat. "Slide over."

She gnawed on her bottom lip, but by the time

he opened the passenger door, she was sitting in the driver's seat, clutching the steering wheel with both hands.

"Don't be nervous" he said. "Just relax."

"That's easy for you to say."

He chuckled. "No, it's not. I've never let anyone drive this car before." He loved the roadster, mainly because he didn't have anything else to love. That realization had come straight out of the blue and stuck hard. Love. That's what he'd wanted since the flood. Since his family had died. He'd thought he'd found it with Lucy, but her shallowness, falseness, had left him emptier than the orphanage had.

A grimace filled Shirley's face. "You haven't?"

"No." He ignored other thoughts attempting to come forward and pointed to the pedals on the floor. "Put one foot on the clutch and slowly press it down to the floor."

He waited until the clutch was fully engaged and then told her to put a hand on the shifter. When she did, he covered her hand with his. Gliding the shifter, he said, "See how easily it goes from gear to gear? It won't do that if you don't have the clutch all the way in. You have to make sure it's all the way to the floor before shifting."

She nodded, and he guided her hand through the gears one more time, this time explaining each gear. Afterward, he removed his hand. "Now you try it. Start with Reverse."

She went through the gears, naming them just as he had.

"Looks like you're ready to me."

Taking a deep breath that had her breasts rising, she nodded.

"Then start the engine, put it in gear and let out the clutch."

She squeezed her eyes shut.

He laughed. "Keep your eyes open and on the road."

She opened her eyes, took another deep breath and then started the car. As the engine roared to life, she shifted and let out the clutch. The car jerked and she let out a little yelp, pushing the clutch back in.

"It's all right," he said. "The car is still running and that's good. Just ease your foot off the clutch more slowly, while gently pressing down on the gas pedal."

It took a few tries, but before long, they were cruising along the road at a moderate speed that allowed her get comfortable. "You're doing great," he said.

"This is unbelievable!" She giggled. "I'm driving."

"Yes, you are!"

"How many other people have you taught to drive?"

He laughed. "None."

She grimaced, then grinned as she quickly looked his way. "I don't think you should have told me that." She laughed again. "I had no idea it was this easy."

Curious, he asked, "Doesn't anyone in your family have a car?"

"I don't have a family. Pappy was the last. That's why I had to go live with the Swaggerts. They had cars, but nothing this nice. My father had a Model T. Pappy drove it for several years, but it quit working years ago."

Knowing she had lived on a farm, he asked, "How did you get to town?"

"Walked. It wasn't that far. Or caught a ride with one of the neighbors. Pappy had a bad leg. Hurt it before I was born. After my father died, Pappy crop-shared our land to the Swaggerts. That's how they got it, said they'd already paid him to farm it for the next five years. Their lawyer said they had papers to prove it, so they tore down the house and planted corn." She shrugged. "That's all it is now. A cornfield."

The fact he'd told her to go back to Nebraska curdled his stomach. No wonder she was so determined to stay. She didn't have anything to return to. He knew what that felt like.

"Oh, no. No." Her arms stiffened. "There's a car coming at us."

They hadn't seen another car since leaving Julia's, but there was one now, a distance up the road, but coming at them.

"What if they hit us? If I hit them?"

"You won't," he assured. "Just stay on our side of the road and keep the steering wheel straight."

She let out a mumbled trembling sound as the car drove closer.

"You're doing great." He continued to assure her all was fine, and waved at the driver as the other car drove past. "See. It was fine."

Her eyes shimmered. "It was. I did it."

"Yes, you did, and it wasn't even hard."

"Oh, yes, it was." She huffed out a breath. "It was terrifying."

There wasn't a single thing about her that wasn't charming. "Well, you did great." He gestured to the intersection coming up. "Take a left up there. There aren't any houses on that road yet."

"I hope that means there won't be any cars." She slowed and took the corner perfectly.

The road ahead of them now was long and straight. "Give it more gas and shift into the next gear," he said.

"But then I'll go faster. I don't think I want to."

"Yes, you do. Trust me."

She shot him a quick and wary glance.

He laughed. "It's fun. This car was made to go fast. That's why I bought it."

She gripped the wheel so tight her knuckles turned white, then gave the car more gas, and at the precise moment, she shifted into the next gear.

"Perfect!" Pride filled him. She'd listened to every word he'd said about paying attention to the whine of the engine to know when the next gear was needed. "You're an excellent driver, Shirley Burnette from Nebraska."

She laughed. "Thank you, Walter Russell." A moment later, she added, "From Los Angles. You are an excellent teacher."

Glee filled the air as they both laughed while she sped along the road, her blue scarf fluttering in the wind.

"Dear heavens, but this is fun!"

"I told you!" he said. "This car is made for driving."

"Will it beat Wilson's next Saturday?" she asked.

"You can bet on it!"

A grin took over her entire face. "How fast does this car go?"

"I'll show you, once you're done driving."

She slowed the car, downshifting with perfection, and then let the roadster slowly roll to a stop. With a sigh, she said, "I've had enough. Got more knots in my arms than if I'd been pitching hay all morning."

Once again, he chided himself for ever pointing out her accent. It was charming and wholesome. Things he now appreciated. "All right. We'll let you rest for a bit." He opened the door and climbed out.

Rather than scooting across the seat, she climbed out, and they met at the driver's door.

"Gotta stretch for a minute," she said, shaking her arms and legs. She then took the scarf off her head and ran both hands through her hair. "I can't believe it. Can't believe I know how to drive!"

He couldn't believe how beautiful she looked. With her curls bouncing around her head and her cheeks flushed red. The desire he'd been holding back for hours, days actually, struck again as his eyes settled on her lips.

She stretched her arms into the air. "I really know how to drive."

Impulse took over and he grasped her waist. "Yes, you do," he said while slowly lowering his face to hers.

With full control of his actions, he watched her, giving her time to pull away.

Her gaze shot between his eyes and his lips, but she didn't pull away. Heat flared inside him as she slowly licked her lips.

He kissed her lightly, gently, and closed his

eyes as she strained forward, her lips pressing more firmly against his. Her lips were soft and warm, and yielded to his as his mouth fully covered hers.

In that instant, everything else disappeared. It was just them. Him and her. The sweet smell of her, a mixture of flowers and sunshine, filled him as he pulled her closer. The enchantment he'd experienced since meeting her fully engrossed him. Overtook all of his senses, and he deepened the kiss, wanting to see how much bigger, brighter, that enchantment could be.

Unmeasurable. That's what it became as her arms looped around his neck and tugged his head downward so their lips met with even more intensity. It grew even stronger as her fingers dug into his hair and the entire length of her pressed against him.

# Chapter Thirteen

Shirley wasn't exactly sure, but imagined she must be somewhere between heaven and earth. Her feet were still on the ground, but they were the only things. The rest of her had entered a place she'd never been before, a world where only she and Walter existed and every part of her felt the wondrous sensations of his lips on hers.

Dear all that was holy, but she could stay right here forever. Kissing him. She pressed herself even harder against him and hoped time would stop. His arms, wrapped around her waist, held her tight, and his lips, his mouth, filled her entire system with a heady tingling warmth.

The kiss ended as perfectly as it had started. She felt as if she was waking up after a wonderful dream, bubbling with happiness.

Walter lifted his head and looked down at her. His entire face was smiling, especially his eyes.

"Are you ready to see how fast this car can go?" he asked.

She bit her lip as the happiness inside her grew even stronger. Nodding, she said, "Yes."

He kissed her again. Briefly, but firmly, then nodded at the car. "Get in."

She released her hold on his neck, and rather than walking around the car, because Lord knows her legs were shaking too hard for that, she climbed in the driver's door and slid across the seat. Her scarf was balled up in her hand, and rather than putting it back on, she tied it around her wrist as he started the car.

The cunning grin he shot her way made her laugh, and she grabbed ahold of the car door.

"Ready?" he asked.

"Oh, yes, I'm ready." She was ready for anything, and it felt amazing.

He laughed and shifted the car into gear. The speed at which they took off forced her back against the seat. She laughed. "Who taught you how to drive?"

"No one," he shouted over the whistle the wind made as it blew around the windshield. "My first job with Arthur was an errand boy, and the second day I worked for him, he told me to take his car and deliver some papers to the courthouse."

The wind whipped her hair into her eyes. She

held it back so she could see him. "And just like that, you learned to drive?"

"I wouldn't say it was just like that." His eyes sparkled, and he winked at her. "But I made it to the courthouse without hitting anything."

He laughed, and so did she. Full of happiness. He was amazing, and so was driving this fast. It was exhilarating, filled her with a sense of freedom she hadn't known was possible.

"Do you like it here?" she asked. "California?"

It was a moment before he nodded. "Yes. I do."

"I do, too. The more you show me, the more I like it." She'd planned on liking it all along, but had never planned on liking him this much. Yet she did.

"Good! Think Wilson will beat us next Saturday?" He was still shouting above the whistling wind and the roar of the engine.

"No!" she shouted in return. "We're gonna win!"

Walter laughed and continued to drive at a breathtaking speed. She continued to enjoy it, lifting her arms over her head and laughing with glee.

Somehow, before long, they ended up near the ocean. This time the water was on her side of the car. "How did we get here?" she asked, gazing out over the vast blue wonder.

"The road circled around—we're heading back

into town from another direction." He pointed toward the ocean. "Want to stop and walk in it again?"

"Oh, yes! Could we?"

"Of course."

They not only walked in the ocean again, they found more seashells, and then ate at a café that overlooked the water. After that, he took her to an amusement park that was full of things she'd never known existed. There were big tanks of colorful fish to look at, carnival rides and games, and so many other things she grew dizzy trying to see everything as they walked around. The entire place was a marvel.

Walter tried to convince her to go on an airplane ride, but she staunchly refused. There was no earthly explanation for how those contraptions stayed in the air, and she wasn't about to go in one; however, she did ride on several other rides, those that stayed firmly on the ground.

They stayed there for hours, and though so many things were simply spectacular, Walter was by far the most magnificent. The way he laughed and teased her, and held her hand.

The dreamlike day continued when he purchased a variety of food and then took her back to the beach, where they watched the sunset while drinking sodas and eating meat rolled up inside a flat flour bread he called a tortilla.

"Whatever it's called, it sure is delicious," she said, popping the last bite into her mouth.

He'd already finished his and was sitting beside her with his arm crossed over his bent knees, gazing across the water. The setting sun had sunk so low in the sky that its reflection made the once-blue water now look shades of red, orange and even black in places. The sky was streaked with reds and fading blues.

"Do you like sunsets or sunrises better?" he asked.

She pondered that for a moment, having never really thought about liking either one more. Both were pretty. "I'm not sure."

"One offers reflections," he said. "The other promises."

"That's true," she said, looking at him rather than the sunset. "I've never thought about it that way."

He shifted, looking her way, and then reached up, touched the side of her face with one finger. "Which do you like more? Memories or promises?"

The memories he'd given her would live inside her forever, she knew that, but something about the way he was looking at her right now made her heart skip a beat. As if he was offering promises, as well. The allure of that had her leaning toward him. "Can I say both?"

"Yes," he said softly. His hand cupped the side of her face as he leaned close enough for their lips to meet.

A thrill shot through her from head to toe, and she closed her eyes as his lips took her back to that place where she felt suspended between heaven and earth. It happened almost instantly, and she leaned closer, pressed her lips more firmly against his.

She wasn't sure what made her part her lips, but when she did, and Walter's tongue slipped into her mouth, she marveled at the intimacy. How he tasted like soda, and how, as his tongue twisted with hers, a heady, hot coil of fire formed deep inside her.

The warmth spread, and she wrapped her arms around his neck, holding on for dear life as her most private of all body parts started to throb in an extremely noticeable and unique way.

By the time Walter ended the kiss, she was thoroughly breathless and aching in ways and places she'd never ached before. He wrapped an arm around her and pulled her up against his side.

"It's almost set," he whispered.

She glanced at the horizon, where the sky met the ocean, and leaned her head on his shoulder as the last bits of the great orange ball of light sank out of sight. If someone were to ask her what the most wonderful day of her life had been, without hesitancy, she'd answer today.

Walter kissed the top of her head. "Do you want to drive again?"

"Yes, but not in the dark." Her mind was still too high in the clouds to ever find their way back to Julia's.

He laughed. "I guess that means I'm driving."

She loved the sound of his laughter, and how it made her want to giggle. "It does."

He helped her to her feet and carried her shoes and his back to the parking lot. She threw away their soda bottles and then put on her shoes while he put on his. He held her hand as they walked to the car, but rather than going to the passenger side, he led her to the driver's side.

Opening the door, he gestured for her to slide in. She did so, but he caught her by the shoulder before she was all the way to the other door. It felt a bit awkward at first, sitting in the middle of the car, but not after a few moments. Like she had on the beach, she rested her head against his shoulder as he drove.

Their arrival at Julia's saddened her. There was so much about the day that she didn't want to see end.

"I'll walk you to your cabin."

"You don't have to." They had climbed out of

the car, and she glanced at the pathway that led into the woods. "I'll be fine."

"I'm sure you will be, but I want to."

She wanted that, too. "All right."

They talked about inconsequential things as they walked, like the trees and weather. He said it rarely snowed along the coast, and she said it rarely didn't blizzard come winter in Nebraska.

"I remember that," he said. "The snow."

Confused, she asked, "You do?"

"The flood I told you about, that had been in Nebraska."

"Really? You lived in Nebraska?"

"Yes. Over by North Platte. The orphanage was in Fremont."

"That was the orphanage Pappy used to threaten to send me to." She laughed. "Not that he ever would have." It amazed her that they had that in common. And it made her happy—not that he'd endured so much as a child, but that they had an even stronger connection.

"We're here," he said, nodding toward the cabin. "I'll light the lamp for you."

They walked inside, and he lit the lamp, then kissed her briefly. "Good night, Blondie."

His whisper was so soft, so sweet, she couldn't do anything but stand there and watch him walk back out the door, closing it behind him.

That night may have been the very first night

that her mind didn't go off in numerous directions. Instead, it remained focused on Walter, on their wonderful day, and stayed right there until she drifted off to sleep.

Nothing within the court system happened quickly. Walter wasn't surprised that he didn't have a ruling on Shirley's case; however, he was frustrated by the direction it appeared to have taken. His refusal to offer representation to several other women who had contacted him, but hadn't worked at CB's, resulted in them finding other lawyers who were now attempting to piggyback on his case. Overall, it had gone from a can to a bucket of worms. Judge Wallis said he'd been inundated with submissions. Some appeared to be legit, others possibly not, yet had to be researched before being dismissed.

Wallis had called him in to say that, with so many serious crimes on the docket, it could take months before this one was settled.

That alone reminded Walter why he had chosen not to be a trial lawyer. Trials could be dragged out for years. The only good thing about this case taking that long was that, by then, Shirley might have given up on the idea of becoming a singer. He didn't like himself for having such thoughts. But they were there. Had been since he'd heard her singing at the Pig's Tail. He'd ignored them, because he'd told himself he was only her lawyer, but since kissing her, he couldn't ignore them any longer. His first bout of becoming embedded in showbiz had soured him to ever being an insider again.

Showbiz included a singer.

There were some good people involved in showbiz—he knew several—but for every good one, there were a dozen bad ones. He knew many of them, too. Those who thought the world revolved around them, that they were above everyone else, even the law. Lucy had brought them into his life, and she'd expected him to make sure they were above the law. He'd refused, and had separated himself from them even before she'd died. That was a world he refused to enter again. Not for anyone.

The diner was open for the lunch hour when he pulled up to the curb. Walking past the window, he scanned the room through the glass, not sure if Shirley would be waiting tables or in the kitchen.

He opened the door, and over the clinking of forks and the murmur of small talk, he heard a familiar laugh. She was at the counter, and a hot flare of fury rippled through him as he recognized the man she was waiting on.

Karl VanBuren.

Lucy's *accident* had occurred after she'd left Karl's house. Their affair had been going on long before then. Long before he and Lucy had gotten married. It had been on and off since the first movie she and Karl had starred in together. The one that had made her a star.

VanBuren still was a star. That, his fame and his money kept him from being blacklisted like others who had done far less than him. After his third divorce earlier this year, he'd boasted that divorce was becoming more popular because of him.

No charges had been brought against him because VanBuren had already paid to have Lucy's death ruled an accident, and there hadn't been anything that could have been done about it.

With anger as fuel, Walter made a beeline for the counter. Someone caught his arm, and he twisted, ready to shake them off.

"Easy there, big guy," Julia said. "You know my rules."

He took measure at the seriousness of her tone, at the anger flaring inside him. His gaze snapped back to the counter, but this time he saw Shirley and the frown on her face.

"Shirley's nothing like those who came before her," Julia said before releasing his arm and walking away.

She was a 120 percent right about that, and he needed to be thankful that she'd stopped him from making an ass of himself, but VanBuren was the worst kind of a piker, a coward. He was as smug as hell and truly didn't care about anyone other than himself.

"Hello," Shirley said, stepping up in front of him. "Do you have bad news? Did the judge rule against us?"

He shook his head. "No. He hasn't made a ruling yet."

She let out a sigh. "That's good, isn't it?"

"Yes, it's good." He nodded to the tray of empty plates in her hands. "Are you waitressing today?"

"No, just collecting dirty dishes to wash." She glanced behind her. "You don't like that man. I can tell."

He didn't, for good reason. "I want you to stay away from him."

"He's just a customer."

"No, he's not."

"Because he's a movie star? They come in here all the time. Look around, the place is full of them from the studio across the street. Jack, Helen and Grace just left a few minutes ago."

He knew actors from Jack McCarney's studio ate here daily, but Karl didn't work for Star's Studio. Jack didn't hire scum. "He told you he's a movie star?"

"No, Rosie did, but there's nothing to worry about. Julia has strict rules about not seeking auditions from customers." She shifted the tray in her hands.

Before she could glance at Karl again, Walter asked, "Do you need help?"

"No, but I'm sure Julia won't mind if you come into the kitchen and tell me what the judge said while I wash these. Alice is helping me and Rita is helping cook. They'll both want to know, too."

"All right." He took the tray from her. "Lead the way."

VanBuren had been staring at them, still was, but Walter ignored him. Not saying a word would irritate the bastard far more than a confrontation.

After setting the tray on the counter in the kitchen, Walter told the women about his meeting with the judge, and explained how things might take longer than he'd first suggested. They were disappointed, but perked up when he said the only thing they needed to continue to do was stay clear of speakeasies.

He left shortly afterward because the place was hopping and the women busy. VanBuren had already left, too, and Walter told himself to forget about Karl. Julia had been right. Shirley was nothing like Lucy had been.

Before driving away, he considered finding something to do until the diner closed, but he couldn't fiddle away hours, not with the workload that was piled up at his office. The new movie theater being built downtown had studios scrambling to get movies filmed and ready to be shown. Jack McCarney had drawn the lucky straw. His movie would be the theater's opening premiere. Walter was glad about that. Jack deserved a break. Not only did he create excellent picture shows, he was a downright good person. One of the few in Hollywood.

By the time Saturday rolled around, Walter was champing at the bit to see Shirley. Wilson called him first thing in the morning, said to park next to his roadster and use the private door to enter the stadium. He also said not to worry about Alice and Rita, that he was sending a car over to pick them up so Walter wouldn't have an excuse to not bring his Packard.

Walter had said there wasn't a chance in hell he'd not drive his car. He didn't tell Wilson, but he'd also paid a young man Mrs. McCaffrey knew to wash and buff the Packard until it sparkled like a jewel.

He pulled up in front of the diner just as the closed sign was hung in the window. Rosie waved at him and then opened the door. "She's up at the house, getting ready!"

He waved, pulled away from the curb and then into the driveway. As she had before, Shirley hurried down the steps, meeting the car as it rolled to a stop. Her white-and-red-striped dress highlighted her sleek curves, emphasizing her narrow waist and slender hips. A white beaded headband encircled her head, riding low on her forehead, but it was the grin on her face that he noticed the most.

He opened his door and stepped out of the car. "Climb in."

Her grin increased as she bopped around him and slid onto the seat. She didn't slide all the way over to the passenger door, and that suited him just fine.

"Excited for the game?" he asked while reversing the car.

She hooked her hand around his arm. "Not as much as I am for the race."

"Me, too."

They laughed together and continued to do so for the rest of the day. And night.

The Angels won again, and just as he'd known it would, his Packard left Wilson's roadster so far behind he and Shirley were already sitting in the booth and sipping champagne at Manchester's by the time the others arrived.

"How many horses do you have under that hood?" Wilson asked as he sat down at the booth.

"More than what's under your hood," Walter said.

Wilson picked up his glass. "Well, ladies, it's a

good thing I have looks and money, because once again, this meal's on me."

When Charles arrived at the table, Wilson again ordered for everyone, going with oyster stew, clams, crab legs, pork chops and chocolate soufflé for dessert. As last time, Walter's greatest enjoyment of the meal was watching Shirley experience things for the first time.

Dragging his attention off her was almost impossible, even to answer Wilson's request to go up the road for dancing after eating. "Not tonight," Walter said.

"Come on, Walter old boy, these dames can't sit home every night. The judge will understand that."

Walter wasn't thinking about the case as much as he was thinking about being alone with Shirley. That had become his goal. To spend as much time with her as possible. Alone time. He kept thinking about her singing, how good she was and how that affected how much time they had to spend together.

"We could go to the pier," Wilson suggested.

The shine that instantly appeared in Shirley's eyes had Walter nodding. The pier was next to the amusement park they'd visited last week, and always sported entertainment and dancing. It would also be an easy spot to sneak away for some alone time. "Sure," he said. "We could do that."

"Ducky!" Rita said. "I've heard the pier is the cat's meow!"

A short time later, once they were in his car, Shirley said, "We don't have to go to the pier."

"Yes, we do, you'll like it."

"But you didn't seem very excited about it."

"Only because I was hoping you and I could be alone for a while," he answered honestly.

Under the yellow hue of the streetlights, he saw her cheeks blush.

"Oh," she said, biting back a smile.

He winked at her and gunned the engine, pulling away from the curb ahead of Wilson.

Shirley's heart had been thumping all day, but had increased speed when Walter mentioned alone time. She would never have said anything, because she truly liked Rita and Alice and Wilson, and being with all of them was fun, but she truly wanted to be alone with Walter.

They parked next to Wilson's car, and all five of them took a wooden board walkway that ran along the sandy shore to where a crowd filled a huge, long and wide pier that went out into the ocean. Electric lights on tall poles shone a warm glow in all directions and cast shadows onto the water. Loud voices and boisterous laughter could be heard above the band spewing out a fast beat for the couples dancing.

People covered every square inch, including the side railings, where men and women alike were perched on the top rail like flocks of birds.

"Come on, dolls," Wilson said, tugging both Rita and Alice toward the dance floor. "Let's cut a rug!"

"Is he going to dance with both of them at the same time?" Shirley asked.

"Looks like it," Walter said.

Wilson twirled Alice under his arm first, then Rita, then all three of them started moving back and forth in a line, kicking up their heels.

Walter stepped onto the dance floor. "Let's join them."

She hesitated. "I've never—"

"Now's the perfect time to learn!"

There was no time to question her abilities; he simply pulled her onto the dance floor, spun her and grasped her waist from behind.

"Just follow my lead," he said in her ear. With his hands guiding her, he instructed, "Back, back, side, side. Now, forward, forward, side, side. And back, back again, side, side..."

Shirley wasn't sure how he managed to teach her so quickly, but her feet slid across the floor in perfect timing with his, and within no time, she was dancing without his instructions.

Walter spun her in a complete circle, then half again until they were facing each other, then he took one of her hands and grasped her waist with the other so they were face-to-face. "You got it," he said as they glided across the floor. "You're dancing."

She was dancing. With him. Just like she'd dreamed of doing. Except she felt as if she was a foot off the floor, merely floating on air.

The song the band played was one she knew, had heard it on the radio, and she couldn't help singing along as she and Walter sashayed across the dance floor.

He was so very handsome, and she adored being with him. Not just because of the all the wonderful things he'd shown her, but because she liked him. Really liked him. Liked him more than she'd ever liked anyone before. Other than Pappy.

She'd loved Pappy.

Love.

A shiver rippled down her spine.

Love was the reason her mother's dream of being a singer ended.

She glanced up, caught Walter looking at her. His eyes weren't shining. There was pain in them. Showbiz. Singing. He didn't like it. That's why he didn't want to come here.

Her throat locked up, and she stumbled.

Walter's hold tightened as he tried to help her catch her rhythm again, but it was lost. So was the song. The music. Her ears heard nothing but a ringing sound as a raw, inner pain filled her.

Her hand slipped off his shoulder as a shiver made the hair on her arms stand up. She couldn't love him. She couldn't love anyone. Not right now. Especially someone who didn't even like singing.

"What is it?" he asked. "What's wrong?"

"N-nothing." She took a step back, separating herself from him. "I—I've had enough."

He frowned. "Are you all right?"

"Yes." Her heart pounded. With fear. She'd come here to become a singer, not fall in love. Not with someone who— "I need to leave. Can we leave?"

"Sure, but what's wrong?"

"Nothing is wrong," she insisted. A dozen excuses raced through her head. He'd believe if she said her feet hurt, or that she was tired, but those were lies, and she'd never cottoned to lying. Not about anything.

He led her through the crowd of people, elbowing to make enough room for them to pass. She kept telling herself that she hadn't fallen in love with him. If that was to ever happen, her falling in love, she'd know it right from the start. It wouldn't just show up out of nowhere. Most certainly not while she was in the middle of the dance floor. Love wasn't like that. It couldn't just sneak up on a person like a cold.

Or could it? Her mother had arrived in Roca with a singing troupe, a troupe that left without her because she'd fallen in love.

No. Oh, no. That couldn't happen.

The crowd was behind them, nothing but a dark boardwalk in front of them. Walter grasped her shoulders. "Something is wrong. What is it?"

She couldn't look him in the eye. "Nothing. I just…" Taking a deep breath, she finished, "Need to go home. I—I need to go home."

# *Chapter Fourteen*

Shirley smothered a yawn, shook her head and delved back into the sink full of dishes before her. The diner was closed, but Julia baked desserts on Sundays for the following week, and needing something to keep her mind straight, Shirley had volunteered to help.

Walter was the reason she was so tired. Every time she'd closed her eyes last night, his image had been right there. Smiling. Laughing. Kissing her.

That image was still there.

There had to be a way for her to figure out if she loved him or not. She didn't want to. She wanted to become a singer.

That dream was all she had of her mother. Of Pappy. She'd told the Swaggerts that she would become a singer, and even though they'd laughed at her, she'd stuck to her guns. She'd told herself that, too.

"You've been awfully quiet today," Julia said, setting an empty kettle on the counter. "Did something happen last night?"

Shirley shook her head. "Nothing more than what Alice and Rita said." They'd been at the diner earlier, crowing over how much fun they'd had yesterday, from the ball game to the pier, and everything in between.

It had been fun. Everything she'd done with Walter had been fun. But she wasn't here to have fun.

Julia picked up a towel and dried a mixing bowl. "Why didn't you want to talk to Walter when he called earlier?"

Shirley shrugged. "Ain't got nothing to say."

"The two of you have a fight?"

"No." Tears stung her eyes. She hadn't cried since Pappy died and wasn't about to now.

"I'll take over," Julia said. "You go over to the house and call Walter. He said he has something to show you."

She didn't want him to show her anything else. Still fighting the tears that threatened to fall, Shirley threw the washcloth into the sink. "I came here to become a singer. A singer."

"Yes, you did," Julia said. "And you will."

Her eyes burned hotter.

"I've heard you sing. You're good, really good, and once the case is ruled on, there won't be anything to stop you," Julia said. "Except for yourself."

Shirley sucked in a breath of air. Was that true? No, Walter could stop her, if she let him. That's what had stopped her mother. She couldn't let that happen to her.

Couldn't let love happen.

"Is there anything you want to talk about?" Julia asked.

"No." Thankful for all Julia had done, and continued to do, Shirley apologized. "I'm sorry..." She huffed out a sigh. "I'm just confused."

"Understandably so." Julia laid the towel on the counter. "Things moved fast between you and Walter. That happens sometimes and it catches us off guard. I fell in love with an actor a few years ago, and thought he loved me, but he only wanted my property."

Shirley's spine quivered. "You did? What happened?"

"I told him to get lost as soon as I discovered the truth. It wasn't easy, but this property is all I have. The rest of it had already been sold off, and if I lost this, what would I do?" Julia let out a false laugh. "Get a typing job? I don't even know how to type."

"Neither do I," Shirley said, even though typing had nothing to do with singing. She was pondering what else Julia had said. The part about falling in love, but choosing her property over the man she loved. "Do you regret it? Making the choice you did?"

Julia shrugged. "Honestly, some days I do. This diner puts money in the bank, but…" She shook her head. "Then I meet a girl like you, like the others, and am glad I made the choice I did because I'm able to help others, and that feels good."

Shirley's insides sank. If she chose singing over Walter, and it didn't work out, she wouldn't have a diner to fall back on. She wouldn't have anything except washing dishes to fall back on.

A knock sounded on the back door. Shirley's heart skipped a beat, hoping it wasn't Walter. She wasn't ready to face him. Not yet. There was still too much she had to figure out.

Julia pulled aside the curtain and then opened the door. "Mr. Johansson. Can I help you?"

"I came to speak to her," the owner of the Pig's Tail said.

A shiver rippled through Shirley as to why he would want to speak with her. He'd been adamant about none of them ever visiting his joint again. None of them had gone there, but he was here, so that meant something had happened.

Julia looked at her, and Shirley shrugged.

"It won't take long," Mr. Johansson said.

"What won't take long?" Shirley asked with a good case of distrust tingling her spine.

"I wouldn't do this, except that my brother is in a real tight spot." He took off his hat and stepped inside the kitchen. "I told that lawyer of yours that I'd have hired you if I could, but with the circumstances as they are, I can't. But you are one hell of a singer, and that's what I told my brother. He wants you to come see him today. Right away."

"Your brother?" Shirley shook her head, telling herself it didn't matter. She couldn't sing for any tavern owner. That much she'd already promised. "I can't."

"Wait a minute." Julia pointed at Eric. "Your brother who owns the radio station?"

"Yes. Earl. His regular girl was in a car accident last night and is in the hospital. He needs a stand-in right away. He wanted Eva, but as you know, she quit and I haven't found another singer to take her place."

"What exactly does Earl need?" Julia asked.

"A singer. Friday, Saturday and Sunday nights from eight to eleven."

"On the radio?" Julia asked.

Radio? Shirley couldn't deny the sense of excitement that bubbled inside her when Mr. Johansson nodded.

"I thought of you right away," he said. "It's

not a speakeasy so it wouldn't interfere with the case. Would it?"

"No, it wouldn't," Julia said, looking at her. "That's the station we listen to every night."

Shirley's heart stopped while her mind spun in so many directions she couldn't catch a single thought long enough for one of them to make sense. It wasn't a speakeasy, but she'd promised Walter... But she'd promised herself, too.

"Tell your brother she'll be over to see him within the hour," Julia said.

"I'll go call him right now." Mr. Johansson grabbed the doorknob, opened the door and left.

"Julia," Shirley said, not sure what she should say, "I don't know—"

"This is it." Julia grabbed her shoulders. "Your big chance. Another one like this won't just happen. Not a radio gig. Any place that can't afford a live band pipes music in from Earl's station. Even some who can afford it play his station. There are hundreds of singers who would die for this opportunity. I pride myself for not putting my nose into anyone else's business, not with any of the girls who have come here over the years, but this is different. This is a one in a million chance."

Someday, she might remember exactly what happened between the time Eric Johansson had left the diner and her, wearing the purple dress and singing one of the songs she'd sung in Julia's living room night after night, into a big silver microphone. Just not right now. She was too focused on singing like she'd never sung before. It was a fast-paced song, one that could steal a person's breath if they weren't prepared. It was about being kissed for the first time, and because she knew that feeling so well, she was able to fully embrace singing the song. The happiness that filled her was so great she thought of her mother and Pappy. Therefore, as she finished the final chorus, she did what she and Pappy used to do. Made up silly words. "Bobbity-bobbity-do!" she sang into the microphone as the music ended.

Earl, who was as tall and barrel-chested as his brother, frowned for a moment, then started clapping. So did Julia, Rosie, Rita and Alice, as well as the piano player.

"I like that!" Earl shouted as his smile grew. "That gibberish at the end. It goes perfectly with your accent. Sing me another song."

The man at the piano handed her another sheet of music. Luckily, it was another one that she'd practiced. It was about dancing under the moonlight, which, again, she could relate to. The song was just as fast a pace as the first one. At the end of this one, right before the music ended, she added, "Dip-dip, dippity-doo!"

Earl rubbed his thick, black mustache before clapping this time. "I really like those little taglines at the end. It's different. Catchy. Do you do those on all your songs?"

Considering this was the first time she'd truly auditioned for anyone, she nodded. "Yes, sir."

"Well, it works for you. Really works." Earl sat back in his chair. "Eric told me you were good, that he wanted to hire you, but I had to hear for myself, and have heard enough. Can you start tonight?"

Her heart pounded with excitement, yet Shirley didn't know if she should nod or not. She owed Walter so much, but she owed herself, too, and Pappy, and her mother.

"We have a few questions first," Julia said. "Things to discuss."

Walter steered the Packard into the parking lot of Earl Johansson's radio station so fast the wheels squealed. This explained last night. The dancing. The band. The reason she wouldn't face him afterward. She must have been planning this for some time. And kept it from him. No one just gets a radio gig out of the blue. With the rise in popularity of radios the past couple of years, singers, male and female, dreamed of getting a gig singing for one of the stations. She must have been auditioning day and night.

He was a sap. Hadn't seen this coming any more than he'd seen Lucy's deceptions.

Anger. Disgust. Pain. It was all there. Inside him. Festering.

He glanced at the seashell on the seat. He'd been so excited to show it to her he'd nearly run all the way to her cabin. Only to find it empty. It had reminded him of the many times Lucy had lied to him, had said she'd be one place but had been at VanBuren's.

He'd gone to Julia's house then, and the look of guilt on her face had reminded him of the last time he'd gone to Karl's. The night of Lucy's death. Julia had told him to calm down, to listen to what she had to say, but the radio had been on, and he'd heard it. The radio. The person singing.

Blondie.

He'd seen red. Still was.

Was she trying to get herself killed? Or just found joy in deceiving him?

He climbed out of the roadster and slammed the door shut.

She was inside all right, in a small glass-paned booth, singing a snappy tune as a curly-haired blond man beat on piano keys. The man on the piano saw him first, then she did. Her expression told him more than he needed to know. She wasn't any happier seeing him than he was her.

She kept right on singing and his anger rose. Lucy would do that when he'd found her. Defy him. Go right on smoking.

A door behind him opened. "Earl say you can be here?" a male voice asked.

Walter kept his eyes on Shirley as he barked, "I'm her lawyer."

"Oh, well, she's on the air for two more minutes, then will have a five-minute break."

*No. Then she'd be leaving.* Walter didn't say that aloud, even though it was the truth.

The moment Shirley stepped away from the microphone, he pulled open the door. "What are you doing?"

"What does it look like?" she retorted.

"I'm going to get a glass of water," the man at the piano said, shooting to his feet and then out the door.

Walter grabbed the door before it closed. "Let's go."

She bowed her head and took a step, but then stopped and shook her head. "No."

Fury filled him. "Doesn't honesty mean anything to you? Promises?"

Her head snapped up and her eyes narrowed. "Honesty!" she shouted. "What about your honesty?"

He shook his head at her anger and her question. "Mine? What about my honesty?"

She glared at him. "Did Eric Johansson tell you he wanted to hire me?"

"Yes."

"Why didn't you tell me that?"

"Because it doesn't matter." It didn't.

"Doesn't matter? Doesn't matter? Well, it does to me!" She threw her arms in the air. "I promised I wouldn't sing at a speakeasy, and this isn't a speakeasy." Pointing at him, she continued her tirade. "You aren't going to drag me out of here. Not this time. I came to California to sing, and that's what I'm going to do. Sing. And you can't stop me. No one can stop me. No one will take that away from me!"

Attempting to talk some sense into her, he started, "The case—"

"Is your problem!" she shouted. "You're the lawyer. Not me. It's your job to win this case, not mine." She pointed to the door. "Leave. Now. Leave me alone!"

She sounded just like Lucy had, and he was responding just like he had back then.

Disgust filled him.

He should have known this would happen. With her talent, her spunk, there would be no stopping her. He was the one who had to stop. Just be done. Done with her. Without a word, he walked out of the room, out of the building, got in his car and drove out of the parking lot. If Judge Wallis chose to use this against her and the case, that was his prerogative and would be her problem. Not his. He should have never gotten involved in the first place.

Walter drove home, determined to stay there. He'd put aside work for too long. Work clients paid him for. Clients who not only appreciated his work, but listened to his advice.

He forced himself to walk straight into his office, and pulled out the paperwork he needed to complete and file for Jack McCarney's movie. Something solid and real to take his mind off Shirley. Get his life back in perspective. Where it should have been all along, rather than chasing after a choice bit of calico.

The anger churning inside him was so sickening he slammed a fist onto his desk so hard the phone jangled. He jumped to his feet and ran a hand through his hair. What the hell was he doing? He hadn't been able to fully concentrate on anything but her in weeks, and tonight was different in only one way.

It was worse.

This was the exact reason he'd focused his practice on contracts. They made it impossible for people to break promises. They were legally bound not to. Theodore had promised to not do anything rash, and had broken that promise. Lucy broke damn near every promise she'd ever made him. Why had he expected anything different from Shirley?

No one could save someone who didn't want to be saved. Not even from themselves.

Walter was still telling himself that weeks later. Had almost convinced himself he didn't care what happened to Shirley. Judge Wallis still hadn't ruled on the case. He hoped that would happen soon so he could end it all. Officially. Put the final nail in the coffin.

The phone on his desk rang, and he ignored it, as he had the past few weeks. When it continued to ring, he stood and walked to the door, ready to tell one of his law clerks to answer the damn thing.

Seeing the empty desk in the front lobby, he remembered his clerks had already left. It was Friday night. The entire office building had been empty for hours.

Another ring from the phone sent the never-ending anger inside him to boiling point. He grabbed the phone.

"Walter, old boy, is that you?"

Not again. Wilson had called every week, asking if he'd be at Saturday's game.

"I know you can't make it to the game tomorrow," Wilson said. "Not with the way our little Blondie is hitting it big."

A red-hot stake struck him square in the chest.

He still thought of her as Blondie, and didn't like the idea of others doing the same.

"The girls and I are going over to listen to her tonight," Wilson said, "and thought you might like to tag along."

Walter had heard the radio station had grown in popularity since Shirley started singing there. It was the talk of the town, the way she ended each song with sexy gibberish. That's what he'd heard, but he hadn't gone anywhere to listen to it, and didn't plan on doing so, either. However, he was duty bound to say, "The case hasn't been ruled on. Rita and Alice know they shouldn't be in taverns."

"We're not going to a tavern. The radio station had speakers installed outside their building for the people gathering in the parking lot."

"Since when?" Walter hadn't heard about that.

"Tonight's the first night," Wilson answered. "We just had dinner at the diner and are heading over to the station."

Walter hadn't been at the diner since that Sunday, when he'd heard Shirley's voice coming through the radio in Julia's living room. He hadn't so much as driven past the radio station since that night, either.

"I have work to finish." Whatever had been between him and Shirley was over. He hung up the phone, and returned to his office, fully intent on working until the wee hours of the morning. Long after Shirley would have sung her last note.

An hour later, the array of thoughts filling his head, centered around Shirley and a parking lot full of people, were too strong to bury.

He pushed away from his desk and grabbed his jacket. She still was his client, at least for the time being, and that meant he still had her best interest at heart. The station was downtown, where there were plenty of seedy people. Especially after dark.

The closest parking spot he could find was more than two blocks away from the station. He spotted Wilson's car while walking toward the parking lot. Piano music played, but there was no singing. There were people, though. Everywhere. Shoulder to shoulder like at the pier.

Walter looked around, taking in the people standing, sitting on and in cars and walking around. His insides quivered as he recognized faces. Among the average people, there were actors, producers, reporters and business owners. A crowd of who's who in Hollywood.

The big round speakers on the corners of the building crackled as the music blaring from them slowly faded away. For the amount of people gathered in the lot, a near silence filled the air, as if everyone had their ears tuned in.

The speakers crackled again as the announcer

came on. "Thank you, Merlin Ransom, KWJT's piano master!" After a moment of static, the announcer's voice returned. "I'm Alan Frank, and will be with you all night. First, I'm sending out a thank-you for tonight's sponsor, Wagner Brothers Studio. Located at the corner of Wesley and Hampton, Wagner Brothers is responsible for bringing you some of the biggest and best movies in the theaters across the nation. Some of the finest actors, too. And tonight, they are bringing you LA's newest singing sensation!"

The crowd erupted with applause.

"That's right, folks, Blondie is here, and in a moment, she'll be singing a song put together just for you! So sit tight, or jump to your feet to cut a rug! Either way, Blondie's here to put some dippity-dip in your step!"

Blondie. Walter shook his head against the ire that tightened his jaw. He should go back home, but something inside him had him edging his way through the crowd, closer to the speakers, as applause broke out again, as well as shouts and whistles.

The next sound that came through the speakers made his heart do things it may have never done before. Her voice made his heart swell with warmth. He'd missed her. Missed her so much.

He closed his eyes for a moment, focused on her singing, on what it did to him.

She was so good. Beyond good. Talent like hers was exceptional. Even here. In Hollywood.

And he was in love with her.

He opened his eyes and bit back the smile that tried to form.

In an odd way, it felt good to admit that. That he'd fallen in love with her.

He couldn't have stopped it if he'd wanted to. The song she was singing was as full of life as she was. Fast, fun, and sung with a spunky Midwestern accent that made the ditty about dancing the foxtrot all the more charming and captivating.

That's what it did to the crowd. Captivated them. People were dancing, clapping, cheering. His smile broke free when she ended the tune with, "Dippity-do-do, dippity-do!"

Having seen it before, he could imagine her smile as a tiny giggle came through the speaker. The crowd cheered and clapped so loud he had to strain to hear the announcer say Blondie would be back in thirty seconds with another song just as entertaining.

Hugging the wall, Walter walked along the building. If he was hoping to find a quiet spot, there wasn't one. Especially when she started singing again. This time the clapping and cheers were so loud he couldn't hear the first half of the song.

She ended that one with gibberish again, and

then sang two more songs before the announcer spoke about sponsors. Not only Wagner Brothers, but those who were sponsoring tomorrow night's show, and how others could contact the station to become a sponsor. He then announced Blondie would be back right after the piano player gave them a song to get their wiggle on.

Walter stayed the entire time, through the piano player, and all of the songs Shirley sang. More than a dozen. She made each one of them entertaining, and her endings evoked a joyous glee from the crowd.

The station shut down after her last song; the big speakers went completely silent. People dispersed slowly, their boisterous elation floating in the air as they walked and drove away, honking and waving at one another.

Walter stayed put, not far from the door, which was locked; he'd watched people trying to open it several times throughout the night. That concerned him. He scanned the parking lot, wondering how she got back to Julia's each night.

It had to have been more than an hour before someone unlocked the door. Walter stepped out of the shadow cast by the overhead awning as the door opened.

He heard her gasp, or maybe that had been him. She was wearing the simple blue paisley dress from the first day he'd met her, but looked more beautiful than ever. He wanted to grab her, kiss her, hug her, never let her go.

The sadness in her eyes as her gaze met his nearly gutted him.

"Move on, buster." A burly man with more hair on his face than on his head blocked her from walking out the door. "Now, or you'll wish you had."

"It's all right, Reggie," she said, stepping around the man. "I know him."

"Who is he?" the man asked.

She let out a long breath. "My lawyer."

Walter took a step closer. "Yes, I am." Eyeing the Reggie fellow, he said, "I'll give Miss Burnette a ride home tonight."

Reggie looked at her in question.

Walter held his breath, but never took his eyes off her.

"It's fine, Reggie," she said. "I'll see you tomorrow."

The man shook his head. "I'll walk you to his car." He glanced at the empty parking lot. "Where is it?"

"A couple blocks up the road," Walter said, taking her elbow.

Reggie walked behind them the entire way and watched as they climbed in and then drove away. Walter wasn't sure if he was impressed or irritated that she had a torpedo. Both, most likely. Impressed that she wasn't walking the streets alone at night, irritated that she needed a hired thug to protect her.

"Did the judge rule on the case?" she asked.

He turned the roadster around the corner before glancing at her. "No."

"Then why are you here? Why'd you come to the station tonight?"

Why indeed? He let out a sigh, contemplated what to say. "Did you sign a contract with the radio station?"

"No. There was no reason. I'm only filling in for their regular weekend singer. She was in a car accident."

He may have heard that someplace, at a point when he'd been telling himself he didn't care. "For how long?"

"Six weeks."

It had been four weeks since he'd seen her, but he hadn't been counting. Not on purpose. He just knew that was how long it had been since he'd laughed. Since he'd thought about a bright and happy future. Since he'd felt whole again. She'd done that to him, made him feel whole again.

Then she'd taken it away as quickly as she'd given it.

That thought disgusted him. Not at her, but at himself for putting so much faith and hope in someone else. That had been the one thing he hadn't done before. Not even with Lucy. He sure as hell hadn't done it when he'd left the orphanage.

So why had he with her? Why had he hoped?

Hope. A smile tugged at his lips. She'd told him to get himself some the day they'd met. Maybe she'd actually given him some.

# Chapter Fifteen

Shirley breathed through her nose again, trying to settle the erratic beats of her heart. It had started pounding the moment she'd seen Walter outside the door. Sitting this close to him, close enough to smell the cologne that brought back images of kissing him, made her heart pound harder. She had missed him so much the past few weeks that she'd cried herself to sleep at night. Something she hadn't done since Pappy had died.

She regretted telling him to leave that day, but she'd had to know if her dream could come true. What she'd really discovered was what life was like without him.

Hell. That was the only word she could use to describe it.

Singing every weekend helped. Learning new songs and singing them, one after the other, for three hours straight. But three hours wasn't much when there were twenty-one other hours where her mind did little else but think about him. Even while learning new songs, he'd been on her mind. Sometimes, she had wished he could hear her. Other times, she wondered if she truly wanted singing, wanted to go through life alone, more than she wanted him. If singing was worth it. If anything was worth not having someone to share it with.

"What will you do after the six weeks is over?" he asked.

She shrugged. "I haven't thought about it."

"Why not?"

*Because she was too busy thinking about him.* She shrugged again.

"Don't you like it?" he asked.

"Yes. It's what I came here to do. Singing on the radio isn't like singing in a joint. It's just me and Merlin. He's the piano player." She pointed that out in case he didn't know. "It reminds me of singing with Pappy. The fun we had."

"That comes through loud and clear," he said.

She'd been trying hard not to look at him, but had to sneak a peek. "What does?"

"Your enjoyment," he said without taking his eyes off the road. "The listeners pick up on that, and it makes them enjoy the songs more, too."

"How do you know that?"

"I was there. I saw the parking lot full of people."

"That was Earl's idea," she said, still in awe over how many people she'd seen outside the door earlier tonight.

"You don't like it?"

"I don't mind, it just worries me a little that someone might find out my real name."

"Your real name?"

If she could tell anyone the truth, it was him. After all, he was the reason. "Julia came with me to the audition. All of the girls did, and Julia told Earl she didn't want people flocking to the diner to get a look at me, so insisted that no one could know my real name or where I live. She said it wouldn't be good for the case, either, so, remembering that you'd called me Blondie a couple of times, I said that's the name Earl could use." She bit her lip, worried that he might not like that.

"You chose that name?"

She nodded. "Because of you." She probably shouldn't have admitted that, but it was too late now.

He scratched the side of his head. "Who does know your real name?"

"Just Earl and Merlin, and Eric, Earl's brother, and Wilson because Alice let it slip, but both he and Eric promised not to tell anyone."

"Are you still working at the diner?"

"Of course. Singing on the radio doesn't pay very much."

The frown that covered his face made her spine tingle.

"It should," he said.

"Not when you're just filling in." Money hadn't been the reason she'd wanted to become a singer. Her dream had been the reason. Singing made her happy, just not in the same way as he had.

He pulled into Julia's driveway, and when he turned the car off, asked, "May I walk you to your cabin?"

Her heart, still racing, nearly leaped out of her chest. "If you want to."

"I want to."

She waited for him to walk around and open her door, and when he didn't release her hand after she'd stepped out of the car, she folded her fingers around his hand. The heat of his palm against hers jolted her insides into life in a way only he evoked.

"I've missed you, Shirley," he said as they entered the trail to the cabin.

"I've missed you, too, Walter," she admitted before she had a moment to think about it. Actually, she'd have said that even after thinking about it. It was the truth. She had missed him more than she'd ever missed anyone.

"I'm sorry I didn't tell you that Eric wanted to hire you," he said. "I didn't mean to be dishonest. I didn't think it mattered."

She hadn't ever told him why she wanted to be a singer. Hadn't told anyone. "Singing is the only thing I have left of my family. That made becoming one more than a hope. More than a dream. It was something I had to do." It was hard to explain exactly how much singing had meant to her. "No matter what. If I didn't, they'd be gone forever." She stopped walking and faced him, needing to tell him something else. "I'm sorry I told you to leave the radio sta—"

Walter's finger pressed against her lips, stopped her from finishing. He shook his head. "I should never have acted the way I did that night, and I'm sorry. It's no excuse, but I'd been lied to so many times in the past, experienced so many broken promises, that I immediately thought that's what you were doing, too. I wasn't willing to walk down that path again."

Her heart ached for him. For promises broken. Lies told. She touched the side of his face. "I didn't think I was breaking a promise. It wasn't a speakeasy."

"No, it wasn't, and you didn't break your promise." He squeezed her hand. "I was also afraid. Afraid something would happen to you. More than one person has died chasing their dreams. I didn't want to watch you walk down the same path others had."

"I took the dangers you warned me about seriously." With a smirk, she added, "I have no desire to become a real singing angel."

He grinned. "I have no desire for that, either. You could have told me about the radio gig that night on the pier."

She shook her head. "I didn't know about it that night. Eric didn't come see me until the next day."

"Then what was wrong that night?" He folded his fingers around her hand on his cheek. "Why did you want to leave so suddenly?"

She had to tell him the truth. "Because I was scared."

"Of what?"

She drew in a deep breath. The last four weeks had been so lonely, and scared or not, she couldn't let that go on. "You."

He frowned. "Me?"

The moonlight shone down on his sandy-brown hair, making it sparkle. Her heart clawed its way into her throat, blocking her airway. He was so very, very handsome. The most handsome man on earth. The most wonderful, too. Swallowing her heart, she nodded. "Yes. You."

"Why?"

"Because of the way you make me feel. I'd never felt that way before." She shook her head. "This way."

"I've never felt this way, either," he whispered. When his lips touched hers, she wrapped her arms around his neck and held on, knowing his kiss would lift her right off the ground. It did. It was also the most demanding kiss he'd ever given her, almost as if he couldn't control himself.

She couldn't, either, and used her tongue to force his lips apart. The taste, the heat of his mouth sent her soaring even higher.

Their kissing intensified, until they had to part because they needed to breathe.

She was gasping for air and his chest was heaving when he grabbed her hand. "Come on."

They darted though the woods like they had the stadium parking lot. Holding hands, laughing, running side by side. Tonight was as exciting as that day had been. Full of exhilaration, they leaped onto the stoop of the cabin at the exact same time and laughed at how the boards thumped beneath their feet.

Walter pulled her into his arms and kissed her again. The happiness inside her was so bright, so bold, she wondered if the sun had suddenly broke rank and decided to shine in the middle of the night.

His hands were on her hips, holding her firmly against him when he dragged his lips off hers. The heat that blossomed deep inside her whenever she thought about kissing him was so strong it ached. Burned.

He kissed her, but then pulled back again.

There was a smile on his lips, but it didn't reach his eyes. He gave his head a single shake. "I should leave."

Shirley studied him for a moment. The last four weeks had given her plenty of time to think, and living with women who lived a much freer lifestyle than she'd lived had taught her plenty. However, there were things she'd known about for years, and had thought about plenty the past few weeks.

"I don't want you to leave," she said.

"I don't want to, but I need to, before—"

Giddiness bubbled inside her. She knew exactly why he felt he should leave. Pressing the entire length of her body against his, she whispered, "I was raised on a farm, Walter. I know all about the birds and the bees."

His chuckle was low and tickled the skin on her forehead as he kissed it. "It's a bit more complicated with people than with animals."

"Only if we make it more complicated," she said. That was precisely what she'd thought about, a lot. The sharing of their bodies. She knew that didn't always mean you truly loved someone, but she did want to be with him. That way. Because she did love him. Always would. More than anything else.

He shook his head, but the shine in his eyes told her exactly what he was thinking.

"Don't leave," she whispered, her lips barely touching his. "I don't want you to."

His kiss was tender, precious, so was the way he whispered, "Are you sure?"

The promises in the kiss they'd just shared left her with no doubt. "I'm sure." She took a step toward the door and, twisting the handle, smiled at him. "Very sure."

She led him inside, but rather than simply being a little cabin in the woods, it was as if the tiny space had been transformed into a place where dreams came true.

Walter lit the lamp while she sat down on the bed and removed her shoes. He took off his coat and hung it on the back of the chair. She stood and slid her fingers beneath his suspenders, tugging at the elastic until his body touched hers.

His kiss was so affectionate she sighed at the beauty of it, then pushed his suspenders over his shoulders.

"I've dreamed of this," he whispered, running a hand down her side.

She giggled, not embarrassed to admit, "Me, too."

No one would have ever called her a nervous ninny, and she wasn't this time, either. In fact, she had never felt more confident that she'd made the right decision. They took their time, removed clothing one piece at a time, his and hers, and explored one another, first with their eyes, and then their hands and lips.

By the time they were lying on the bed, bare skin touching bare skin, excitement buzzed inside her and her pulse beat faster than a jazz tune.

"You are so beautiful," Walter whispered, kissing her temple as his hand roamed across her belly. "So perfect."

"I'm far from perfect." She tilted her head to the side as he kissed her neck. "But I'll let you believe that if you want to."

He chuckled. "I do believe that."

She gasped with delight as he kissed one of her nipples.

"Let me show you," he said, kissing it again.

It seemed as if he spent hours showing her exactly how beautiful he thought she was, and how precious. Slowly and tenderly, as if her body was some kind of fragile keepsake.

It wasn't. She showed him that when they joined together for the first time. The sensation of him sliding inside her was such a joyous, fulfilling moment that she dug her nails deep into his skin and wrapped her legs around him. There, in his arms, united, she knew exactly who she was and what she wanted.

"Are you all right?" he asked, his voice full of sincerity. "Did that hurt?"

The insignificant snap of pain wasn't worth

mentioning. "I'm more than all right," she answered, pulling his face down to kiss his lips.

He began to move inside her, filling her with more wondrous sensations. Just as he'd done with dancing, and driving, and everything else she'd experienced with him, he gradually, thoughtfully, taught her how to do this, too. To share all she had, all she was, with him.

She allowed herself to take, and to give, with unabashed openness, and strove harder with every moment that passed, driving onward toward an unknown destination that beckoned her, promised more and more. When pure pleasure stole her ability to think, she shouted Walter's name and then gave in to a release that was beyond anything she'd ever known. Truly sent her into another dimension.

Walter was there with her, and she clung on to him as they collapsed deep into the mattress.

She opened her eyes, looked up at him as he braced himself on his forearms, keeping most of his weight off hers. The happiness inside her was incomparable to anything else as he kissed the tip of her nose.

"I told you, you were perfect," he said.

She giggled. "Maybe I am, after all."

Walter rolled off her and pulled her against his side. He'd known the aftermath of making love, the pleasant hum that vibrated through his body, but this time, it was different. The euphoria living inside him was magical, and he could damn near believe it would stay with him forever. Those final moments of thrusting inside her, of her body clenching around him, of her breasts pressed into his chest, had transported him past the act of making love and into some eternal realm where no one had ventured before, except the two of them. Together.

He kissed the top of her head as she flipped a leg over his thigh and stretched an arm across his chest, snuggling in deeper.

She kissed his shoulder blade. "I have never felt so wonderful."

Neither had he. His entire life had been superficial compared to this. This went deep. Clear to the core of his very being. Nothing he'd experienced had prepared him for it, either. That's where his mind had been. In the past. On what had happened rather than what could happen. The future was what could give him everything he'd ever wanted, not the past. Why hadn't he realized that?

A grin formed. *Why* didn't matter. *How* did. She'd opened his eyes and his heart, and he was going to keep them open.

He kissed the top of her head again. "Do you like singing at the station?"

"Honestly?"

"Yes, honestly." No matter what she said, he'd find a way for them both to have the future they wanted.

She sighed. "Yes." Tilting her head until their gazes met, she grimaced. "But you don't, do you? You don't like singing."

"I like you."

Her smile never waned, but she shook her head. "I like you, too, but that doesn't answer my question."

He looked up at the ceiling. It didn't seem right to talk about Lucy at this moment, but at the same time, he wanted her know. To understand. He let the burning air in his lungs out slowly. She was talented, so very talented, yet he knew, in the end, talent had little to do with it. "It's not that I don't like singing. It's that I've lived in the show-business world, and it's not all sunshine and roses."

She frowned. "But most of your clients are in show business."

"Yes, they are, and I'm cautious about who I agree to represent."

Removing her arm and leg off him, she sat up and pulled the sheet up, clutched it to her breast. "Because of your wife?"

He scooted up and rested his back against the headboard of the bed. "Yes." Then, rather than make her ask, he continued. "Lucy was in show business when we met, already deeply embedded. A star. I'd only been an outsider looking in until then, and after we got married, I saw a world that…" He shook his head, searching for the right words. "That made me sick."

She laid a hand on his thigh. "Why? What did you see?"

"The worst of the worst." It no longer turned his insides raw to think about it, and that, too, was because of her. She was the reason he was now able to face the past instead of run from it. "I was flattered at first, that a movie star, a famous one, wanted more from me than my legal services." He shook his head at how blinded he'd been. "It was a whirlwind. Within weeks, we were married, and shortly thereafter, I found out why. She was having an affair with an actor. They were starring in the same movie, and his wife was suspicious. They both knew a scandal could ruin their careers, and needed ironclad contracts to make sure that didn't happen."

Her blue eyes were full of compassion. "She told you that?"

"No, his wife did, and she told me what else he was supplying Lucy with."

"What was that?"

"Opium. He had a den in his house, still does. I confronted Lucy, but because I'd already created their contracts, she thought that protected them from everything. I told her no contract could protect her from dying. That didn't faze her. She thought she was invincible." Disgust, as well as sadness, filled him. "I hauled her out of his place so many times. In a stupor, so drugged she couldn't even walk, and looking like hell. After she'd sober up, she'd thank mc, promise that it wouldn't happen again. I wanted to believe her, but something would always happen. A party. A premiere. I'd find myself alone, and knew where I'd find her."

"That had to have been awful," she whispered.

He nodded. Awful wasn't even the word. It had been beyond hell. "I couldn't walk away. I kept thinking about Theodore. Thought if I got her out of there, kept her away, something bad wouldn't happen. That I could prevent the inevitable from happening."

"Her death?"

"Yes." He shook his head. "Despite the reports, Lucy didn't die in that car accident. She was dead before her car went over the cliff. She'd died from an overdose at Karl VanBuren's home. He, or his henchmen, put her in her car, and drove it up the hill and…and pushed it over the edge." He wrapped his hand around hers. "She had been clean for a month, and I had brought a bouquet of flowers home to her, but she wasn't there. I drove straight to VanBuren's, and knew he was covering something up, but didn't know exactly what until the police found her car."

"You must have loved her so very much," she whispered.

The truth. The entire truth was now crystal clear. "No," he answered. "Maybe if I had, things would have worked out differently. Maybe if we'd loved each other, things would have worked out differently, because she didn't love me any more than I'd loved her. She wanted me for what I could do for her as a lawyer, and I…" The truth wasn't pretty. Now, looking back, Lucy had been nothing more than a client to him. It hadn't started out that way; he'd thought he'd grow to love her, especially once they had a family. That's what he'd wanted, a wife, a family, but a wife was the last thing Lucy wanted to be. "Theodore had been the only client I'd failed, and I'd sworn that wouldn't happen again. That I'd never fail another client."

She squeezed his hand. "Theodore wasn't your client. He was your friend. You weren't a lawyer when he died."

Leave it to her to point out the one distinction he'd overlooked. The catalyst that had driven him for years. He'd still failed. There was no denying that.

She bit her bottom lip. "Karl VanBuren was

the actor at the diner that you told me to stay away from."

"Yes, he was. And he's not the only one with a smoking den or who's having affairs. It's all part of the industry." He was part of that industry, too, despite what he told himself. "Lucy had wanted an ironclad contract, and I'd given her one. Even in death. Her contract stipulated that any details concerning any scandalous event would never be released. The studio abided by that. They paid the police and the reporters, made sure everyone only heard one story. That her car had accidently gone over the cliff and tragically ended the life of one of America's brightest stars." Disgust tightened his throat. "And because I'd put that in Karl's contract, too, he was absolved from having anything to do with her death."

Empathy filled her face. "Oh, Walter, I'm so sorry. I—I don't know what to say."

He traced the side of her face with the tip of one finger. "You don't need to say anything. I just wanted you to know the truth." He now knew it, too. "When I arrived here at the cabin that night and you weren't here, were at the radio station, I was afraid the past was repeating itself."

She leaned forward, kissed him softly. "And I'm sorry that I told you to leave the radio station that night. I've regretted it from the moment you walked out the door."

He ran a hand over the silky skin on her shoulder and down her arm. "I've missed you since the moment I walked out that door, because you are much more than a client to me." He'd been so foolish to not realize that. "So, so much more." He grinned as his heart filled with joy. "Have been since the moment I saw you sitting on the pavement. You've been the only thing I've been able to think about since that day."

Her eyes sparkled as she grinned. "So you're glad I didn't go back to Nebraska like you told me to?"

He kissed the tip of her nose. "Very."

"I am, too, because I've thought of you every moment since that day, as well." She released the sheet, let it fall away from her pert, enticing breasts. "Including right now."

It seemed impossible, how the sweet burn of arousal roared back to life inside him. "What are you thinking about right now?"

She took his hand and laid it on one breast. "An encore."

It was more than an encore. It was a performance. One of his best, if not *the* best.

The afterglow was heavily weighted with satisfaction as Shirley's warmth and softness melted against him. This. Holding her. Loving her. Was exactly what he wanted.

Wanted forever.

But was that possible? She was one hell of a singer, and that was her dream. Could he put that ahead of his fears, knowing what he knew? Dreams faded, talent wasn't always enough and evil existed. None of that would change.

"Walter?" she whispered.

He nuzzled her hair with his nose. "Hmm?"

"You won't leave, will you?" She snuggled closer. "If I doze off, will you still be here when I wake up?"

His car was at Julia's, and everyone would know where he was when they saw it. Yet, right now, he truly didn't care. "Yes, I'll be here when you wake up."

"Good." She let out a long sigh. "I'll be here, too."

He smiled and pulled the sheet up over both of them. He'd wanted love for years, but had convinced himself it was as make-believe as the eight hundred movies Hollywood produced every year. She'd changed that. Made him believe it was out there, and that he could have it. Fulfilling that dream for both of them was up to him, but what if he failed again?

He fell asleep to that thought and awoke to Shirley's sweet curves pressed firmly against him. The tiny giggle she let out as he slid a hand over her hip, down her rump, brought him fully awake.

She rolled onto her back and opened herself for him, welcomed him as the earth did the sun that was rising outside the window. He took her slowly and purposefully, coaxing her body into full awareness, even while his screamed for release. Ignoring his own need, he stretched out the act of making love with her for as long as possible, until she was fully spent. Then he focused on his own orgasm, gave it rein to peak and let loose so completely it had him thinking about love all over again.

Afterward, he pressed his forehead to hers. "Sleep well?"

She smiled. "Yes. You?"

"Like I haven't for years." That was true. He felt more energetic than he had in years. He kissed her one more time and then leaped off the bed. "Ready for breakfast? I'm starving, how about you?"

She laughed and climbed off the bed. "Actually, I am hungry." After a quick glance at the window, she said, "The diner isn't open yet."

"I know a place that is." Then, remembering she still worked at the diner, he asked, "Do you have to work today?"

"No. Julia gives me Saturdays off." Grinning, she asked, "Where's the place that you know is open this early?"

"My house." He wanted her to see it. See

where, in the not so far-off future, she would be living. Grabbing his clothes, he said, "Mrs. Mc-Caffrey makes pancakes that melt in your mouth, and squeezes the juice from the oranges off the trees in the backyard every morning." He lifted an eyebrow. "You do like pancakes and orange juice, don't you?"

"Yes, but what will your housekeeper think? Me showing up with you so early in the morning?"

"That you're adorable."

# Chapter Sixteen

Shirley was the one who thought Mrs. McCaffrey was adorable. Plump with pure white hair and twinkling green eyes, Walter's housekeeper was nearly the spitting image of her own grandmother, Mammy, rest her very soul.

Walter was right about the pancakes; they melted in her mouth, and the orange juice was so sweet she licked her lips after every sip, made sure she didn't miss a drop. The scrambled eggs and sausage were just as delicious.

When she couldn't eat another bite, she stood up to clear the table of dirty dishes, but Mrs. Mc-Caffrey would have no part of that. The woman nearly chased both her and Walter out of the kitchen with a broom.

He had given her a tour of his house while Mrs. McCaffrey had been cooking breakfast. It was beautiful, as close to a mansion as Shirley had ever seen. She told him that again as they walked down a long hallway with white-and-gold wallpapered walls.

He stepped in front of her. "I'm glad you like it." Grasping her waist, he gave her a solid, sweet kiss.

Her arms were around his neck when their lips separated, and she felt the heat of a blush on her cheeks. It was silly, especially after what they'd shared last night. A night that would forever remain the most wondrous one of her life. The sensation of walking on air was with her today, like it had been when they'd danced together, and she wondered if her feet would ever touch the ground again.

Reminding herself they weren't alone in the house, she glanced over his shoulder at an arched doorway that led into the front room that had three divans as well as half a dozen green-upholstered chairs and several side tables. A big seashell sat on one of the tables.

Remembering that day at the beach, when he'd told her about hearing the ocean inside a seashell, she released her hold on his neck and walked into the room. Unable not to, she picked up the big shell and held it to her ear.

"Do you hear it?"

"I hear something," she admitted. "A swooshing sound."

"That's the ocean."

She laughed, knowing that was impossible, and set the shell down.

He laid a hand on the shell. "It's a conch shell. I found it years ago. The first time I went to the beach."

Her throat swelled. She now understood so much more about him, about his past, and why he didn't like showbiz or anything to do with it. He hadn't said so, but that had to include singing. Turning about, she caught sight of something tucked inside an alcove on the far side of the room. "A piano? Do you play?"

He chuckled. "No."

"Then why do you have a piano?"

His grin was adorable, and a bit sheepish. "Because it came with the house."

She laughed and walked toward the piano. "That's as good of a reason as any, I suppose."

"Do you play?"

She touched a key, then another. "No, but I always thought I'd like to."

"I'll hire a teacher to give you lessons."

"Why would you do that?"

"So you can play it," he said. "You love music."

She did, but there was more to it than that. There was more to everything. More than she'd ever imagined there would be. She'd never imagined she could be this happy, either, or that she could love anything more than singing.

His hands slid around her waist and he pulled her back against him. "Want to go for a drive?"

She closed her eyes and leaned against him. "Where to?" Not that it mattered. She'd follow him to the moon if there was a way to get there.

He kissed the side of her neck. "I want to show you another place."

"All right." She spun around so he could give her another kiss before they left.

Once in the car, he drove downtown to where the buildings reached the sky. She still liked that about them. How immense they were.

"Where are we going?" she asked as they waited for a line of people to cross the street at a corner.

"My office. I thought you might like to see it since I am your lawyer."

Laughing, she shook her head. "I never thought I'd have a lawyer."

"Because you don't like them?"

She laid her hand on his arm. "Didn't like them. I changed my mind about that. At least about one of them."

He gave her a wink as he started to drive again. "I'm glad."

She had changed her mind about that. Could she change it about other things, too?

His law office was on the first floor of the three-story brick building and had several rooms, one of which had more books than she'd ever seen all in one place.

"Whose office is this?" It was by far the biggest. Besides the shelves full of books and a big desk with a chair and typewriter, there were other chairs and a long leather couch.

"Mine," he said, closing the door behind him.

The glint in his eye made her heart skip a beat and her womanhood throb. Her breath caught in her lungs at the desire that suddenly filled her. "It's a very nice office."

He pulled her to him. "With a very nice couch."

Excitement made the throbbing increase. "What do you do on that very nice couch?"

His hand slid down her thigh, and then grasped a handful of her dress. "Up until now, I've slept on it a couple of times."

She probably shouldn't want what she wanted, but she did. "Is that all?"

He lifted her skirt and ran his hand over the bare skin of her thigh and higher. "Yes, but I think we should change that."

Pressing her hips into his, feeling the bulge between his legs, she bit her lip, hard. "By doing what?"

He slid a finger beneath her underwear. "Whatever you want."

She nearly melted right then and there. Stretching upward so their breathing mingled, she said, "I want whatever you want."

They wanted the same thing, and spent a good part of the afternoon on the couch in his office having fun. So much fun that, by the time they left, she looked forward to visiting his office again.

Walter sat outside the booth where Shirley sang and Merlin played the piano that night, and the next. She truly was spectacular, and her love of singing was undeniable. It was on her face, in her voice, and filled the air with an energy that literally encompassed the entire studio. And beyond. There was once again a crowd outside in the parking lot.

"She's something, isn't she?" Earl Johansson said as he stepped out of the room on the other side of the booth.

Walter nodded. "Yes, she is."

Earl sat down beside him. "She's bringing in sponsorships left and right."

Walter leaned forward, planted his elbows on his knees and watched as Shirley, eyes closed, sang into the microphone. There was rapture on her face. Similar to what he'd seen while they'd been in bed together.

"And," Earl said, "as of last night, our ranking hit number one. Best damn radio station in California."

Walter's gaze never left Shirley. He returned the small wave she sent his way as she stepped away from the microphone. She poured herself a glass of water from the pitcher sitting atop the piano and drank it while shifting through a stack of song sheets. Picking one out, she handed it to Merlin and walked back over to the microphone.

"I can believe it." Walter could believe it; she was a starlet like no other.

It took over two hours for the parking lot to clear after she'd sung her last song. Reggie made a sweep of the lot, making sure no one lagged behind, then walked them both to the Packard.

Walter drove to Julia's place, walked Shirley to the cabin, and even though they both had to get up for work in the morning, he spent the night.

Early the next morning, while it was still dark, he kissed her goodbye, and during his drive home thought about the future he used to dream about, and was once again. He also compared it to the one Shirley wanted, and if they were compatible.

To his surprise, Judge Wallis called shortly after Walter had arrived at his office later that morning.

"I've made my ruling."

Nothing in the judge's tone gave him an inclination as to what that decision might be. "I'm on my way," Walter said.

He was already at the courthouse when Mel Cartwright arrived, along with a lawyer Walter had heard of, but also had stayed clear of. Jamison was the type of lawyer that gave attorneys a bad name. If there was an underhanded way to win, Jamison was all about taking it.

All three of them were led through the courtroom and into the judge's chambers by a bailiff. Once they were seated, in his no-nonsense manner, Judge Wallis began his spiel.

Ultimately, the girls won, with no repercussions or stipulations on their parts. Cartwright, however, was ordered to pay past wages of an accountable amount beyond the wages he'd previously paid them for the hours they'd worked at his establishment.

Although he was more than happy about the ruling, Walter made a point of assuring any monies stolen out of their purses was also included in their restitution.

Mel slapped the arm of his chair. "I didn't steal any money from them."

"Someone from your establishment did," Walter said. "It's in the depositions I turned into the court."

"And it's in my ruling," Judge Wallis said,

looking at Jamison. "Your attorney can point them out to you, unless you want me to."

Jamison's jowls wobbled as he nodded. "I will, Your Honor."

"The payments are to be delivered to Mr. Russell's office no later than noon tomorrow," Judge Wallis said. "I hope you understand, Mr. Cartwright, that this isn't an end, but a beginning. Every employee of all establishments in this city is to be paid a fair wage, without underlying stipulations or obligations."

Mel mumbled under his breath.

The judge's somber gaze turned even darker. "I could have taken this a step further, Mr. Cartwright, brought in federal agents. I chose not to because nightlife is a part of our city. However, it will be more regulated, leastwise until the feds figure out prohibition isn't working. Then we'll have a new set of guidelines to follow."

Walter agreed with that, and couldn't help but wonder if an end to prohibition would make things better or worse. They'd find out sooner or later. The entire country would once Congress quit debating it and took a vote.

For now, he was going to rejoice in the fact the girls had won.

Walter drove straight to the diner from the courthouse and told the girls. They were ecstatic, as he'd known they would be, but because the diner was about to open for lunch, he didn't stay long. Julia said they'd have a celebration after the diner closed that evening. He agreed, planted a kiss on Shirley's lips, walked out the back door and drove back to his office. He was glad they'd won, but now that it was over, he had one more issue to take care of.

# *Chapter Seventeen*

Shirley was happy that they'd won the case, but it just wasn't as significant as it once had seemed. Leastwise to her. She was glad Mel had been ordered to fairly pay them for the hours they'd worked, and was certain that Alice and Rita would never fall into working at a place like CB's ever again.

She wouldn't. That was a given.

Walter squeezed her hand, and she smiled at him, even as her stomach bubbled. Vivian, the regular singer, was healed, and would be coming back to the radio station next weekend, which meant she'd be done singing, unless she signed the new contract Earl had given her this morning. She hadn't told anyone about it. Earl had stopped by before, dropping off songs for her to learn, so no one had questioned his visit. Even if the others had questions, there hadn't been time to ask them. Earl had left only a few minutes before Walter had arrived with the news about the case.

"I'll bring your restitution payments over tomorrow," Walter said. "Any money stolen from your bags will be included."

He'd arrived after the diner had closed and they all sat around a table, having just finished the celebration meal that Julia had insisted upon cooking.

"I feel as if we need to pay you something," Rita said. "We'd never have recouped our money without your help."

"We'd still be working at CB's without your help," Alice said.

Shirley nodded, looking at him, thinking about how he'd changed her life. Continued to change it every single day because, with each sunrise, she fell deeper in love with him, and reflected upon that with each sunset. Her love for him.

He shook his head. "I told you in the beginning you didn't owe me anything, and you still don't. I'm just happy that it's over, and that we won."

"Hear, hear," Julia said. "I knew this is how it would turn out. Cartwright didn't have a chance against you."

Everyone agreed with that, and Rita asked if it would be all right for everyone to go to the Pig's Tail for a celebration drink.

"That's not up to me," Walter said. "You each

have to choose what's best for you." He looked at her then. "That's what everyone has to do."

Shirley's insides quivered. She jumped to her feet. "You all go ahead. I'll clean up."

"No, we'll all clean up," Rosie said. "Then go have a celebration drink."

Shirley nodded, but had no intention of going to the Pig's Tail.

When the others departed, Walter asked her, "You sure you don't want to go?"

"I'm sure."

"All right." He wrapped an arm around her. "Do you want me to walk you to your cabin?"

"Yes." She'd told Earl she would have Walter look at the contract, but wasn't certain she even wanted him to know about it. She understood why he didn't want to be a part of showbiz. Didn't want anything to do with it. Yet, at the same time, it felt as if she was giving up a part of herself if she didn't sign Earl's contract.

"There are no stipulations about going to speakeasies in the final ruling," he said as they started along the path to the cabin.

"I know, and I'm sure they will all be fine."

He nudged her with his shoulder. "What about you? Are you fine?"

There was so much she loved about him. He truly made her happy, even when she was utterly confused. "Yes." She nudged him back with her hip. "Are you?"

He laughed, and kissed her temple as they walked. "I'm about as fine as I've ever been. Finer."

"Finer." She laughed. "Is that even a word?"

"Yes, it's used all the time, as in the *finer* things in life." He stopped walking and twisted so they faced each other. "And I'm looking at the finest."

His hands slid up her sides until his thumbs rested just below her breasts. She drew in a deep breath at how he could make her forget everything except him.

"I'm curious about something." He kissed her forehead and then her cheek.

Trying hard to concentrate, she asked, "Curious about what?"

He kissed the tender skin in front of her ear before whispering, "About what color underwear you're wearing." He kissed that spot again. "Pink?" He kissed the side of her neck. "White?" Then kissed the base of her neck. "Beige?"

She was melting, would soon become a puddle right in the middle of the trail if he kept this up.

His thumbs brushed over her nipples. "Are you going to keep me in suspense?"

It was either moan or giggle. She attempted to go for a giggle, but it came out at the same time he kissed her shoulder, so it was laced with the moan.

"Is that a hint?"

Not so long ago, she'd thought this was the last thing she'd ever want, to be so madly in love with a man that nothing else mattered. Now, she had to wonder why she hadn't wanted this. She cupped his face with both hands and brought her lips up to his, but didn't let them touch his. "What color do you want them to be?"

Before he could answer, she let go and dashed around him. Running toward the cabin, she shouted over her shoulder, "Pink. I think."

Laughter echoed behind her. "You think?"

He snagged her around the waist as she jumped onto the cabin's stoop, and spun her around for a solid kiss. That quickly proved to not be enough for either of them. Their actions intensified; their kisses became hot, demanding, forceful.

Arms and legs entwined, they stumbled inside the cabin. He kicked the door shut, spun her around and grabbed a fistful of her dress, tugged it upward as his mouth found hers again.

Back pressed against the wall, her body shivered with need as she found the waistband of his britches, then the buttons, undid them.

He grasped her tap pants, tugged them down.

She kicked her underwear aside while pushing his pants down over his hips.

The heat between them boiled with need, hers and his. Their mouths devoured each other as he lifted her up against the wall.

Wrapping her legs around his hips, she threw her head back as he slid inside her. She was so hot, so ready, intense pleasure instantly rippled through her. Clinging to him, she rode the waves of his lunges, gaining pleasure in the swift rhythm he set.

His hands had ahold of her bottom, lifting her up and tugging her down in time with each of his thrusts. Her breathing was uneven, her pulse pounding, and when her time came, she gave in to it with the freedom of a bird soaring through an open sky.

He plunged into her at that very moment, deeper, then deeper again, as his entire body went rock hard and he released a guttural sound. She found his mouth, kissed him with the last bits of energy her body had to offer, knowing his strength was enough for both of them.

This. Assurance that she wasn't alone, would never be alone, was the basis of life. Love. Unconditional love. She'd found it. Here in California. In his arms. That's what she wanted forever and ever. Until death do they part.

She opened her eyes as their mouths separated. His chest was heaving, sweat glistened on his forehead and a full smile filled his face.

"You really are perfect," he said.

Laughing, she kissed him. "So are you."

He disengaged and then, with her legs still wrapped around his hips, carried her to the bed. They lay there, side by side, staring up at the ceiling with their legs dangling over the edge, sucking in air and waiting for their breathing to return to normal.

Twisting his neck to look at her, he grinned. "So what color were they?"

He still sounded breathless. She certainly was. Too euphoric to think about anything, she closed her eyes. "Pink. I think."

"Me, too. I think they were pink."

It was hours later when she felt him leave the bed. The sun wasn't up yet, but the sky was bright enough that she could see, and watched as he snuck around the room, finding his clothes.

She waited until he sat down on a chair to put on his shoes before she sat up.

He looked over. Grinned. "I was trying not to wake you."

"I know. I saw that."

After slipping on his shoes, he stood, walked to the bed and kissed her. "You saw?"

"Yes."

"Did you see me stub my toe?"

Biting back a smile, she nodded.

He kissed her again briefly. "Next time I won't be so quiet about it."

Last night, while in his arms, sharing a love that filled her beyond all else, she believed that was all she needed; now watching him prepare to leave, she wasn't so sure. They couldn't spend the rest of their lives in bed. The envelope containing the contract from Earl was in her suitcase sitting near the wall. Her throat tightened as she looked that way. Suddenly, she wanted him to know about it, and that she wasn't going to sign it, but if she didn't sign it, didn't sing, what would she do? She didn't want to work at the diner forever.

"You don't have to be up yet. Go back to sleep." He tugged a suspender over his shoulder. "I have an early meeting, and then have to complete some things for Jack and deliver them to Star's Studio."

A thought struck her. "Did you know that Helen goes to work with Jack every day? She brings Grace with her."

He nodded while pulling up his other suspender. "Yes."

"She types for him."

He frowned slightly. "I know."

She scooted to the edge of the bed. "You could teach me how to type, and I could go to work with you." Learning to type wasn't a dream she'd ever have, but—

His laughter interrupted her thought. "I know

what you're thinking." He grabbed his suitcoat off the chair. "And the answer is no."

"No?"

He walked back to the bed. "Yes." He kissed her forehead. "No, you aren't coming to my office with me every day."

"But—"

He lifted her chin with one finger and kissed her lips. "Go back to sleep, Blondie. I'll see you at noon, with your payment from Mel, including the twenty-two dollars and eighty-six cents he stole from you."

Chuckling, he walked to the door.

She tossed aside the covers and jumped out of bed, but he'd already shut the door. Was gone. She couldn't follow him naked as a jaybird, and by the time she collected her clothes, she figured it wasn't worth it. He hadn't even given her a chance to explain. Hadn't given her the chance to tell him about the contract and to say that she wasn't going to sign it. That she was going to do what her mother had done. Give up singing for love. It would have only taken a minute. He could have spared that.

Unless he hadn't wanted to spare even a minute because there was nothing about showbiz he wanted to hear. Helen, typing for Jack, was showbiz.

Shirley huffed out a breath. She hadn't thought

about that, but everything in Los Angeles had something to do with showbiz. Some way or another. That's why she'd come here.

Later, after she'd weeded the garden and was ready to go to the diner, her frustration turned into hurt.

She opened the suitcase and took out the contract. It was her dream, more than her dream. Her own radio show. The reason she came here, until she met Walter and fell in love with him.

Why had she done that? The one thing she'd sworn she wouldn't do. Because he was so handsome? So charming? So perfect? Anger at herself and him rose up inside her.

Perfect? She'd give her dream up for him, but he wouldn't even talk about giving her a job typing? That's not perfect. It's not even fair.

By the time the diner was ready for the noon rush, Shirley had worked up a good bout of anger. At herself and him, for making her fall in love with him. She had half a mind to find a job typing for someone else, just to prove to Walter how good she was at it. Or could be. It wouldn't solve anything, but it might make her feel better.

The daily lunch special was egg salad sandwiches, and she was in the middle of peeling another dozen eggs when Rosie entered the kitchen carrying baby Grace. Helen was behind Rosie, and they laughed as they all rushed over to have a turn to hold Grace.

Helen looked lovely with her brown hair pinned up beneath a fashionable felt hat, and happy. She'd been happy ever since Jack had hired her to work at the studio. Typing.

A fresh bout of ire struck so hard Shirley wanted to throw the eggs at the wall rather than peel them. Or throw them at Walter. She might save one for that. To throw at him next time she saw him.

"Oh, that baby bonnet is so cute on her," Alice cooed, bouncing Grace in her arms. "Where did you get it? Did you sew it?"

"No, I didn't sew it," Helen said. "Jack bought it. He bought several, and Gracie looks adorable in each one of them."

"I should sew some for her," Alice said. "I love sewing."

"Maybe that's what you should do," Julia said. "Open a sewing shop."

Rosie and Rita agreed, gushing about the new waitressing uniforms Alice had sewn for everyone.

Shirley experienced a bit of guilt at not joining in on the conversation. But she couldn't, not with all that was troubling her right now. She finished peeling the eggs, and then, wiping her hands on her apron, walked over to the group. "My turn to hold Grace."

Alice handed over the baby, and Shirley's heart welled as the baby smiled up at her. She couldn't help but wonder what it would be like to have a baby like Grace. The baby was Jack's niece. Helen had brought Grace to California—to Jack—from Chicago, and Jack had given Helen a typing job so she could bring the baby with her every day. Shirley sighed. Why couldn't things work out as well for her as they had for Helen and Grace?

Greta poked her head in the door. "Two more specials." Her grin increased as she added, "Shirley, Walter just walked in."

Shirley patted Grace's back. "Good for him."

All eyes landed on her, and the stunned silence that followed made her insides sink.

"What's wrong?" Rita asked, holding out her arms for the baby, indicating it was her turn. "Is Mel not going to pay us?"

"You're all so courageous," Helen said. "Escaping a raid, and then winning a court case."

Flustered all over again, Shirley handed the baby to Rita. "There was nothing courageous about it."

"Except for Walter," Alice said.

That was about her last straw. "Walter!" Shirley snapped. "The man who won't even give me a typing job."

"A typing job?" Alice frowned. "Why would you—"

"Alice," Julia interrupted. "Go tell Rosie that Jack and Helen's sandwiches are ready."

Helen took Grace from Rita. "We better go back out to our table."

Shirley sighed at the gloom she'd caused to fill the room. Frustrated, she marched over to the sink.

"What about your gig at the radio station?" Alice asked after handing plates out the door to Rosie.

"It's done this coming weekend." Shirley dumped soap flakes in the sink and turned on the hot water. "Vivian's coming back."

"Maybe Earl will—"

"No," Shirley interrupted.

Silence filled the room for a moment. Shirley ignored it, focusing on a pile of dishes.

"Do you think Walter brought us our payments from Mel?" Alice asked.

"Ask him, not me," Shirley replied.

"No," Julia said. "Let him eat his lunch in peace, just like all the other customers."

A short while later, when the counter beside her was empty, Shirley spun around. "Aren't there any more dishes?"

"Greta and Rosie must be stockpiling them under the counter," Julia said.

Shirley glanced at Alice, who was mixing up another batch of egg salad, and at Rita, who was slicing cucumbers. Tossing aside her dishrag, she walked toward the door. "I'll go get them."

She didn't want to step through the door, knowing Walter was out there. A part of her said it was foolish to be so upset with him—she didn't even know how to type—but the other part of her couldn't make light of the fact she was willing to give up her dream for him and he'd laughed at her. Said, *"No, you aren't coming to work with me."*

Drawing a breath, she pushed open the door. Walter was there, all right, at the far end of the counter. He grinned at her.

Lifting her chin, she marched out the door and behind the counter.

"Hey, Blondie," a man sitting at the counter said.

She shot a glare his way, and instantly recognized the black-haired man.

"I've heard you on the radio," Karl VanBuren said in a low, raspy whisper.

"No, you haven't," she hissed.

"Oh, yes, I have. You and I could do a lot for each other." He winked. "Do a lot together."

She'd had one nerve left, and he'd just snapped it. She grabbed the glass sitting in front of his plate.

* * *

Walter had jumped to his feet when he'd realized Karl had spoken to Shirley, and was rounding the counter when she threw a glass of water square in VanBuren's face.

Karl leaped to his feet.

Walter grabbed Karl's arm. "Get out of here."

Water droplets flew in the air as Karl shook his head. "Blondie here—"

That's all Walter heard. All he needed to hear. He drew back an arm and planted his fist on Karl's nose.

As VanBuren sailed backward onto a table behind him, Walter hooked Shirley around the waist and hoisted her off the floor.

She kicked and tugged at his arm, trying to break his hold. "Put me down."

"In a minute." He hauled her through the kitchen door, past the women staring at both of them and out the back door.

Once outside, away from the door, he planted her feet on the hard-packed ground and kept her there by grasping both of her upper arms. "What the hell was that all about?"

Her face was beet-red and she was huffing air. "He called me Blondie!"

"So?"

"So?" She hit him in the chest with both hands.

"I didn't like it. And I don't like you right now, either."

"Me? What did I do?"

"You wouldn't even consider giving me a typing job!" She smacked his chest again. "Just said, *No!* I might be good at it."

He was stunned. When she'd mentioned that this morning, he'd thought she'd been referring to his couch, and what they could do on it all day. He'd liked the idea, but he'd never get any work done. Not in a million years would he have imagined she was serious. He tugged her forward, looked her square in the eyes. "If you set your mind to it, you'd be the best typist in California, but, honey, you don't want to type, you want to sing. That's why you came to California."

She pulled her gaze away from his and looked down at the ground. "I'm done singing after this weekend."

His heart constricted with pain for her, even as anger at the radio station flared. She was the best singer they'd ever had, ever would have. Earl knew that. Everyone knew that. Including him. "Not if you don't want to be."

Confusion flashed in her blue eyes as she looked up at him.

The teardrop slipping out of one eye nearly gutted him. She loved singing. It was a part of her. Of who she was. His ire at Earl increased.

She'd already made the station a bucket of money. They should be begging her to stay.

He ran his hands down her arms, over her wrists, and took ahold of her hands. He wasn't going to let her give up. Not on her dream. "I'll go to Earl, negotiate a new contract—"

"Earl's already offered me a new contract."

The sadness in her tone sent a shiver up his spine. "He has? Where is it?"

She sighed. "Inside, in the kitchen, but I'm not going to sign it."

"Why not? Are the terms that bad? I can negotiate them."

She shook her head and her lips quivered as a smile partially formed, but not quite. "The terms don't matter. They're worthless. It's all worthless without you. That's why I wanted a typing job. I can't work for Julia forever."

Walter had thought he'd already hit his lowest, but he hadn't. It had just happened.

## *Chapter Eighteen*

⁓⁓⁓⁓

**W**alter released her hands and cupped her face, held it in front of his. "You won't sign Earl's contract because of me?" Why he needed that clarified made no sense. He already knew the answer. Already knew what a fool he'd been.

She lifted her chin slightly. "You hate showbiz."

At this moment, he hated himself that the thought she had to give up her dream because of him had ever crossed her mind. "What's your name?"

She frowned.

"What's your name?" he asked again.

"You know—"

He tightened his hold on her face.

She sighed. "Shirley Burnette."

"That's right. And what has Shirley Burnette dreamed of becoming her entire life?"

She shook her head.

He stared at her, waiting.

"A singer."

"That's right. Shirley Burnette is who you are, and a singer is what you are. And Shirley Burnette, the best damn singer in all of California, probably the world, is the woman I love."

His throat was on fire because, of all the people on this earth, she was the last one he'd ever want to hurt, yet he had. "I'd blamed Hollywood, blamed showbiz, for everything that hadn't worked out the way I wanted it to for years. Then I met you. You turned my world upside down, challenged me in ways I'd never been challenged and opened my eyes. Let me see things all over again. Showbiz didn't kill Theodore or Lucy. I was blaming it because of what I'd lost. The emptiness I felt. Until you came along and filled that void. You gave me hope. Hope that, someday, my long-lost dreams could come true."

He should have told her all this last night when lying in bed, holding her, it had all become crystal clear. But he hadn't. He'd thought he'd get a few things in order first. He should have known better. This was Shirley, his spunky little starlet from Nebraska who had a mind of her own.

That was just one of the things he loved about her. "My dream includes you. Your happiness. Your dreams. I'll teach you to type and hire you, if you can honestly tell me that's what you want.

Above all else, including singing and a contract with Earl, that you want to be a typist." He let go of her face and took a step back.

She frowned and shook her head. "No, I don't want to be a typist." Tossing her hands in the air, she continued. "I want to sing. I want a contract with Earl. It's what I've always wanted, but I also want you. No. I want you more. You're my dream now. Singing is just…not as important. Those weeks when you weren't around, I was empty. Even while singing. It wasn't worth it, and I don't want that again."

"I don't want that again, either." Walter grasped her waist. "Those were the worst weeks of my life."

"Mine, too." Her hands slid around his neck as she tilted her chin up so their lips could meet, gently, sweetly. There was nothing hurried or demanding about it. Just a pure sharing of love.

That kiss may have been the most precious gift anyone had ever given him. He reached up, touched her cheek. "I love you, Blondie."

Happiness shone in her eyes, in her smile. "I love you, Walter. So very, very much."

He ran a finger under her chin. "I'm sorry about this morning. I honestly thought you just wanted to go to work with me so we could spend the day on the couch."

She laughed. "You did?"

"I did."

She shook her head. "I should have thought of that." She shrugged. "So what are we going to do?"

He pulled her hips tighter against his. "We are going to get that contract of Earl's, take it down to the station, where I'll negotiate the best terms any singer has ever received."

"He's already offering me my own show."

"Then I'll make him give you two shows."

She laughed. "You probably will."

"I will." He reached around and cupped her behind with both hands. "And then we'll stop by my office and check out the couch."

She bit her bottom lip for a moment. "Are you sure? Are you really, really sure?"

He kissed the side of her neck. "I'm really, really sure."

She giggled. "I mean about the contract. Me, singing. Showbiz."

Meeting her gaze, he nodded. "I'm as really, really sure about that as I am the couch."

Walter had never been so excited to go to a movie premiere as he was that following Saturday night.

Whistling, he straightened his bow tie, brushed the lapels of his jacket with both hands and then left his room. He'd picked Shirley up earlier, so they could get ready here, at his house. The last he'd seen of her was when she'd entered the bathroom. "Come out, come out, wherever you are," he said, walking down the hallway.

Giggles filtered up the steps.

"She's down here," Mrs. McCaffrey shouted. "Waiting for you."

More alive and carefree than ever, he hopped onto the banister and slid all the way down the staircase.

Jumping off, he wobbled slightly at the sight before him.

The most beautiful woman on earth.

"Doesn't she look lovely?" Mrs. McCaffrey asked.

"Yes," he answered, unable to say more. He was too stunned.

Shirley stood near the front window with the sun shining in behind her. The shimmering dark blue gown fit her like a glove, outlining her perfect curves, yet was simple enough that all of his attention went to her face and the smile she wore.

"Gorgeous." He stepped into the room. "You look absolutely gorgeous."

"Thank you." She blushed and gave him a slight nod. "You look very dashing yourself." Her eyes sparkled. "I do hope you didn't rip your pants coming down the stairs that way."

He spun around and hoisted up the tails of his tux. "Did I?"

She laughed. "Looks good to me."

He held out his elbow for her to wrap her arm around and then nodded toward his housekeeper. "Hold down the fort."

Mrs. McCaffrey chuckled and opened the front door for them to exit. "I always do."

He patted Shirley's hand looped around his arm as they walked to the car. "Thank you for attending this premiere with me. It means a lot to have you with me and to be there for Jack."

"You're welcome," she said. "I'm excited to see Jack's new movie, and I'm happy that Vivian was able to come back a week early. She's very nice and we've worked out a schedule for our shows that works perfectly for both of us."

The premiere was downtown, at the new State Theatre. Finding a place to park was easy enough, but getting in the building was another story. The line stretched down the sidewalk for over a block. Reporters with cameras strolled along the line, taking pictures of people they recognized and others they assumed were famous, or on the up-and-coming list.

Walter slid a hand around Shirley's hip, pulled her closer to his side as one particular reporter noticed them. Stocky, with a nose curved like a hawk's, Lane Cox was known for turning over every rock while working on a story.

"Walter." Lane flipped his camera out of the way to shake hands. "Good to see you." He tipped the brim of his flat hat at Shirley before he said, "I have a piece about your case against Mel Cartwright in tomorrow's paper."

"If you wrote it, I know it'll all be true," Walter replied.

Lane nodded, then leaned closer. "Heard about Karl VanBuren's nose. He's claiming it was a set accident."

Walter felt Shirley shiver slightly. "Well, he is always acting. Perhaps it was."

Lane laughed. "If you ask me, it was about time someone popped him in the snout." Then whispered, "He looks like hell. Both eyes are black and his nose is swollen twice its size. Jake Perry got a photo of him leaving the doctor's office. The studio bought it off him for five hundred bucks." Lane winked. "But Jake never sells his negatives."

The flare of happiness inside Walter wasn't because of Karl's injuries. It was because he no longer cared one way or the other about the actor. There were a lot of things about his past that he no longer cared about. Not in any way, shape or form, and that felt good.

Changing the subject, he said, "I'll look forward to reading your piece about Jack's premiere tonight."

"It'll be on the front page. I've heard good things already, but will hold my opinion until the movie ends." With a tip of his hat, Lane moseyed down the never-ending line of people.

Walter turned to Shirley and gave her a wink. She smiled and leaned her head against his shoulder for a brief moment. This was the only thing that mattered to him now. Her. And their future. Together.

Once they entered the building, he pulled her out of the stream of people. "We'll say hi to Jack and Helen after the movie."

"There certainly are a lot of people here," she said. "They're packed in tighter than the stockyards before the train rolls into town."

He chuckled, loving how she did that. Described things to a T. He found a tray-bearing waiter, lifted off two glasses of champagne and handed one to her. Before she took a sip, he clinked his glass against hers. "To us."

"To us." After taking a sip, she grinned. "Shouldn't we be toasting Jack or his movie?"

"We will later."

They mingled for a time, and then found a pair of plush seats, where they had a good view of the screen. As they conversed with others around them while waiting for the movie to begin, Walter spied Judge Wallis and his wife. A wave of joy filled him, thinking about what was yet to come.

"What are you smiling about?" Shirley asked.

"No reason," he said. "Other than I'm happy."

Shirley stared at him for a moment, then planted a fast peck of a kiss on his cheek. "Me, too." She was. Couldn't possibly be happier than she was at this moment. Walter was the very core of that happiness. Everything else, including singing, was superficial compared to him.

Unlike her mother, she hadn't had to choose. She had it all. Thankful, she looked up and smiled. She was sure her mother and Pappy were looking down, smiling back at her.

The theater was as grand as Walter had promised it would be, and as the lights went out, he winked at her. She wrapped her arm around his and watched as the velvet curtains parted.

The movie was wonderful. There were parts where she laughed, along with the hundreds of other people in the theater, and times when she cried, sniffling into the handkerchief Walter silently handed her, especially at the ending, when the two soldiers both made it home to their families through a blizzard in time for Christmas.

Afterward they stood in line to congratulate Jack and Helen. When their turn arrived, Shirley hugged Helen, who wore a stunning gold dress and looked like royalty. "That was amazing!" she told Helen. "I laughed and I cried. Then laughed and cried again."

"Me, too," Helen said.

Walter and Jack were talking about the snow scenes in the movie, and Shirley saw a hint of confusion cross Helen's face when she looked at Walter. Most likely because of the other day, when she'd been in the diner. The day Shirley had been mad over him not giving her a typing job. She and Walter laughed about that a lot.

Shirley waved at Helen as Walter led her away from the line.

"Where to now?"

"Down that corridor." He gestured toward a long hallway. "There's a dinner party."

At the end of the corridor was a huge ballroom, with flowers on every table and crystal chandeliers hanging from the tall celling. "Everything about this place is gorgeous."

"It is." He scanned the room, then pointed to a table near the center. "That's our table."

Upon arrival, Jack introduced her to the other couples, including Judge Wallis and his wife, Evelyn. Sitting at the same table as them made Shirley nervous at first, but both the judge and his wife were so pleasant she soon got over that and enjoyed their company.

They were served lobster and steak, and she

quietly said a prayer of thanks that Walter had already shown her how to eat the lobster. The last thing she'd want to do was look like she'd just stepped off the train.

Shortly after the meal ended, Walter asked, "Are you ready?"

She'd rather be alone with him any day. Every day actually. "Yes."

The judge and his wife rose from their chairs at the same time. Shirley took a moment to shake their hands, tell them how nice it had been to meet them.

Smiling brightly, they both told her the same.

"He seems like a very nice man," she said.

"He is," Walter agreed as they walked down the corridor.

His grin was so big, so bright—almost as if he knew a secret that she didn't—a shiver tickled her spine. "Where are we going now?"

His eyes were nearly dancing with sparkles. "The beach."

"Dressed like this?"

"Yes."

Happiness bubbled inside her all over again. "I love the beach."

"I know."

"And I love you."

They stepped outside the building, where a big

marquee sign spelled out the theater's name in huge letters that reached the top of the building. Walter stopped under those lights and kissed her, right there in the middle of the street for all to see. "I know that, too, and I love you."

The night was warm, and the breeze that flowed over the windshield was refreshing after being inside the theater with so many people. Walter parked in the same parking lot that he had the first time he'd brought her to the beach, and they sat on the edge of the pavement and removed their shoes, just like that day. Tonight, they left their shoes there rather than carrying them.

The skirt of the lovely blue gown that she'd purchased with her retribution money—that had included the twenty-two dollars and eighty-six cents stolen from her bag—swished around her ankles as she walked through the sand. She couldn't help but stop every now and again to bury her toes.

"You love burying your toes in the sand, don't you?" he asked.

"Yes, I do. It's amazing."

"You are amazing." He led her to the shoreline and turned to walk along it, letting the water gently wash over their toes.

"The hem of my dress is getting wet," she said, laughing.

"We can walk in the sand."

"No. I don't mind. This is too wonderful." And romantic. The moonlight cast upon the water twinkled as brightly as the stars overhead, and the swoosh of the waves rolling ashore made the sweetest music.

The outcropping of rocks they'd sat on before was a short distance ahead when Walter stopped. She stopped, too.

He took both of her hands, kissed her gently and then knelt down.

She looked at the sand, wondering if he'd seen something, but then a tingling sensation rippled from her toes all the way to her heart.

"Shirley Burnette," he said, looking up at her. "You have changed my life. Changed it for the good, and I want you to keep changing it, keep making it better for all my years to come."

Tears prickled the backs of her eyes as he released one of her hands, and then dug something out of his pocket.

A ring.

She pressed a hand to her mouth, unable to speak.

"Please say you'll marry me," he said. "Make me the happiest man on earth, today and every day forward."

Her knees trembled so hard she sank down on them, stared at the sand as her mind swirled with disbelief.

"Blondie?" He lifted her chin with a knuckle. "Is it too soon? I know it's happened fast, but I love you so much."

She nodded, then shook her head. "I wasn't sure if you'd want to get married again, after—"

He pressed a finger against her lips. "I love you. Love you far more than anything on this earth. And that love is strong. So strong my past no longer matters to me. None of it. But my future. Blondie, the future I see is as full of promises as the sunrise. Bright, wonderful promises. That's all I can think about now. A life full of tomorrows with you."

Her heart was pounding, her lashes wet with tears of joy, tears of promises. She looped her arms around his neck. "Yes! Yes, I'll marry you!"

They kissed.

Hugged.

Laughed.

Kissed again.

Then he slid the ring on her finger. "When?"

"When?" she repeated. "I don't care. Whenever you want."

"How about right now?"

"Now?"

He stood and helped her to her feet. "Judge Wallis and his wife are standing by the rock cropping, ready to marry us."

"Here? On the beach?"

"It's your favorite place."

She had no words. And for her, that was a first. All she could do was squeal with delight and hug him. Kiss him.

Then run beside him to the outcropping of rocks where Judge Wallis performed a ceremony that made her Mrs. Walter Russell.

Shirley Russell.

She truly did have it all. More than she'd ever dreamed.

But her loving husband wasn't completely done yet. Once they were in the car, he started driving along the coast. She twisted the diamond ring on her finger, loving the feel of it, of what it meant. "Where are we going now?"

"On our honeymoon."

"Honeymoon?"

"Yes. I've rented a beach cabin an hour's drive up the road," he said. "Where we will stay, just the two of us, for the next four days."

"You did? A beach cabin! I love it!"

"I knew you would," he said. "Mrs. McCaffrey took clothes and food up to it for us this morning, so we won't have to leave for anything."

She laughed and squealed. Life truly couldn't get any better. Just couldn't. She recalled that moment, not so long ago, when the train had rolled into Los Angeles. She'd known then that the City of Angels was where she belonged. And had been right.

Throwing her arms over her head, she shouted, "Look out, Los Angeles, Shirley Russell is here to stay!"

# *Epilogue*

⁓⁓⁂⁓⁓

Sitting close beside him, Shirley tightened her hold on Walter's arm as she felt the car make a corner. "This is crazy!"

His laugh mingled with the sounds of traffic. "We are almost there."

"Where is there?" The blindfold prevented her from seeing anything, but she knew they were downtown. "We're close to the radio station. I know we are."

"Are you peeking?"

She giggled. "No." That would ruin his surprise. She had no idea what it might be, but that only made it more fun. He loved surprising her, and did so regularly. Everything from bringing home a box of chocolates, to taking her for a night out on the town, or the beach for the entire day. Of course, their wedding and honeymoon would forever be her favorite surprise.

"You certainly have a good sense of direction," he said.

"I was born with it. Good thing, too. Nebraska had so many cornfields that without a good sense of direction, I'd have gotten lost just walking home from school."

Walter laughed.

"It's the truth," she insisted. "Cornrows all look the same, and when that corn gets tall, a person could get so lost not even the coyotes could find them."

"I know it's the truth." He stopped the car and shut off the engine before kissing the top of her head. "I just love how you explain things."

She loved him. So much. Being his wife had proven to be even more than she'd ever dreamed. Her life was more than she'd ever dreamed. And it was about to get even better. She had a surprise for him, too, was just waiting for the right moment to tell him her secret.

"Ready?" he asked.

Lost in her own thoughts, it was a moment before she asked, "To take off the blindfold?"

"Not yet. We have to get out of the car first."

"All right." They were downtown, the sounds of traffic filled the air, and she wondered if he was taking her to a movie. It was the middle of the afternoon, but that wouldn't matter. Not to him. That was another thing she loved about him.

He helped her slide past the steering wheel and step out of the car. "Right over here," he said, guiding her sideways. "You'll have the perfect view."

"Perfect view of what?"

"You'll see."

The excitement in his voice increased her curiosity. This was the first time he'd blindfolded her and drove her someplace. But knowing him, it wouldn't be the last. She laughed, knowing that was true.

His hands settled on her shoulders, and his chin touched her shoulder from behind as he said, "On the count of three, I'm going to remove your blindfold."

Anticipation peaked. "How about on the count of one?"

Chuckling, he agreed. "All right. One!"

The blindfold was gone, and the brightness of the afternoon caused her to blink several times. Then she saw it. "Oh, good Lord!"

"Like it?"

She stared at the billboard that had been erected on top of the radio station. It was huge, and of her.

"Blondie, Radio's Most Popular Singer. Live in Concert, Weekly." Walter pointed at the billboard as he read aloud the words printed in big bold letters.

The word *Blondie* was bright red and at the top, right next to the huge picture of her singing into a microphone. The other words were printed in black, and across the center and bottom of the billboard.

She was on a billboard.

Her.

A billboard.

Dang, if that didn't beat all. Pappy would never have believed that. *I did it, Momma*, she said to herself. *Made your dream come true. Our dream.*

She turned, looked at Walter. "That's why you had that person take pictures of me last month."

His grin went from ear to ear. "Yes, it was Earl's idea, and I agreed with it. You are the most popular singer on the radio."

She enjoyed singing and would for a long, long time, but it was him that made her happy. Him that she loved. Loved beyond all else.

He hooked her around the waist, pulled her close. "I'm so proud of you. Proud to be your husband. Blondie's husband."

She slid her arms around his neck. "I'm proud to be your wife. The wife of the most renowned attorney in all of Los Angeles." The moment she'd been waiting for had arrived. Excitement flared inside her. She drew in a deep breath. "And I'll be proud to be the mother of your child when he or she arrives in seven months."

Walter went stiff. "Seven months?" he asked, slowly stretching out the words.

She bit her bottom lip and nodded.

The shout he let out was probably heard on the other side of town. He picked her up and spun around in a circle, while asking, "A baby? Our baby?"

Clinging to him, she laughed. "Yes. A baby. Our baby."

Shirley closed her eyes as he held her tight, kissed her. Their love was so great it would last forever, and that love would prove to their children that it was possible to have it all. No matter what they were, or where they came from, every dream could come true.

Theodore Owen Russell was born six and half months later. When he turned sixteen, he became an errand boy for the most prestigious lawyer in California, his father.

Amelia Ann Russell was born two years after Theodore. By the time she turned sixteen, she was already singing duets with the most famous radio singer nationwide, her mother.

\* \* \* \* \*

# MILLS & BOON

## Coming next month

### A MIDSUMMER KNIGHT'S KISS
Elisabeth Hobbes

'It smells wonderful,' he said, cupping the rose in the palm of his hand and bringing it to his nose.

'May I?' Rowenna asked.

This time Robbie did not hold the flower out at arm's length, but kept it where it was so he could smell it at the same time. Rowenna leaned in towards him. She rested one hand on Robbie's shoulder. The other took hold of his wrist to steady it as she had done when she smelled the lavender. She buried her nose in the petals and took a slow, deep breath, then sighed with pleasure, closing her eyes and inhaling again. Her face was close to Robbie's, tilted a little to one side, with only the flower between them. He could count the individual eyelashes that seemed to reach all the way up to her arched brows. Her lips were the same deep shade as the rose he held, almost as soft as the velvety petals, but much fuller and more enticing.

'Beautiful.' He sighed.

'It's so strong it makes me feel lightheaded,' Rowenna said.

She opened her eyes and looked at him over the top of the flower, the long lashes widening to frame eyes that were now heavy with sensuality. Her lips curved into a wide smile and Robbie's heart began to beat faster.

He was starting to feel lightheaded himself, but that was nothing to do with the scent of the rose. Lightheaded, and more than a little reckless.

'I don't mean the flower,' he murmured.

He folded his hand over the rose and lowered it, noticing in the back of his mind that his hand was trembling. He bent his head down a little more until he was close enough that his mouth was next to Rowenna's. Close enough that he could feel the softness of her cheek against his. Close enough to whisper and be perfectly certain that no one else who might venture to this part of the garden would be able to hear the words that were meant only for her ears.

'I mean you.'

And he kissed her.

*Continue reading*
**A MIDSUMMER KNIGHT'S KISS**
Elisabeth Hobbes

www.millsandboon.co.uk

# LET'S TALK
## Romance

For exclusive extracts, competitions
and special offers, find us online:

- facebook.com/millsandboon
- @MillsandBoon
- @MillsandBoonUK

**Get in touch on 01413 063232**